"Those who favor suspense novels will have a ball with *Sharp Practice.* . . . The shades of *Psycho* will inevitably be evoked, and with good reason. . . . There is, of course, the required socko climax with an unexpected twist. What raises *Sharp Practice* high above the standard shocker is its sophistication."

—*The New York Times*

"A thriller-suspense-horror story containing some of the best action scenes extant. Farris has an uncanny knack for making terror a household word. For sheer technical skill, few novels of recent years can match *Sharp Practice.*"

—*Fort Worth Star-Telegram*

"The best horror-story opening chapter since *Rosemary's Baby.*" —*Lewiston Journal*

"As psychotic as *Psycho.*" —*The Kirkus Reviews*

SHARP PRACTICE
was originally published by Simon and Schuster.

Books by John Farris

The Captors
Crisis at Harrison High
The Girl from Harrison High
Happy Anniversary, Harrison High
King Windom
Shadow on Harrison High
Sharp Practice
The Trouble at Harrison High
When Michael Calls

Published by POCKET BOOKS

SHARP
PRACTICE

a novel by
JOHN FARRIS

PUBLISHED BY POCKET BOOKS NEW YORK

SHARP PRACTICE

Simon and Schuster edition published 1974

POCKET BOOK edition published October, 1975

*The song, "My Blue Tears," copyright, ©, 1971, by
Owepar Publishing Co., 1007 17th Avenue South,
Nashville, Tenn., 37212.*

L

**This POCKET BOOK edition includes every word contained
in the original, higher-priced edition. It is printed from
brand-new plates made from completely reset, clear, easy-to-
read type. POCKET BOOK editions are published by POCKET
BOOKS, a division of Simon & Schuster, Inc., 630 Fifth
Avenue, New York, N.Y. 10020. Trademarks registered
in the United States and other countries.**

Standard Book Number: 671-80098-1.
Library of Congress Catalog Card Number: 74-8991.
This POCKET BOOK edition is published by arrangement
with Simon & Schuster, Inc. Copyright, ©, 1974, by John
Farris. All rights reserved. This book, or portions thereof,
may not be reproduced by any means without permission of
the original publisher: Simon & Schuster, Inc., 630 Fifth
Avenue, New York, N.Y. 10020.
Front cover photograph by Eric Meola.

Printed in the U.S.A.

SHARP PRACTICE is dedicated to
Edward Colton—
who lost a lot
of sleep over it.

In letting of blood three main circumstances are to be considered, who, how much, when?

Robert Burton,
The Anatomy of Melancholy

Part One

VICTIMS

THE LIGHTS WERE already coming up onstage when he slipped into his aisle seat in the Royal Shakespeare Theatre. The music for Sir Rudy's production of *Troilus and Cressida* was atonal, sharp and painful as broken glass in the eardrums. The set consisted of horizontal levels like raw slabs dripping stalactites of concrete and a number of vertical transparent shafts in which simple lifts rode slowly up and down. Each lift contained a character from the play, some of whom, like Ajax, would not make their entrances for several scenes. The lighting was a dusky saffron in the foreground, like a foggy sunrise, and a brutal, swirling battlefield-red on the cyc.

Down front, on the thrust stage, two hollow chrome balls rose magically from the stage floor and were captured in dramatically crossed spots. They revolved slowly on slender poles: Troilus appeared, then Pandarus, who was feigning exhausted sleep.

The Thursday matinee audience, many of whom were off the tour buses, applauded generously. Undoubtedly they were current with the notices, nearly all of which had been lavish in praise of Sir Rudy's production. Through the centuries *Troilus* had failed as history, comedy and tragedy. Now it was failing as science fiction, but the critics were inclined to blame Shakespeare and not Sir Rudy.

Troilus, a burly actor in a khaki jumpsuit and a rakish red beret, jumped down from his perch, unslinging an AK-47 assault rifle. He looked desperately unhappy about something.

"Call here my varlet, I'll unarm again: why should I war without the walls of Troy, that find such cruel battle here within? Each Trojan that is master of his heart, let him to field; Troilus, alas! has none."

2

In the dim background Valery appeared, rising in one of the tomblike shafts.

From his seat near the rear of the stalls he could just make her out. Her normally expressive eyes looked wild and frozen. An eerie effect, he thought, trying to ignore both the irony and the way his heart was kicking up. But at least the effect was in keeping with the madness of Cassandra, and Cassandra's brooding presence had been well established in the opening scene. Sir Rudy definitely had his wits about him.

He managed to stay with the play until Valery/Cassandra's entrance in the first act, her initial ravings chillingly amplified throughout the house.

"Cry, Trojans, cry! Lend me ten thousand eyes, and I will fill them with prophetic tears."

It was Shakespeare at his worst, just words to fill a page. But in spite of her youth Valery possessed the talent —or the instinct—to act against the speech. She had the sliding moves of a lynx and there was a feline malevolence in her words. Her madness was tempered by slyness, emphasized by a bloody baring of her teeth at the concluding "Troy burns, or else let Helen go."

With an ominous backward glance she caught her lift on the way down and stood with folded arms and imperious uplifted gaze to a smattering of applause. He'd seen worse exits, since Shakespeare was in the habit of letting a minor character make his way to the wings as best he could after saying his piece.

His own exit before the interval went unnoticed. He had a whiskey on the terrace of the Dirty Duck, then returned to the river.

It was a chilly, blowing day but warm enough when the sun broke through, and there were quite a few boats on the Avon. Feeling a need for exercise, he rented a boat by Clopton Bridge and rowed hard upstream past Holy Trinity Church, Shakespeare's resting place. Upriver the banks were alive with bluebells and laburnum, clumps of rambling rose. He selected a secluded spot by a stand of shimmering willow, rowed the boat ashore and wandered a while, tieless, coat over one shoulder, thinking just enough about how it was going to go without fretting too much over the details. From experience he knew it was folly to worry the details.

By ten of four he was back at the theatre. The lawn, an unsullied green to the bank of the Avon, was speckled with picnickers, strollers, family groups feeding and making a fuss over the swans and their cunning cygnets. He smiled at an elderly couple who drifted through scuffling children arm in arm and with a finny apprehension, like goldfish in nitroglycerin.

At four o'clock there was muted but prolonged applause, and the theatre began to empty. He made his way through the crowds to the theatre's garden, near the stage entrance. There he sat on a low terrace wall beneath the lime trees, a little distance from a group of theatrical-appearing youngsters, probably up from RADA for the day. They preened and cut up for each other and for passersby, perhaps hoping to be mistaken for members of the Royal Company.

He had time for one cigarette before Valery appeared, as she always did, gliding up behind him, snaking an arm around him as she bent over to brush the lobe of his ear with a kiss.

" 'Lo, luv."

"Hello," he said, smiling up at her.

"You're awfully moist—what've you been up to?"

"I went rowing."

"And you missed the last act? *Jimmy*. God."

"He took her hand and guided her in the direction of the car park, aware that they were being observed by the RADA group. Perhaps one of them had recognized Valery and was wondering who *he* was. That gave him a shiver, but he forced himself to be reasonable. Probably they all had eyes for Valery, who at twenty was already a member of Britain's best known theatre company, receiving favorable mention in the notices.

"One act was enough," he said. "I got to see you. And you know I'm not much of a theatre man."

"Look at me," she said. "I'm pouting."

"I thought it was your Portia you especially wanted me to see."

"Well—yes—"

"*Caesar*'s more my sort of play anyhow. I've never understood *Troilus*."

Valery laughed, her good spirits restored. "Nobody else has either."

"Sir Rudy seems to have found an angle of attack."

"Oh, Sir Rudy. I treasure Sir Rudy, and he *is* a genius at doing obscure things in a fascinating way, but his genius —hmm, how did Foxgrove put it?—'His genius lies in an artful distraction rather than in brilliant illumination of essential problems.' "

"Do you suppose that's a compliment?"

"Coming from that sodding Foxgrove it is. Excuse me, darling."

She stopped at the edge of the car park to do a couple of *allongés,* wincing a little in pain.

"Thought I'd pulled a muscle getting on and off the lift," she explained.

"You seemed to manage it very well."

"It's bloody dangerous," Valery said grimly. "We're getting hazard pay, you know, and it took *forever* in rehearsal to learn stepping on and off without fetching up with a wrenched ankle. One miscalculation backstage and someone will be injured yet. Poor Botsford—he's Priam —Bots gets deathly ill riding those contraptions. If it wasn't for a stiff dose of Dramamine before performance he couldn't manage at all. Oh, God, I'm stiff! Wasn't it George S. Kaufman who said that the trouble with Shakespeare is you never get to sit down unless you're a king?"

"If he didn't, he should have."

"This one here? The Austin?"

"Right."

"Miss, may we please have your autograph?"

They were two Lancashire children, freckled as ripe bananas, neither of them older than twelve. Each was holding out program and pencil to Valery. She turned, beaming. She loved it all, he thought, and reveled in the glory of performing without being too much of a bore about it. Probably because performing was as natural to her as flight to a bird. Totally a now girl, she had a tawny, youthful mane, eyes like dark stars, and lips of bitter orange. Looks plus certain intangibles—the perpendicular elegance of a born winner. And he had Valery, he thought.

"Did you enjoy the performance?"

"Oh, yes, miss," he girl said. Her brother just gazed at Valery. He had one foot poised slightly behind the other, as if he were preparing to bolt as soon as Valery turned her eyes on him.

" 'To April,' " Valery recited as she wrote, " 'and come back soon.' "

She handed back the girl's program and smilingly held out her hand for the boy's. Her smile had a little too much voltage for him to bear and she knew it. She spoke gently to him.

"May I have your name? Gilbert? I'm very pleased to know you, Gilbert. I hope you enjoyed *Troilus*. Wasn't too difficult for you, was it?"

"Oh, no'm." He looked at his sister rather helplessly, then back at Valery. "Which one was you, miss?"

"Oh, Gilbert," his sister murmured, finding that unpardonable. "Come on, now."

"I acted Cassandra," Valery said, signing the program with a flourish.

"Oh, the mad one," Gilbert said. "I do recognize you now."

"I hope you'll both come back to Stratford for *Romeo and Juliet*. We're in rehearsal this month. I'll be Juliet."

The children walked away, heads together, comparing the signed programs. Valery slid into the car a little breathlessly. "Oooffff. Weren't they lovely children? I'm still not all that used to signing programs, but I adore their asking. What time do you make it, Jimmy?"

"Quarter past four. What time are you due back?"

"Promptly at seven thirty. That does give us—loads of time."

She clung lightly to his arm as he maneuvered the Austin out of the emptying car park, never taking her eyes off him. "Do you know what I'd like to do?"

"Can't imagine."

She sneered sweetly at him. *"That* too—oh, yes—oh, very definitely. But first I think I'd like to get on the train for London and discover you all over again. Sitting there in the carriage with your annotated Yeats. Pretending not to notice me."

"I thought I gave you a friendly enough glance."

"Oh, yes. That's what did it. I was mad for you right off."

"Ought to have said something."

"Me? Pick *you* up?"

"It would have been less painful in the long run."

"Ohhhh, darling, are your toes still giving you trouble?"

"That's all right. You were kind enough to drop your case squarely instead of at an angle."

"I didn't want to break your bones, just attract your attention. My God! Will you listen to that."

"What? Something with the car?"

"No, it's my *stomach.* I'm perishing for food."

"There's a surprise. You eat scratch meals for days or you don't eat at all."

"You can't imagine how furiously *busy* I've been! Oh, please, James, please, couldn't we stop just long enough for tea somewhere?"

"Reach behind the seat."

"What for? You mean back here? Jimmy! How marvelous. A hamper."

She put the hamper beside her on the seat and rummaged. "Cheese! Biscuits! A whole broiled chicken? You shouldn't have, you know I'll stuff myself like a boa constrictor. Is this wine? Château Haut-Brion? I don't know a thing about wines, but the bottle is certainly impressive. Look at the date! That's the year I was born. You comic."

"It was a great year. For *Graves* and for women."

"Ha, ha, ha. Well, I shall just nibble. I don't want to stodge my performance tonight."

"Or *my* performance this evening."

"Get on," Valery said, curling her lip at him. She balanced the little cheese board on her lap and cut into the Cheddar, larding it on a biscuit. "Umm, delicious! I'll just be a moment opening the wine."

"Try not to give the bottle a shaking."

"Oh, I know *that* much. But isn't it rather elderly after twenty years?"

"It's just at the peak of its greatness. Tomorrow would be too late."

"Well, I'm honored." Valery finished off the cheese and biscuit, carefully opened the Haut-Brion and poured two glasses half full. "Is this suitable with breast of chicken?"

"It would be suitable with week-old porridge."

Valery clutched her glass between her knees as she ate. They had cleared the worst of the traffic now, most of which was bound for Birmingham and London. Within a few minutes they were on a trunk road south through the Cotswolds.

"I wonder if I shouldn't have given Boyland a ring?" Boyland was her new agent. He was trying to move her quickly into films.

"Isn't he in Cannes for the Festival windup?"

"Oh, God, that's right. Well, he should have called me yesterday at the latest. It's been almost a fortnight since I tested. My luck to have lost the part."

"Your luck has been phenomenal. Don't worry."

"I suppose Brian is still testing girls. Boyland said they would be doing a lot of testing. I might hear by Tuesday, then. Don't you think?"

"Shouldn't be surprised. Will it be so terrible if you don't get it?"

"But I *want* it!"

She seemed so wounded at the thought of losing the role in the film that he reached over immediately and squeezed her knee. Valery smiled and looked contrite.

"I shouldn't be bringing up all this when we've so little time together."

"I don't mind talking about—"

"No. That's the end of it. I don't want to talk any more about bloody acting and bloody Stratford and bloody films and bloody career. I want to devote the next three hours to being your bit of stuff."

Valery held his hand and caressed it, ran her tongue lightly over the salt hollow of the palm. Then she placed his hand beneath her short skirt and, like a puppet master, directed it to do intimate and erotic things. She braced bare feet against the firewall, then twisted in the seat and nipped the lobe of his ear.

"I *am* your bit of stuff now, aren't I?" she said. She took a shuddery breath and forced her knees together, but a gluteal rhythm was well under way.

"You'll have me driving up a tree."

"You look all hot and bothered, luv. More wine?"

"At once."

At a T junction near Chipping Camden he turned off onto the B road to Durning Wold. The road twisted more deeply into the whaleback hills, following a river through woodland and pastures of spring grass, past tall hedges blooming with Rosa mundi.

The sun was setting behind Lycoming Hill when they drove through a gap in the box hedge and followed the drive around to the front of the gabled brownstone cottage, which, after the custom of the region, was set sideways to the lane. There were two thirty-foot copper beeches in the dooryard, both trees occupied by a flock of daws. An apple orchard beyond a stone wall filled the rest of the vale.

The blue tor of Lycoming not only shut off the sun and brought early dusk to the cottage, its height and breadth afforded complete privacy. The main buildings of the farm of which the cottage was a part were located a few hundred yards down the lane, and it was rare for anyone to pass by during the day; occasionally a cow wandered down from the high meadow.

Valery got out of the car with the empty wine bottle in one hand. She had drunk most of the wine herself; she was slightly unsteady, yawning, filled with expectant tremors. She smiled ear to ear and leaned elaborately against the car.

"Oh, James, I'm daft about it."

"Why don't you go in? I'll dispose of the bottle for you and bring the hamper."

Valery pitched the bottle to him and wandered up to the door, chuckling to herself.

He carried what trash there was to the pit beyond the well house. There he paused for a smoke, knowing full well what Valery would be up to inside.

When he returned to the cottage Valery was waiting for him just inside the door. She had turned on a small lamp, but the cottage was still heavily in shadow. Even so, he was excitedly aware of the fine texture of her skin as she came naked into his arms.

"Jimmy—now—right now—here—quickly—can you manage?"

"Don't you want to—?"

"I don't want to lie down. I don't want to get all comfortable first. I want to be taken. Standing up. Do it, Jimmy!"

He fumbled a bit with his clothes. She tried to help him. As soon as they were both naked he took her, as she wanted, with his back braced against the wall, all of her mounted weight in his arms and on his strong thighs.

"My God, my God, it's so good!" she cried all too soon, and with a final vehement clenching that threatened to lock them permanently together. Her heart pounded and her breath sighed past his ear.

When they were able to, they disengaged tenderly and

leaned against the wall. His arm was around her waist, and she rested her head in the saddle of his shoulder.

When she could speak again Valery said, "But you—you didn't—"

"Don't worry about me."

"I feel so selfish. I've been thinking about you and *wanting* you for almost a week—then I drank all that wine. I was so randy I almost came in the car, you know. But I will make it up to you, darling. I'm a long way from being done."

"It's chilly in here. Why don't you turn down the counterpane? I'll light the fire."

"Yes, I'd love a fire." Valery was still short of breath and thoroughly chapfallen. "But I mean it when I say I'm not done."

She walked across the room to the bed alcove, still unsteady, giving a leather chair a bump with her hip in passing. She paused to pull her long hair away from her face, then bent over the low bed to fold back the counterpane.

Instead of linen the bed was neatly covered with a double thickness of polythene. Valery stared at it for a few moments, running her tongue over her lower lip where a tooth had almost drawn blood, listening to the chatter of birds in the bushes just outside the mullioned window. Now, why on earth did Jimmy prefer to sleep on polythene? Awfully clammy next to the skin. Or could it be a water bed? No, she saw mattress ticking underneath.

"Jimmy?" Valery sensed him behind her and she turned. "What's—?"

He was closer than she had thought. Arm's length. There was a professional-looking carving knife in his hand. A thin wedge of blade, perhaps fifteen inches in length. It looked horridly sharp. Jimmy was still naked, but he'd pulled on a pair of thin leather gloves.

Her mind was muddled from the wine and the flash flood of orgasm, but the heat of her initial passion had left her body, and Valery now realized just how cold it was in that sunless cottage. Her teeth chattered. She recalled everything she'd read about the other two in the newspapers. Each girl had been struck down with a carving knife, then wrapped in a securely stapled polythene cocoon.

Valery looked deeply into Jimmy's eyes. The wine came up in her throat in a soured column, but she blocked it. Otherwise she had no control over her body. From the neck down she was turning to stone.

"You can't be him. I don't believe it. No. No, no, no, Jimmy, no, God, I'm going to dieeeeeeeeee, oh, Godddddddddddddddddddd. Help me. Help. Please. Oh, don't. I'm afraid of knives. I'm so afraid of knives, Jimmy!"

"My name isn't Jimmy," he said.

Her lips continued to move beseechingly, but she made only whistling and whining sounds. Her legs were pressed against the bed. She was so pale he could look down and see all of the delicate veins in her breasts. She began to tremble violently, coming to a frozen stop between spasms. She ground her tongue with her teeth.

He was fast with the knife. Valery didn't see it, because her eyes were glazed and fixed on a point somewhere beyond his right shoulder. In her shocked condition she might not have felt the blade striking hard and deep through her solar plexus—and just that quickly, as the blade traveled upward through her body and sliced the spinal cord two inches below the neck, Valery died.

He quickly caught her as she was falling straight back to the bed and gave her a turn onto her side, so the exposed bit of blade wouldn't cut the polythene. Then he backed away, because there was the usual excremental problem. But nothing unexpected this time: no last convulsion and messy gout of arterial blood. He had learned just where to place the knife. The air hostess (What was her name?—Ewa. They'd had so little time to become acquainted) had kicked about in an unnerving manner, so violently that he thought he'd missed killing her with the first stroke, and he was about to pull out the blade and cut her throat when she hemorrhaged, and all motion ceased.

There'd been quite a bag of blood, however, and he'd done a hasty job of disposing of Ewa, without finesse; he'd only cared that she be discovered quickly.

Valery bled slowly from the mouth. It ran under the angle of her jaw and began pooling on the polythene, so he went to work quickly, bundling her up, using the big stapler. Within ten minutes he'd finished bagging Valery.

He drew the spread up over the body, drank a pint of stout, which he barely tasted, then spent thirty minutes in the shower cleaning himself, scrubbing, scrubbing vigorously.

AT HALF PAST midnight an ashen log breaking in the fireplace awakened him, and he sat up stiffly in the chair in which he had slept.

As soon as he had verified the time he went directly to the bed, pulled down the spread and looked at Valery. Her eyes, dusty and lightless, reminded him of the way she had looked during the opening scenes of *Troilus*. The bleeding had stopped of course. There was slight condensation on the inside of the polythene bag. Perhaps it had something to do with the cooling of the body in death or the escape of intestinal gas.

Tonight's performance at Stratford was long over. Another girl had gone on for Valery, and undoubtedly Valery was on report, or whatever they called it when an actor failed to make a show without a proper excuse. But in the morning they would all know what had happened to her. Poor thing, she had such talent, they would say. Such a brilliant future. I'd like to get my hands on that bleeding madman! And the police—they'd soon be swarming over Stratford, asking their questions. Yes, I suppose I was her best friend in the company. She had someone new, she told me that much. When did *you* see her last? Well, Inspector, she was in a frightful hurry to be outer here after curtain calls, skimmed off her makeup and into her dress and it was whoooosh! through the door. Did she say she was meeting someone? Not to me, sir, I'm just the wardrobe mistress. But, then, they all meet their men after a show, don't they? And you, did you see her with anyone? Yes, I did have a glimpse of Valery in the car park with a gentleman, can't really say what he looked like. About as tall as you or me. Wore a cap, he did, bit of a brown color. Sunglasses. Sorry not to be of more help. And the children: It's *her* picture right here in the *Express,* Mam, she's the one signed our programs! Perhaps we should ring up the police, then. Don't remember much about *him,* do you, Gilbert? Do try, children. It's very important. Well, I should say he's about Dad's height. Six one? Not heavy. No. Nor very thin. Medium. Fairish, wouldn't you say, April? Oh, yes, I'd definitely say he was fairish. He sat in the car while she signed our programs, so actually— Bloody hell, we're not getting anywhere with this one either. The press will crucify us, Inspector. Should say they've done an excellent job of that already.

Outside he backed the rented car to within a few feet of the cottage door and went inside for the body. Valery took up most of the room in the boot, but it wasn't like trying to pack the air hostess away, she had stood an inch below six feet and had weighed a robust hundred and fifty pounds. And that quantity of blood, he'd been afraid of puncturing the bag. . . .

This time it was all so easy. There was a welcome mist and fog as he drove into Oxford and to the close beside the dry cleaner's shop. The cleaner's delivery van was parked against the dock by the side door and there was a dim light burning. He parked behind the van, got out, and unscrewed the bulb in the fixture. The van stood between the doorway and Broad Street, but he doubted anyone was wandering about. Of course coppers would be punting around, even though it wasn't what one would call a high-crime area. These days coppers were everywhere, he'd never seen so many. Well, he had only himself to blame for that, but the increased police watch was beginning to tax his ingenuity.

As he'd thought, no attempt had been made to change the lock on the door despite what the papers were calling "the climate of fear" in Oxford. Undoubtedly not too much had been made of the missing keys. Oh, they'll turn up, Meg, you've left them in your other coat. Use my set, why don't you? He found the right key for the lock on his third try and let himself into the long, narrow shop.

The key in the lock had automatically deactivated the infrared burglar alarm inside. Another light, shaded, was burning above the counter at the front, but even if he stood under it stark naked cleaning his teeth it would be difficult to make him out from The Broad.

The closeness of the shop, the vapors of carbon tet and other powerful cleaning agents stung his eyes. He left the rear door wide open, popped up the boot of the Austin and lifted out the body of Valery St. James.

She had stiffened considerably and he found it difficult to carry her. Lugging her in, he bumped her head hard against the jamb; for some reason that brought on cold sweats. He put Valery down on the floor while he made room for her on the mechanical rack that looped around the shop from the cleaning machines to the counter.

At dawn the route men would be on the dock to load the van, one of them operating the rack with a foot pedal, handing down the billowy bags of suits and dresses to the other for loading. What's this? Sweet Jesus, he's done it again! Somebody fetch the coppers . . .

Not as original as having the corpse found floating down the Isis during the middle of a crew race—that had taken a bit of doing—nevertheless the discovery of Valery should prove to be a stunner.

Getting Valery properly hung up seemed to take far too much time, and though he was a strong man, his arms ached and sweat ran down his ribs before he was finished.

The final touch was the announcement card.

Plain white card, block letters in ink. He took it from his coat pocket and Scotch-taped it firmly to the poly-thene bag.

> HELLO!
> MY NAME IS VALERY.
> ISN'T IT SAD
> TO FALL IN LOVE
> WITH PRETTY JOE?

Nothing else to do, then, but pitch the key ring to a shelf below the counter, set the automatic lock on the door, screw the bulb back into place. The boot of the Austin had to be shut; to his sensitive ears it made an unholy *thump* in the misty close. He jumped into the car and within a minute was well away from there.

But it *had* been easy, he told himself. Each time it was easier, because it no longer seemed possible that he could fail. (Perhaps one got a more powerful high from heroin, but he doubted it. And he wasn't about to acquire the filthy habit to find out.)

He wondered if Valery would be the end of it? Were they all likely to get the message straight this time?

Actually he hoped they wouldn't. Because he was al-ready savoring the expectation of doing it all over again.

JORAM THORNTON SURPRISED herself by getting up in plenty of time to catch the 6:45 train from Paddington Station. Bev had offered to drive her up to Oxford, but Joram was still a little unstrung by the carefree way Bev had run amuck in London traffic in her tiny Triumph, and heavy weather was threatening throughout the south of England. Joram had visions of the two of them strewn across the roadway after a skid or a collision, so she was able to beg off while staying on her cousin's good side, always a touchy feat of diplomacy.

"But Jory, honey, we might not get to see you all again before you go off to the kawntinent," Bev complained in her newly acquired mid-Atlantic accent, or what she thought was mid-Atlantic. But because of a stubborn Texas drawl, Joram placed her cousin's accent a little farther west—about the middle of the Mississippi River. And the idiom had been bred into her. "I'll tell you the truth, I could just take a gun and *shoot* Richard for getting involved in that tacky little country, Culotte, or whatever they call it."

"Kuwait, Bev."

"Well, I don't care. Honestly, we could have had such a mahvelous holiday together, and now it's spoiled."

"We won't be leaving before the end of June. Richard might make it home by then. Or the three of us could go. It'd still be fun, Bev."

"Hugh wouldn't like that *at all.*"

"Hugh thinks the world of you, Bev."

"Wellllll—" Bev said doubtfully, and let the matter drop. "I wish you'd stay a couple more days anyway. We just scratched the surface. I wanted you to meet Countess Vespugli. You know my opinion of all the royalty that's running around over here, but she's so down to earth and

17

so much *fun*. Besides, if *I* were you, I wouldn't be in such a hurry to get back to Oxford."

"Why not, hon?"

Bev's eyes widened. "Because of *him*."

"Because of——? Oh, you're talking about the murders."

"Uh-huh. Pretty Joe. All those poor girls in baggies, and his little messages. 'Compliments of Pretty Joe.' Oh, Lord, that just gives me cold shivers, Jory. I don't even like to *think* about you being alone up there while Hugh's doing whatever it is he does."

"Hugh does research, Bev. And Pretty Joe likes his women under twenty-five."

Bev squinted judicially at her. "You could pass for twenty-five in the dark."

"It would have to be *very* dark, but thanks anyway, Bev."

"I mean it, I don't know how you've managed to keep your figure so good for so long. Your side of the family certainly has wonderful bone structure."

"And your side has all the money."

"Oh, well, I'd rather have looks than money, and that's not a word of a lie." Bev's face-lift, done in Switzerland three months before, had failed to take, and she was still sulky about this mishap.

"Maybe Hugh and I will get down next weekend for a show," Joram had said, and they let it go at that.

Going home on the train she was aware of the interest of a donnish-looking young man (younger, probably, than her son), and she wondered if he would attempt conversation. Perhaps suggest a drink later on, and then——? It still happened to her, and for the most part her admirers were young. Undoubtedly they had mother fixations, but at least they wanted her for something, bless the good bones Bev had envied. She gave the young man an open glance, ready to smile, but he cracked a book and seemed absorbed in penciling the margins.

Joram smiled anyway, at her reflection in the glass. She had to admit the urge wasn't really there any more, just the desire to be courted and flattered. She hoped she would never lose that; if she did, she was ready for the blast furnace.

She had six years on Hugh, who was—unarguably—in his prime, but there were days when she was willing to pass herself off for forty-two or forty-three. With a certain tenderness she recalled her fortieth birthday. Ah, forty had made her miserable, and forty-five was an ordeal, but at fifty it seemed ridiculous to give more than an occasional yearning glance at the past, and criminal to idealize it. At least she didn't have poor Bev's problems. Wrinkles by the yard and pots and pots of suet.

It was raining hard by the time the train pulled into the shed at Oxford. Cabs would be at a premium, Joram thought, standing up to reach her case. She was a little sorry she hadn't let Hugh know last night what time she was getting in.

"May I help you with that?"

She smiled automatically. "It is heavy, thank you."

This close she could see him much better. He might have been a graduate student, but he looked, in general, slightly threadbare and quietly harassed. First- or second-year lecturer probably, hungry and hopeful of a fellowship. So many of them never made it; the system was harsh and there were too many candidates, too many highly qualified teachers even in the most esoteric fields. He had a bony, wistful handsomeness, introverted eyes, a thin straggle of blonde beard that clung to the jawbone from ear to ear.

The elderly couple who had shared the compartment with them were first off. Joram stepped down from the carriage and the young man followed with her suitcase.

"I have a car—if I could drop you?"

"Oh, I'd appreciate that," Joram said without stopping to think. You didn't just go off with strangers in Oxford these days, no matter how earnest and puppy-harmless they seemed.

It had been four weeks since the actress, Pretty Joe's

last victim. And as in other cases of multiple murder committed by the same man, the full moon seemed to set him off. WILL HE KILL AGAIN? the London tabloids were speculating. Wonderful scare stuff, but—

He saw the sudden change to caution in Joram's eyes.

"Oh, it's my wife meeting me with the car, you see—so there's nothing—I assure you—"

"I wasn't worried," Joram said.

"You are Mrs. Thornton, aren't you? Mrs. Hugh Thornton?"

"Yes, I am. Have we met?"

"Oh, no, but I've chatted with your husband recently at a pour at The House. And then my wife and I noticed the two of you one evening in the covered market."

"Oh, I see. Are you at Christ Church?"

"Yes. Oriental Studies is my field."

His name was Ronald Adlord, and as Joram had suspected, he was lecturing. Carrying far too much of a load while trying to keep up his research, having to attend to all the other duties—counseling, administrative work, entertaining—which counted so heavily if he hoped to become a Fellow. Working himself to death on a salary that wouldn't exceed fifteen hundred pounds a year.

He'd been up to London in pursuit of a grant that would give him a year to finish his study of elite groups in seventeenth-century Japan, and he was worried sick that he'd muffed the interview. The joys of the academic life, Joram thought.

His wife and two babies were waiting for him in a scruffy Mini-Minor, and the poor girl looked so embarrassed by circumstances—there really was no place for Joram to ride—that Joram wished fervently she had opted for a cab, no matter how long the queue. Instead, she solved the problem gracefully by taking the two children on her lap and amusing them as best she could on the way.

Ronald held Joram's case awkwardly on his own lap, spoke sharply to his wife when she stalled the engine, then tried clumsily to make up. He got a thorough frosting for his efforts.

He spent the remainder of the ride to her banbury house talking about Hugh, overpraising Hugh's two-volume work on the Tudors. Joram wondered when he'd been able to steal time to skim through the books. It was obvious that the young lecturer admired Hugh and envied his success. Hugh was a former Christ Church Rhodes Scholar and Supernummary Fellow; he was enjoying all the privileges of The House during his sabbatical. Ronald Adlord probably thought Hugh would be able to do him some good with the Dean. Despite two venomous looks from his wife he fished nakedly for an invitation to the Thorntons'.

Joram smiled and played with the babies and said nothing at all.

"Oh, he's drooled on you," the devastated girl said when Joram handed over the teething baby, "he's ruined your beautiful coat."

"This old thing? Don't you worry about it." The pastel Acquascutum raincoat was both new and expensive and the girl knew it. She was almost in tears.

Her misery was compounded when she took in the elegant 18th-century house that the Thorntons were renting for Hugh's sabbatical year. Joram wanted to say a comforting word, but she couldn't think of any.

Ronald took Joram up to the door beneath his leaky umbrella, offered a bleak smile in return for her thanks and ran back down to his car, where a gust of wind destroyed the umbrella. He savagely threw the remains of it into the back and got in. One of the children was crying. The Mini-Minor drove off at a balky pace as the wife mismanaged her gear changes again.

Mrs. Merton opened the door for Joram. "Oh, my goodness, here you are already and I've not even got a start on the dusting." She took Joram's suitcase and set it by the stairs.

"I was hoping to get home before the worst of the storm," Joram said, taking off her rain gear.

"Will you be joining your husband for breakfast? I'll just be a moment setting another place."

"Coffee's all I want, Mrs. Merton. Oh, do you suppose you could do something about this stain on the lapel of my coat? It's teething drool, of all things."

"I've had plenty of experiences with drool stains, Mrs. Thornton. I'll just take the coat along to the pantry before the stain has a chance to set."

Joram followed her as far as the breakfast room, hoping that Hugh had been able to get his shell off the river before the deluge. But she didn't find him at breakfast.

It was eight twenty-three. By this time Hugh ought to have been drinking his second cup of coffee while he leafed through the last pages of the *Times,* getting ready for a brisk ten-minute walk to the Bodleian. Hugh was rarely even five minutes off his daily schedule, so Joram was perplexed by the sight of the paper lying folded and untouched beside his breakfast plate, also untouched.

"Mrs. Merton? Hasn't my husband come in yet?"

The housekeeper appeared in the doorway to the kitchen, dabbing at the spot on Joram's Acquascutum with a piece of sponge.

"No, and he's very late this morning. That isn't like him —now, is it?"

"And he hasn't called?"

"Not since I arrived. I've kept his eggs warmed, but there's no saying how they'll taste. Shall I bring your coffee?"

"Yes, thank you, Mrs. Merton."

Joram stood staring through the bow window at the rain in the garden. Only illness or emergency could alter Hugh's routine. Up at six, at the boat club by six thirty, an hour of hard sculling no matter how terrible the weather was. Depending on whether he drove the car or rode his bicycle, she could be sure of seeing him at breakfast no later than quarter past eight.

Illness, she thought apprehensively. "Mrs. Merton, have you called upstairs? Could Hugh still be in his room?"

"Didn't think of that. Why would he still be lying abed at this hour? Oh, you don't suppose—?"

But Joram was already headed for the front stairs. She went up them at a trot to the third floor, turned left to Hugh's room. The door was closed but not locked. She went in, seeing instantly that he was not there. The coverlet on his bed was turned back, but obviously he hadn't slept in it.

Visions of finding her husband on the floor, dead of a heart seizure, evaporated from Joram's mind, but she was forced to lean against the jamb until her heart stopped beating in such a frightened way.

"Oh, Mrs. Thornton?"

She went to the stairs and spoke over the railing. "Yes?"

"I remember now the car wasn't in the garage when I came."

"I see." Joram walked slowly downstairs and returned to the breakfast room, where she drank her coffee too hot and burned her tongue.

Well, the fact was Hugh had been delayed somehow and hadn't been able to call. If he'd had a chance to get to a phone he would have let Mrs. Merton know about breakfast. A minor accident en route? It was now the height of the morning rush hour, and Joram could imagine the snarls that the downpour had caused in Oxford's always exasperating traffic.

She tried not to dwell on the other possibility.

Joram had often urged him not to go rowing in bad weather, but Hugh had assured her it was not dangerous on the Isis even during a rainstorm, just damned wet and uncomfortable. Should the boat be swamped, he was an excellent swimmer. A man in his prime, fit and strong. Punctual about his twice-yearly checkups, clean bill of health last time, as always. The blood pressure of a man twenty years younger. Hugh had always kept himself in excellent shape, and once he'd had hopes of making the Olympic team in his specialty, the single sculls.

Why not call the boat club, see if he was still—?

Instead, Joram recalled the condition of his bed. Was it possible he hadn't been home all night?

"Mrs. Merton?"

Her head appeared in the doorway. "I've a mind to throw the eggs out and start fresh when he comes."

"Yes, do that," Joram said absently. "Mrs. Merton, did Hugh have his dinner at home yesterday?"

"No. He says to me at breakfast, 'Mrs. Merton, I'll eat at Kefford's tonight. Why don't you get an early start home?' I left about three, I think it was. I was glad to get home, because my Edward's been ailing. All that overtime work—and there's no extra pay for PC's, as you know."

Kefford's was on_ of Hugh's clubs, the rugger and rowing crowd.

"Did Hugh mention who he was having dinner with?"

"That he did not. There, the coat's like new, not a trace of a spot. Lovely color, flatters your eyes, if I may say so. Shall I give it a quick press while I'm about it?"

"Please." Joram took her coffee to Hugh's second-floor study and looked in. The study was dim and slightly musty from his pipes. She opened the drapes over the windows and turned on the old green-shaded student lamp which Hugh had bought during his student days at Oxford.

The notes she had typed up last week looked undisturbed in their folder on the right-hand side of his desk. The manuscript was in two boxes on the left side, and more notes, typed, boxed and indexed—nearly twelve hundred pages so far—took up shelf space within easy reach of Hugh's chair.

He'd been incredibly productive this sabbatical year. The new work, dissecting Elizabethan court politics and analyzing the effects of their labyrinthine power plays on a global level, was Hugh's most ambitious project. He'd allowed himself to talk of a National Book Award this time, but only to Joram.

She found the box of handwritten notes beside her own typewriter surprisingly empty after a week: only a few pages, scarcely a day's gleaning, considering the pace he'd set the last few months. Hugh employed student researchers in some of the other libraries; and one was paid just to solve the mysteries of the Bodleian's catalogue and compile a list of works in print germane to his subject. But Hugh tackled the manuscripts himself. Occasionally there were dry spells when he was unable to locate the precise charter he needed, or the right manuscript among the fifty thousand stored in archaic nooks and vaults in the Bodleian. Many nights he had worked until the ten-o'clock bell that signaled the closing of the great library, only to come home and continue on his own manuscript until well after midnight. It would have made a difficult schedule for a recluse, but Hugh also had his athletics, and he hated to miss a party or a pour.

And he seldom missed any of the women who were attracted to him.

Joram fingered the little sheaf of notes and dropped them back into the box, thinking that she would type them later.

It seemed a reasonable explanation of his absence from his own bed last night. Hugh had taken advantage of her going, just as she'd expected him to. Leaving him for a week to visit Bev in London had been a signal: *Get this affair over with—I'm tired of it.*

Joram didn't know who the girl was. She never cared to know, although sometimes she couldn't help but have an inkling. Usually his choices showed taste and fore-thought, and the resulting affairs left no little messes behind for either of them to be sorry about. But this particular girl had claimed his attention much too long, and Hugh had grown impossibly moody of late. He was also drinking too much, and that worried her. He'd never been less than heroic with her in bed, no matter what demands were being made elsewhere, still—

He never let his girls have the best of him, that was all: if they got too deeply under his skin he let them go. What if he'd finally met one he couldn't bear to let go? Someone who offered all that Joram had to offer, and the premium of a youthful body? No, she refused to consider that. Hugh would never let his passions overcome his sense of fitness or his loyalty. If not for her he'd be an obscure, perhaps broken, man. Instead, he was enjoying the rewards of a distinguished career. It had been a good marriage; it was marriage he still needed.

The doorbell. Hugh? No, he wouldn't ring. She went to the windows and looked out. A delivery van stood at the curb.

In the foyer she found Mrs. Merton with a huge paper vase of cut flowers, gladioli from Cornwall, wrapped in tissue to protect them from the heavy rain. Yes, and there was a card, which she read while Mrs. Merton hurried off to the pantry to rearrange the flowers in a proper vase.

> Darling: Welcome back to the cold and the damp and the warmest heart in England. Missed you. Love, Hugh.

Undoubtedly he'd arranged for the flowers yesterday afternoon, intending for them to be there when she arrived from London. Joram smiled, greatly relieved, forgetting for now that he'd so uncharacteristically missed his breakfast. The flowers were Hugh's own signal. So he *had* spent last night with his bird, but today the affair was over.

"Mrs. Merton? Suppose we try the flowers in the cloisonné bowl. They'll be lovely on the lowboy in the dining room."

Detective Chief Inspector Kilderbee, Thames Valley CID, found the door to Professor Ramsdell's office standing open.

Apparently they'd been mistaken when they told him the don was in. He saw no one but a smashing girl in slacks and a bulky sweater, curled up shoeless in a lounge chair, drowsing. The blinds, half closed, allowed only a murky light into the room, and music was coming from the tape deck on the desk. Something by Mozart, he reckoned, although he couldn't place the opus immediately. Oh, that was it—Symphony Number 40, G minor.

"Yes?" she said without opening her eyes or looking up.

"Pardon me, miss. I'd hoped to find the don here."

Perhaps it was the masculine voice; she sprang alertly out of the chair and switched on a standing lamp. He had the opportunity to appreciate her coloring—auburn hair, hazel eyes that turned almost a pea-soup shade next the vivid green of her sweater—and to correct his first impression of her age. Thirty-three? No, give her a year. Without shoes she was just his height. Altogether impressive.

"I'm Professor Ramsdell," she said.

The Inspector introduced himself. She looked over his identification carefully.

"What can I do for you, Insp—— Oh, excuse me a moment, please make yourself at home." She was already walking to the portable chalkboard that stood by the windows, blocking an excellent view of the Fellow's garden of Paternoster College. The chalkboard was covered with symbols he found incomprehensible. She stood there for a few moments, hands on hips, then made quick erasures and drew more symbols. It all looked

27

vaguely algebraic to Kilderbee. He'd been dreadful at algebra, and was forever in awe of the type of mind that took higher math in stride.

He had the leisure to glance at some of the titles in her bookcase. Many volumes were printed in Cyrillic. *Theorems of Continuous Function,* a thickset book from the University Press, had her name on it. So did *Studies in Lobacevskii's Geometry,* monographs dealing with hypercomplex numbers and canonical matrices. Whatever they might be. Her framed degrees lined the wall above her bookcase. Oxford. Stockholm. Royal Manchester College of Music. She was a Fellow of six mathematical societies at home and abroad.

There was a framed motto to puzzle over. "Intuitive Conclusiveness and Logical Necessity Are Two Different Things." Hmm. Apt in police work also, although he'd never been able to put the thought into so many words.

"Right. Sorry to keep you waiting. Shall I shut off the Mozart?"

"Oh, no, I like it. You're a musician too?"

She smiled. "Not of professional quality. Violin. The Chamber Orchestra—Sundays in Wadham Chapel. Tea?"

"I don't want to take up too much of your time."

"I'm sure we have time for tea," she said graciously, getting out the hot plate.

"What is it you're doing there? On the chalkboard?"

"Oh, I'm merely doing some scratch work in number theory. For relaxation mostly. I may write it up."

"Relaxation. I see."

"This is one of those days when I hardly know what to do with myself. Students are canceling tutorials—everyone's frantically preparing for exams. There, the water will be hot in a moment. What was it you wanted to see me about?"

"An undergraduate named Mary Galashields. I understand you're her adviser."

"Oh—Mary. It's not something serious?"

"There's reason to believe she may have disappeared."

"Oh, *God*. Oh, no. Not again."

"At the moment we have no evidence she's met with harm, but under the circumstances it would be well if we located her as quickly as possible."

"Come to think of it, I haven't noticed Mary around for days. She canceled a tutorial last week. Mentioned she might go home for a while, rest up a bit. Before the big push, you see. Mary's in line for a First."

"Good student, then."

"Yes, very good."

"She packed her bags, all right, but never showed at home. No word from her."

"I can't account for it. Unless she went off with a chum?"

"I'm afraid she didn't do that."

"She may be with some chap, then."

"Possibly. Do you know the names of any of her chaps? Someone she fancied particularly?"

"I can't remember names—my *worst* failing. She was always with a bloke, changed them as often as her linen. You don't suppose *he's* got hold of Mary? That's dreadful."

"As I say, we're merely checking on her whereabouts. Girls do go off, and turn up in unexpected places. No idea they've caused a furor."

"Mary was level-headed. Keen about her studies. Stunt like that, I just don't know, we've all been so bloody security-conscious around here of late . . ."

"Could she have been feeling the pressure of her studies? Decided to chuck the college and not tell anyone?"

"She worked too hard to get here, Inspector. Paternoster isn't lightly chucked, I can tell you that. We're all a bit shagged now, but I think I would have noticed something—in her work, or her attitude . . ." Anne paused, stared at her chalkboard, and Kilderbee was afraid she'd gone off again. But Anne shook her head and looked excitedly at him.

"There *was* this guy—Swedish—she was with him during Eights Week, and not long ago I saw them again at Luna Caprese. Mary looked smitten, no doubt of that. His name, his name! Wait. *Lars*. That's all I can tell you. Lars. Built like a front-row man. Very blond of course. And his college was BNC."

Kilderbee wrote "Brasenose" in his book. "That should help a bit. I'll get someone right on it. Mind if I ring the station?"

"No, the phone's right there, it wants plugging in." The tea-kettle whistled, and Anne went to prepare tea while the Inspector spoke to his headquarters.

"I hope it won't take your men long to track Mary down," she said worriedly as soon as Kilderbee was off the phone.

"I shouldn't think so—you've provided us with a splendid lead. I do want to stress that there's no immediate cause for alarm."

"No. Of course not. It's so unlike Mary, that's all." She gazed forlornly out the windows. "Where is that marvelous June weather we've been looking forward to?"

"Looks like staying this way a while."

"Bloody nuisance, and my car's in dock."

"Beautiful college. Very new, isn't it?"

"The main buildings date from 1950."

"Oh, that recently. Remarkable unity of style one seldom finds in the Oxford colleges. You may not be able to forgive my saying this, but you strongly remind me of an actress—great favorite of mine—she died years ago."

"Marian Holgate."

"Yes, exactly. I suppose it's tiresome being compared to her."

"Not at all, I'm very flattered. She was my mother."

"Oh, your mother. The likeness *is* uncanny." The Inspector finished his tea, placing cup and saucer on the desk. "I'd best be running along. Many thanks for your help, Professor Ramsdell."

Anne turned and smiled radiantly at him. "Oh, Inspector! I realize it must be contrary to regs, but if you're returning St. Aldate's way, could you possibly drop me near the Triple Crown?"

The Inspector was delighted; with the CID stretched so thin, he'd endured a long, wet turn that promised to be interminable, and he had no further prospect of such bright company. "Come along, then."

"I'll just be a moment changing."

Anne snatched a jersey dress and a pair of trendy shoes from her cupboard and popped into the adjacent lavatory to change. She was back within five minutes, giving her hair a flashing comb-out.

"Right, thank you so much for waiting. I'd have been hours late for lunch otherwise. I have no idea what's gone wrong with my car. But I didn't hear middle C, so I took it to the garage straightaway."

"I beg your pardon? Middle C?"

"Why, yes. When a car is running at such a rate that the pistons make two hundred and sixty-one strokes a second, a vibration of frequency two hundred and sixty-one is set up, and one hears a note of pitch middle C in the noise of the engine. That's how I know my car is running properly."

"Musical training comes in handy. You seem young to have taken so many degrees. Written so much."

"I suppose I was something of a prodigy. Somehow I discovered I could solve algebraic equations even before I could talk very plainly. That isn't unnatural, of course: algebra is a language unto itself, but a language of symbols, and no verbalization of problems is necessary."

Anne checked out with the porter at the gate of Paternoster, required procedure for all undergraduates and Fellows now that there was a maniac on the loose. The Inspector drove his own powder-blue Hillman instead of one of the ubiquitous Pandas that belonged to the Valley police. They were quickly on their way to Carfax.

"A man in your profession must enjoy problem solving," Anne said. "Have you ever looked into *Célèbres Problèmes Mathématiques?* I'm sure there must be an edition in English."

"I've never even heard of it."

"It's a puzzle book. All sorts of super brain twisters. Wonderful relaxation."

The Inspector smiled painfully. "I relax in the usual way, I'm afraid. The papers, television, a pint, a bit of music, football. The children on weekends—though I've had precious few of my weekends since this thing began."

"How are you managing to find this murderer? Seems all we get from the *Mail* and the London dailies is the usual load of tat. 'The investigation is proceeding. Leads are being followed up.' "

"That's about all there is to detective work, actually. Interviewing people who might have a shred of useful information."

"Aren't there any vital clues? What's happening in those fabulous crime laboratories we read about in the supplements?"

"Forensic science is often useful, but we've had very little physical evidence to turn over to Scotland Yard. The murderer is one of your exceedingly meticulous psychotics. He's bought no supplies that can be traced, left no marks. Undoubtedly he wears gloves to do the job. We can't say for certain where the murders have been committed."

"Speaking of doing his job, Pretty Joe had had relations with all his victims, hadn't he?"

"Oh, yes. But even though he participated, it was not to his ultimate gratification."

"Couldn't get off without killing them, in other words."

"We think that's the case."

"Is that his motive, then? Psychological impotence drives him round the bend?"

"That's only part of his syndrome, according to the expert testimony we've received."

"But he's bound to make a slip. He can't just go round

plucking women off the street any longer. Everyone in this end of England is too suspicious."

"Suspicious of what?"

"Men. Men one doesn't know."

The Inspector smiled. "What about the men you *do* know?"

"That is a terrible thing to say."

"I'm only saying that if you go round with one eye cocked for someone who strikes you as a bit off, rather odd-looking, then you're missing an important point about this fellow. Pretty Joe, he calls himself. There must be some truth in that. We believe he's a chap who'd be a favorite in any girl's crowd. Very well spoken, terrifically good-looking, all of that. You'd never suspect he was the one till he opted for the knife."

"Think like that, we'll all be bloody paranoid. Looking past our shoulder at every shadow."

"No, he won't suddenly spring out of shadows at you. He's no Jack the Ripper. He's gone to a bit of trouble, at personal risk, to become acquainted with all of his victims. Seems he might have been dating the actress for as long as three weeks before she died."

"Then someone ought to have a fair description of him."

"So far, no. Pretty Joe has had his share of good luck too."

"He must have been hanging around the Shakespeare Theatre that day."

"Yes, he was. The actress left him a comp ticket in her name. We located the couple he sat next to at the matinee. Unfortunately he took his seat after the house lights had dimmed, and he left before the interval."

"How long can this go on?"

"We don't know. It took two years to solve the Cannock Chase murders. I suppose you remember—young girls in Birmingham were being raped and strangled. Fifty thousand men were interviewed before the murderer was found, hiding behind a false alibi. Sex criminals usually repeat themselves. Our chap has a compulsive need to put his victims on display for us, that's one of the nastier aspects of his mania. Possibly Pretty Joe feeds on the thrills that this streak of exhibitionism generates. It may become like a drug to him. If so, perhaps he will make that crucial slip."

"After who knows how many girls have been slaughtered. We've already had refusals from half a dozen top-flight girls we'd hoped to enroll at Paternoster next term."

"Yes, that is a shame. Lot of incidental distress caused by our Joe. We're not at all used to the gaudy crime in these parts; rotten weather's enough for most Oxonians to have to bear. Here we are, the Triple Crown."

"Thank you so much, Inspector. I hope I haven't caused you any delay."

"Not a bit."

"Do let me know as soon as you've heard anything about Mary."

"I shall. Take care."

Kilderbee wasn't quite sure why he'd added the last, but he was feeling quite wistful about the woman on so short an acquaintance. Anne smiled bleakly and hurried through the vertical rain to the lee of the restaurant. She seemed to briefly light up the gray street in passing; you could not be unaware of her, no matter how miserable the rain. The Inspector watched her in the door, envying the chap she'd be lunching with. Then he drove on reluctantly.

"TERRY, DARLING."

"Hullo, Anne. How'd you manage to be on time for once?"

She kissed her brother lightly and sat opposite him on

the padded seat of the banquette. "I hitched a ride with a very nice Inspector of Police, thank you."

"Oh, someone new in your life?"

"As of this morning. Actually he was making an inquiry, one of our girls has turned up missing. No telling yet what it's about, she probably went off somewhere."

"With a proper gentleman, I hope."

"What's happened to your mustache?"

"Good God, I shaved it off long before I flew to the States. Hasn't been that long since we've seen each other."

"Never mind, I do like you this way. That new growth of muttonchop is sufficiently distinguished for a man of your eminence."

"Welcome back, Mr. Camming, delighted to see *you* again, Professor Ramsdell. Will you be having an aperitif?"

"Yes, Otto, and I think we'd best order now, I'm a little cramped for time this afternoon. Sorry, Terry."

"That's all right, I'm still half asleep from the confounded jet lag, or whatever they call it."

"Supersonic flight of long duration disturbs one's circadian cycle. Don't expect to sleep soundly for at least three nights. A glass of Château Chalon, Otto. I believe I'll have the game pie today. Veg? Hmm. Is the asparagus holding up? I don't want to chew my way through a stalky asparagus."

"This week the asparagus is still good, but we've nearly seen the last of it. For you, sir?"

"Whitbread tankard, please. And, I think, a plate of oxtail soup."

"Very good, sir."

Terry lit a cigarette for Anne and she sat back in the seat, beaming at him.

"We have some catching up to do. Tell me about New York. All of it. Is it as unbelievable as I've heard? Did you see anyone throttled in the streets?"

"No. I suppose the violent crime there is worse than London's—at least, it's what everyone in New York talks about. My hosts gave me a map straight off, with certain areas of Manhattan marked out of bounds after dark. Otherwise I went everywhere and saw everything. All the cliché sights, plus the trendy things. Took in an astonishingly good production of *Iphigénie en Tauride*. In Brooklyn, of all places. Do you know the opera?"

"Certainly. First-rate Gluck, for what that's worth. The bass line is stodgy, but some pretty melody—borrowed, I should think. Oh, hell! What are we doing talking about the opera? I want to hear about *Stoner*. Have you settled on an American publisher?"

"I'm letting Simon and Schuster have it. They did a good job with *Perkin,* and they didn't feel I was being either capricious or self-indulgent by wanting to rewrite portions of *Stoner* before the American edition is published. In the meantime they'll bring out my collection of stories, probably this autumn."

"That's super, Terry!"

"Oh, and they took reams of portraits for publicity. I brought some of them back."

Terry opened his attaché case and handed her an envelope containing the photos. Anne looked them over.

"Yes. Excellent. No, not this one, it makes you look too broad and rather contentious. I do like the uncombed look. That's a winning smile, my lad. Where is this you're posing? With the fountain and the huge buildings all around?"

"It's called a 'vest pocket' park. Untold millions' worth of midtown real estate used for lunching or just lying about in the sun. New York has some rather sublime touches, actually, despite the general air of mendacity and the celebrated rudeness. There's the shot goes on the dust cover."

"What is it they say? 'You should be in pitchers, sweetheart. I could make you a star.'"

Terry winced. "I think we've both had enough show biz in our lives."

"Merely joking, darling. Did you have the opportunity to look over Kingman College?"

"I flew down and spent two days there."

"And?"

"Rather nice country. Reminded me of the Tyrol. Their mountains are called the Smokies. Highly descriptive. And the people are grand. They talk—very—slowly—lahk—this, and they're just so—*pleased*—to—meetcha, hope—you're—gonna—*injoy*—your—visit?"

Anne laughed. "Does the situation appeal?"

"I've no idea. The teaching wouldn't be a problem—seminar once a week. Loads of free time to work. I looked over some manuscripts that undergraduates have turned out for the other fellow—a good bit of talent lurking there. It could be—I just don't know."

Anne placed a hand on his. "*I* think it could be just what you're wanting. At the very best it means a stimulating change of scene for a year. Time to forget about the play and the stupid notices. Time to make a start on something new."

At the age of twenty-nine Terry had two highly successful novels to his credit, the first of which had become a famous film. His small percentage of the film's profits to date had earned him close to fifty thousand pounds. And one of the more sought-after young British film makers was currently scripting *Stoner* for a fall start.

With largely glowing notices behind him, Terry had attempted his first play. It was nearly a year in the writing. He then spent several weeks seeing his play through rehearsal at the New Theatre in Oxford, where the trial run was encouraging. More rewriting followed; then came the West End opening.

It turned out to be one of those plays—and there is at least one every season—that encounters its critics in their worst possible humor. Every flaw was dissected with a meat-ax; the good in the play was passed off with some remarkably obfuscatory writing. Foxgrove of the *Evening Standard*: "He has created characters of mysterious substance, steered them with Pinterish reticence through the emotional icebergs that inhabit his stage. His scenes throb with the perdurable terrors of the mediocre and the never-was; there are glints of agonized humor. Talent, yes, there is talent at work here; it all but overfills the stage. Yet Mr. Camming has not managed an effective play."

Foxgrove never did get around to saying why not. Perhaps he had fallen asleep at his typewriter, just as he'd fallen asleep during the second act of *Half Hour*. A couple of the grayer deans had taken exception to what they thought was an unnecessarily destructive portrait of Terry's mother, Marian Holgate. And so it went.

Terry was unused to this kind of treatment; the vitriol had burned deep. Despite Anne's best efforts he had floundered lately. One novel abandoned for good, another try at a play not working out. The invitation to become writer in residence at Kingman College had arrived at a welcome time, Anne thought, and the enthusiasm with which his American publishers had received him seemed to have worked a great deal of good. Before his trip he'd been so down in the mouth of fame (Keats?) that some of the gayer birds of Oxford had been unable to cheer him for any length of time.

"When must you let them know?" she asked Terry over dessert.

"I have a week," Terry said without enthusiasm. From the set of his jaw Anne knew it was not the time to be powerfully persuasive.

"Terry, I'm having a little rave tonight. Mark and his new pash, the Chaucer scholar. And Paul, of course."

"How is Paul?"

"Maddeningly inconsistent."

"Unlike yourself. How do you really feel about him?"

"I adore him. In spurts. Anyway, I'm preparing one of my fiery curries. You must come."

"Backgammon after?"

"Of course. We'll play a chouette. Unless the majority opts for poker."

"Everyone in Oxford knows better than to play poker

with you. I can't say what my chances are of bringing a date on short notice."

"Get on. Madeleine's mooning about the library today, and she asked me twice during her tutorial yesterday when I thought you might be returning. Write a note quickly and I'll see she has it within the hour. Shall we say eight o'clock?"

"All right, love. Madeleine and I will be prompt."

JORAM THORNTON AWOKE from her Valium-induced sleep with a dry throat and a sodden feeling of desperation. Her room was dark; outside a gust of wind drove rain against the windows.

As she listened she heard another sound—glass breaking in the depths of the house.

She sat up, groped for the table lamp and switched it on. She looked at the clock: quarter to six. At three she'd retired to her room with an aching head and a rare case of nerves.

"Hugh?" she called, her voice croaking. To her disgust she sounded like an old lady. She cleared her throat to try again, glancing at the bedroom door. She'd closed it before lying down. Now the door was standing open. Joram still tingled from her abrupt awakening; the tingling was excited by fear. She pushed the comforter aside, a little clumsy in her movements, and got off the bed.

"Hugh? Are you downstairs?"

Joram listened; no reply.

She went cautiously to the door and looked toward Hugh's room. No lights on there, no sounds from the bath. The gloom of dusk in the house further unnerved her. She switched on the hall light over head.

Another fugitive sound; from the kitchen this time? It

might have been a chair or a stool being shoved a few inches across the tiles. Mrs. Merton had left a little before three with a rapidly swelling jaw and a tooth that needed quick attention. She would not have come back. Joram had locked all doors soon after Mrs. Merton's departure.

But there *was* someone in the house; Joram could feel his presence as accurately as a clairvoyant senses a poltergeist. The breaking glass: that meant— For a few moments Joram was too shocked to move. Then she grabbed control, went directly to Hugh's room and opened the top drawer of the wardrobe. She took out a loaded Walther automatic.

Joram had virtually been born with a hunting rifle in her hands, and she knew she was at least competent with the lightweight Walther. It was all Hugh had been able to come up with in England. He'd checked her out with it behind their rented cottage in the Cotswolds. There was one peculiarity of the hand gun he'd warned her about. Oh, yes, it would jam if she held the trigger back too long.

Joram turned on the light above the back stairs and walked down two flights to the kitchen, taking her time. To steady herself she had conjured the image of a quail hunt on the gold-and-umber plains of central Texas. Daddy to her right, Uncle Cal to her left, the brown-spotted dogs coursing out in front . . . Naow, honey, soon as you see that ol' whitetail bird flush cover you get the gun up to your shoulder. Be smooth. Look for him to break either right or left. Then you nail him. Make that first shot count.

Did the Walther have sufficient power to knock a man down? Probably not. But a well-placed slug would give him plenty to think about.

The kitchen was empty. Joram glanced at the pantry, but her full attention was already focusing on the back door to the kitchen. It stood open an inch. From outside she heard the rain muffled sound of the E-type Jaguar's engine. She hurried to the door, all but forgetting the gun in her hand.

She had a glimpse of the red car through the hedges and the rain. Then it was gone.

So it had been Hugh after all. The glass in the kitchen door was intact, and the door had been unlocked. There were only three sets of keys to the house. All accounted for.

The brick path through the garden was covered with sediment. Joram turned on the outdoor flood and saw rain pooling in the mucky footprints. He'd wiped his feet before coming in, but—Joram closed and locked the door again and looked at the kitchen tiles. He'd tracked everywhere. To the sink. To the foot of the stairs. Hugh was not ordinarily so thoughtless. So either he'd come in drunk, or in such a confused state of mind that—

She couldn't frame a reasonable alternative. She followed his tracks to the ground-floor drawing room. The Scotch was out on the bar. He had made himself a drink and carried it to the foyer.

In the foyer Joram found shattered glass on the parquet, smelled the spilled Scotch. Ice cubes had been carelessly kicked aside. *What in God's name?* More traces of mud on the stairs to the third floor. Water from his raincoat hadn't yet soaked into the pile carpeting just inside her door. So he'd come up to see her, and found her sleeping. Why hadn't he awakened her, then? Instead he had gone back down the stairs, where apparently he had lost his grip on his glass.

And when she called, instead of answering he all but ran through the kitchen and ducked out.

Joram sat on the edge of the bed, placing the Walther on the night table. She felt far from secure, but a different kind of insecurity plagued her now. Hugh's behavior was incomprehensible. With the remote-control unit she turned on the television set, found a newscast to keep her company. It was easier for her to think against a background of human voices.

Well, he'd just had it, that was all. He'd been living at much too fast a pace, and some sort of binge was inevitable. For some reason he felt he couldn't face her. She dreaded the thought of Hugh driving around in all this rain in an unstable condition, but his excellent reflexes usually came to his aid even when his mind no longer worked well.

Sooner or later he would be back. There was nothing she could do but wait and make the best of it.

Joram cleaned up the mess in the foyer, then busied herself. She had a drink and a long bath, and another drink. She did her nails and tried her hair a different way. She ate a little something.

After the third drink her mind clicked into the groove she'd sought. She sat before the gas-log fire in the drawing room and read Thucydides in Greek with rapt attention and did her best to ignore the slow passage of time.

THEY'D BEEN INDUSTRIOUSLY digging in Eversedge Road for a fortnight, which meant the nearest parking was two hundred yards away. Inconvenient at any time, but all the rain made it a damned ordeal getting from car to doorstep, particularly with shopping bags. Anne had additional problems managing her umbrella in the feisty wind; she was soaked and fuming by the time she backed into the foyer of the Victorian house where she lived.

"Oh, Isobel! Sorry, dear, didn't see you standing there. Did I give you a poke?"

"No, I'm all right. Still perfectly foul out there, I see."

Isobel McCarry was an editor with the University Press; she lived with her mother in the flat below Anne's. She was a sunny dark-eyed girl who concealed complexity with openheartedness and a classy smile, but tonight Isobel looked unexpectedly sickened, or weary.

Anne took in the travel togs and the suitcases. "Going on holiday?"

The girl smiled wanly. "Yes. I had a week coming, so I decided to take it now. Have you been to Sardinia?"

"Oh, the Costa Smeralda. You'll have a super time."

"Really? That's encouraging. I only hope my flight isn't scrubbed."

"Who'll be looking after your mum? Is there anything I can do?"

"She's in hospital for more of her tests."

"Oh, that is a shame."

"I'm certain it's nothing serious this time either. Thanks awfully, Anne. Where could that cab be?"

Anne collapsed her umbrella and picked up her groceries. "I'd better strip these wet things and get cracking. Have fun, Isobel."

"Certainly shall," the girl said, looking even more doleful. She wasn't in the proper spirit to start a holiday, and Anne felt sorry for her. The rotten weather couldn't account for all of her mood; perhaps it was man trouble. But there was nothing like a week in the Med sun to chase the blues. Nor would she lack for company once she arrived, not with her looks.

Anne trudged up the stairs. She could hear the phone ringing behind the door of her flat as she arrived at the top floor.

She set the groceries aside, plumbed for her keys, unlocked the door, ran inside, grabbed the phone off the hook, gasped, "Yes, do hold on, I'll be right there," returned to the landing outside, picked up her armload of groceries and struggled in, giving the door a kick behind her. She carried the groceries to the kitchen and made a dash to the phone. It was about her typewriter. They'd repaired it and she could claim it anytime, thank you, missus.

"Thank *you*," Anne said, hanging up. She glared at

her bedraggled image in the pier glass but paused long enough to drink a pint of stout from the pantry before cleaning up.

With the flat below her empty, Anne felt at liberty to play David Oistrakh and company as loudly as she wished on her quad speakers. She adjusted the volume, shed her clothes and plunged into a tepid bath. Right, time to complain about the pipes again. Wasn't often she craved a really hot soak, but when she did she wanted it *steaming*. . . . She forgot her displeasure and succumbed to the *portamento* she adored. Ravishing—wasn't he a frigging genius, though? Perhaps, if the curry didn't take forever, she'd have a blissful hour with her own violin before the first arrivals. It had to be Brahms tonight. She had definitely been seduced—right there in her own bath—by David Oistrakh.

Despite all the steps she had to climb, Anne liked her flat for the unobstructed view of the river and meadow from her bedroom windows, and particularly for a spacious kitchen. At one end of the kitchen there was a breakfast alcove and a single floor-to-ceiling window that overlooked a formal garden and an oval pool teeming with trout-size goldfish in its ferny shallows. On rare mornings when she had the leisure to sit and eat a proper breakfast she could look almost directly down into the pool and see the orange fish gliding about, oblivious of the tabby who spent *his* mornings tracking them from the concrete rim of the pool.

As soon as she was out of the tub Anne spent half an hour in the kitchen preparing the prawns for boiling. She washed her hands in baking soda to get rid of the fishiness, then set her table for dinner.

The dining area was off to itself in one corner of a thirty-foot living room, convenient to the kitchen. With an hour to go until dinner, she began to chill the scarce Clos Blanc de Vougeot, which she had belatedly decided was the perfect wine to serve with her curry. Half a dozen calls had failed to turn up Clos Blanc de Vougeot at any of the off-license shops, so she'd coaxed a bottle from the cellar of an oenophilic friend.

Now. Only the mellow glow of candlelight would inspire a suitably cozy mood on such a night. Anne dialed the rheostats as low as possible and brought out a hoard of candlesticks collected from half a dozen countries. By the time she had them in place, candles lit, it was nearly seven thirty.

Anne might deliberate over a selection of vintages for the better part of an afternoon, but she detested buying clothes and usually accepted the first thing the shop assistant handed her when she walked through the door. She'd been known to wear ancient hand-me-downs from second cousins or something out of one of her mother's theatrical trunks. Somehow she managed to look as if she had a designer stashed away, lavishing his genius on no one but Anne Ramsdell. As for her hair, she washed it when it was dirty and cut it when it needed cutting; occasionally, in a fit of concern on a formal occasion, she did something artful with pins or old-fashioned combs. Tonight she couldn't be bothered. She was concerned about rushing the curry sauce and botching it.

She was hurrying from her bedroom to the kitchen when the heavy front door flew open and smashed against the wall, scaring her silly. A couple of candles guttered and were blown out by the draft from the stairwell.

As soon as she was over her fright Anne realized what had happened. She remembered giving the door a careless kick behind her upon arriving home and hurrying to the telephone. Obviously the door hadn't latched properly then, and as soon as someone else came in from the street with a good gust of wind behind him the resulting pressure from the updraft pushed her door open.

Anne listened. The dentist who lived on the ground floor was home, already bellowing at his poor wife. Anne caught her breath and shut her door. Firmly, this time. She continued to be shaky until she had thrown the dead bolt home and put on the chain for good measure.

Excellent way to be murdered in your bed, she thought, and smiled. She relit the candles that had blown out, put Ars Antiqua Paris on the hi-fi, picked up her apron from the back of a chair. Her mind was on the curry sauce again.

She was tying the apron behind her when she shouldered open the kitchen door and ran right into the man standing inside.

Anne had a first awful impression of bigness, of the shining wetness of his hat and coat, of the light reflecting from one staring eye; then she screamed. He cut her off in mid-scream, grabbing her with one hand, stifling her with the other.

"You miserable cunt!" he said.

She got him almost simultaneously in the groin with her knee and in the face with a stiffened thumb. The thumb missed his eye by a fraction, but caused him to jerk his head aside. Pain loosened his grip, and Anne pivoted, throwing a hip into him, trying for the *harai-goshi*. But they were both seriously off-balance, and he was able to grab her by the hair. He fell back against a counter with her, recovered first, hammered her ear with his fist. Anne screamed again with the pain of a ruptured eardrum and tried to shake him with a thrown elbow; he absorbed the blow and clung to her tenaciously, used all his strength to slam her against the sharp corner of the counter. A rib broke and Anne almost fainted from the pain. The fight went out of her. As her hands dropped powerlessly she had tearful glimpse of him lunging at her, tried to duck and was smashed across the face. The blow was hard enough to drive her to the sink on the other side of the kitchen. She buckled there, clinging to the lip of the sink with one hand. An eye was swelling fast, there was blood on her lip and blood in her aching ear. She saw the chopper sharp and cold and angled into the cutting board and knew he was coming up fast behind her.

The pain of the broken rib shortened her swing and

spoiled her aim with the chopper; otherwise she might have buried it between his eyes. But she was able to strike with enough force to sever the fourth and fifth fingers of his left hand and cut deeply into the middle finger.

The shock of hitting him caused Anne to drop the chopper. When she reached for it, he knocked her head back with a quick slap, grabbed her by the front of her high-necked blouse, used his forearms for leverage and jerked her off the floor, choking her as he did so. Blood spurted in her face. Despite the murderous choking, the loss of blood to the brain, she was aware of being carried, aware of the big window just behind them.

Her last conscious thought was the conviction that he couldn't possibly do this thing to her, and then he did it, he hurled her through the window. She fell backward, spread-eagled, in a jagged spray of smashed panes, fell out into the rain without a scream and was gone.

THE BLOOD—OH, God, the blood! What was he going to do about the blood?

He backed away from the shattered window. Rain was streaming in, he could hear shouts in the dark. *What was it, what was it? Imagined I heard someone screaming and then a crash. Did you hear anything, Mrs. Oorthuys?*

He pulled his handkerchief from an inside pocket and wound it around the stumps on his left hand, jammed the hand deeply into the pocket of his trench coat. All right for now, but he felt on the verge of blacking out as he stumbled toward the sink. How could he have been so stupid, panicked so completely? The blood was bad enough, all over the kitchen probably, but he had to have his fingers back. He sank to his knees to search the floor by the light that came in beneath the swinging door.

Couldn't risk turning on a kitchen light now, in another couple of minutes the entire neighborhood would turn out. Get out of there, get out fast!

He located the chopper first, awkwardly unbuttoned his coat and slipped it, handle down, inside his belt. He saw one of the fingers lying nearby and snatched it up, putting it into the other pocket of his trench coat. But there was still the little finger. Oh, the bitch——Christ, she almost killed him! Find the other finger, or you're as good as dead.

At least two dogs were barking harshly, and a woman screamed tremulously, like an octogenarian soprano trying to recall what it was like to hit her top notes. *Oh, my God——look there, there in the pool!*

Ring immediately for an ambulance, Mrs. Oorthuys! Mr. Ross, give me a hand here, sir!

Look up there, the window's all smashed——that's where she come from!

With the back of his hand he wiped perspiration from his clammy forehead. As far as he could tell, the missing finger wasn't on the floor, but he couldn't see clearly any more——shock, he supposed. He stood up and tried to reconstruct the chain of events. She'd chopped at him from this direction, his hand had been raised like so. The finger might well have traveled several feet toward the sink. He looked in the sink, then overturned a bowl of cooked rice, and there it was, curled in with the rice like a fat white shrimp. He grabbed the finger and ran, sobbing in fear.

He was done for anyway, he thought. They couldn't miss the bloodstains. His was a common blood type, but if they had enough fresh blood to work with, the serologists could break it down into subgroups and isolate various factors, thus drastically narrowing down a choice of suspects. Still, he had to keep moving, try to think on his feet, save his skin somehow.

Just make it as far as the car, then there might be a chance.

He'd expected to find the stairs crowded with concerned neighbors beating a path to the top floor, but there wasn't a sound when he cracked the door. He crept as far as the railing and looked below. He saw no one. His good luck gave him the incentive to fight off the nausea and dizziness that was threatening to overpower him and to make his way down the rubber-treaded stairs.

Second floor, ground floor—the foyer was just ahead of him.

Telly was playing in the ground floor flat and the door was slightly ajar. He had to pass it to get to the foyer door, and anyone looking out would surely see him. But there was no time to waste; they'd have heard him on the stairs if they were listening very hard.

So he walked boldly past the door, risking a glance inside as he went by. No one was there—apparently most of the tenants in this and the surrounding buildings were either in the garden or peering out their rear windows. An umbrella hung from the doorknob and he helped himself to it, opened the foyer door, walked through, opened the outer door.

No letup in the rain. Yellow warning lights winked muzzily atop the barricades in the dug-up street. There were no houses on the opposite side of Eversedge Road, only a meadow and then the river. He had difficulty getting the umbrella up with only one hand, but he managed. He walked down the steps and leaned into the wind, keeping the brolly between himself and the row of lighted windows on his right as he continued down the footpath, in no appreciable hurry.

He was listening hard for the first gongs. Dial 999 and scream into the phone a bit, police would be on their way in sixty seconds. But it was unlikely they'd throw a net around North Oxford until they had the drift of the situation. He had to keep his mind firmly fixed on the likelihood of escape.

Say, three more minutes—in three minutes he could be well clear of the area.

He had to stop to vomit in the gutter, and the ordeal left him with next to no physical reserve. By the time he had stumbled the last long yards to his car he heard them coming. He sat inside in the dark, shuddering, heart palpitating, pains shooting up his left arm, and watched in the mirror as the police car went by. Seconds later it was followed by an ambulance.

He started his own car and pulled away from the curb, drove up the street at a timid pace. Unused to driving with one arm, he had to control a tendency to oversteer. Another police car, silent, blue dome lights revolving, hurtled around the turn just ahead, almost skidded on the wet tarmac, then roared past him. He was breathing heavily now through his mouth, hyperventilating. The car radio was on and a female vocalist was crooning something absurdly sentimental, a dance-band number from the forties. He couldn't let go of the wheel long enough to turn it off.

His main concern now was shock, not panic. He knew he wasn't going to bleed to death, but the possibility of adrenal exhaustion was equally dangerous. The lights of oncoming cars seemed to float up to him and his depth perception was unreliable. He might have been flying the car instead of driving it. He just wanted to head in to the curb and fall asleep.

He cut off the Banbury at St. Margaret's, turned right into Woodstock. More than a mile to the A-40 round-about. In his lucid moments he had conceived a plan that seemed very nearly foolproof—*watch the truck!*

Straying over the center line had almost resulted in a collision, but the hooting of the truck's air horn snapped him wide awake.

Time to get rid of the umbrella. He had almost forgotten about it.

There was no other way to manage, he had to hold the wheel steady with his mutilated hand while he cranked the window down and shoved the brolly out. If it lay in the roadway long enough oncoming traffic would rip it to shreds.

Thank God he'd had the presence of mind to bring the chopper along. The chopper was next. *Then* let them try to prove he'd been in the girl's flat.

He'd left the offside window partway down and the rain was pelting in, wetting his face. It helped, but as the roundabout and the Medley turnoff appeared, his vision was dimming again; he felt insatiably drowsy. He began to shout at himself.

"JUST FIVE MORE MINUTES! STAY AWAKE, YOU BASTARD!"

He was across the Oxford Canal almost before he knew it; the bridge across the Thames lay just ahead. It meant stopping in the middle of the bridge to be sure of his aim, but traffic in both directions was light. Changing hands on the wheel again, he worked the chopper from under his coat, nicking his thumb in the process.

Then he was on the bridge, slowing. He couldn't see a thing out there in the dark, but all he had to do was throw the chopper straight and hard, and the river would take care of it. He thought he heard the splash just before he drove on.

Now the dangerous part; there was no way to plan the outcome. But it couldn't be any more dangerous than what he'd already been through—in serious hazard all risks seemed equal.

And if he didn't make it—better than spending the rest of his life in prison.

Lap strap in place? Yes. *Go*.

As the narrow road began to climb toward the village of Medley he stepped on the accelerator. A normally safe speed on these turns was thirty miles an hour; he pushed the Jaguar to forty, forty-five, half a ton. There was a box junction coming up, a wide place in the road. The lights of a cottage winked by off to his right. To his left Sunderland Hill rose steeply, almost from the verge.

He felt the back end of the car going mushy as he gunned around the last curve of the intersection. He stood on the gas again, cut the wheel hard left and held it there, jumped his foot to the brake and rode it.

The Jaguar is a particularly well-engineered car that holds the road in most crucial situations, but this was asking too much of it. The resulting shunt was spectacular. The Jaguar slewed completely around in the intersection, tires screaming, crashed through a low stone wall and the hedge behind it, and plunged into an apple orchard on the other side. The car then rolled over hard, rolled three times down an embankment studded with limestone outcroppings, and came to rest at a thirty-degree slant in a stream bed, pointed toward the road, headlights illuminating the tops of apple trees and the needle-flecked sky beyond.

He smelled the engine and felt its heat; he was afraid of fire. The steering wheel was nearly against his chest. He unbuckled the lap strap, found the offside door crushed and jammed, the window shattered. He fumbled for the cut-off fingers in his pocket, dropped them out the window.

It was too late now, but he thought of his wedding band. Third finger, left hand.

The cut had come below the ring, else the thickness of gold would have deflected the blade. But was the ring still on the finger, or was it on the floor of the kitchen back there in Eversedge Road?

He had to roll down the nearside window and squeeze through it to get out of the car. For some reason, having come through the accident alive, he began to laugh. He crawled up the embankment, laughing hysterically, sprawling full length many times. By the time he had struggled up to the road he was mud head to foot.

He crawled through the gap in the hedge and wall and sat down with his back against the stone, too exhausted to go another foot.

A car was coming up the grade; its headlights would sweep the wall and they would see him. He closed his eyes, holding his mangled hand inside his coat, and waited, no longer really caring what happened to him.

KILDERBEE HAD BEEN spending a not altogether pleasant evening at home, going over the household accounts because his wife had made a botch of them again. Kilderbee's youngest, Richard, was in his third day of Never Speaking to Him Again, because they'd planned for weeks to attend the Air Fair at Biggin Hill on Sunday, and at the last instant Kilderbee had been unable to get away. So he wasn't too disapointed to answer the phone and hear the voice of Detective Sergeant Beer.

"Well, he's been at it again, sir."

"Where?"

"In Eversedge Road. This time it looks as though he may have bungled the job."

Kilderbee felt a jolt of excitement, and it took a lot to get him excited. "She's alive?"

"Was when she went out of here not five minutes gone. Unconscious, though—in rather a bad way."

"Still, if she's able to talk at all, it's a classic break for us. Area sealed?"

"Yes, sir, we're inquiring house to house now. So far no one's seen a thing. Our bloke may have skipped frame."

"Very likely. Car on the way?"

"Should be at your door in a moment, sir."

"Who was the victim?"

"Woman named Ramsdell. Fellow of Paternoster College."

"Good God!"

"Sir?"

"That's all right, Sergeant. Freak of chance—I happened to interview her about a related matter just this morning. I want DC's in hospital standing by with a tape recorder. Have someone in the operating theatre with her if possible. Seal the infirmary grounds with uniformed police. He may realize he's done a bad job this time and attempt to remedy his mistake."

JORAM THORNTON WAS fast asleep by the gas-log fire when the doorbell aroused her. She sat up on the settee in the drawing room, the heavy volume of Thucydides falling to the floor. She looked at her wristwatch and saw that it was five minutes past nine.

The bell again.

She hurried out to the foyer, saw the silhouette of a uniformed man on the curtain that covered the glass to one side of the door. She turned on the outside light and said without opening the door, "Yes, what is it?"

"Thames Valley police, mum."

Joram pulled the curtain aside, looked past him at the police car in the street. She opened the door on the chain.

"Mrs. Hugh Thornton?"

"Yes—"

"I'm sorry to have to inform you that your husband has been in an automobile accident."

"Dear Lord."

"Do you have a way of getting to Radcliffe Infirmary, Mrs. Thornton?"

"Infirmary? He's—"

"Your husband suffered a rather severe injury to his left hand. Otherwise I reckon he'll be all right. The car is a loss, I'm afraid. If you'd care to come with us, we'll see you go to the right place. Hospital does ramble a bit if you've never been there."

"I'm—not dressed. But I'll only be a moment."

"Right, take your time, we'll wait."

She dressed in a daze, trying to construct something solid from the straws of information she'd been given. Crashed the car. Hurt. Not too seriously. Not . . . too . . . seriously.

The rain had stopped, and when she glanced up outside she could see the full moon through thinning inky clouds. Joram got into the back of the police car and they drove away.

"How did it happen?" she asked the constable.

"Apparently he misjudged a turn in the Medley Road. Brakes locked and he went into a skid. Happened in the box junction below Medley village. Are you familiar with the road?"

"Yes, we go to Medley quite often. The pub there, it's one of Hugh's favorites."

"The George and Dragon. Is that where he was going tonight?"

"He—" Joram hesitated only a moment, but it flashed through her mind that whatever she might say at this time could prove to be of critical importance later. There'd been no mention of another car involved in the accident, but it was possible that Hugh was in serious trouble. She decided to lie, and hope for the best.

"Yes. Hugh worked on his manuscript for nearly two hours after supper. My husband is a historian. He said he wanted to run up to Medley for a nightcap—we often do that. But I was translating Thucydides, and I've been feeling run-down lately, so I begged off."

"And what time did your husband leave the house?"

"Oh, it must have been—I think a little before eight." Joram paused, wondering if that was the right answer. The constable wrote it down without comment.

"Was—was anyone else involved in the accident?"

"No, good job he had the road to himself." The constable closed the book he'd been writing in. "Thank you, Mrs. Thornton. We're attempting to get an accurate idea of when the accident occured."

"When did you find Hugh?"

"First notification of the accident was received at eight twelve. We were on the scene three minutes later."

"Oh, I see."

"Bleeding maniac's got loose," the constable behind the wheel murmured.

"Excuse me?" Joram said nervously.

"I was listening to the police calls, mum. Lot of excitement tonight. Pretty Joe struck again."

"That's dreadful. Where did it happen?"

"Eversedge Road. Got himself a don this time."

"A woman?"

"Oh, yes, it's always a woman. She's not dead, however."

"Infirmary was bloody bedlam," the other constable said. "Coppers all over. You all right, mum?"

"Yes. Just a little queasy."

"Harry, drive a bit slower on these turns, can't you?"

Harry steered the car through a gate and down a narrow passage and arrived at the accident department of Radcliffe Infirmary.

"You'll find him inside, Mrs. Thornton."

"Thank you, you've been very kind."

Joram hurried in through the ambulance bay, past two constables standing guard at the entrance. A brisk, smiling receptionist intercepted Joram before she got very far. Joram explained. The receptionist looked up the particulars.

"He's in the operating theatre just upstairs, Mrs. Thornton. Dr. Sheely is in charge."

"Can you tell me how badly he was injured?"

"Your husband was admitted suffering from shock and loss of blood. Two fingers of his left hand were amputated in the accident."

"Oh, God. Poor Hugh."

"Is there someone you'd like me to telephone?"

"I—no, I can't think of anyone. How long will it be until I can see Hugh?"

"Shouldn't be too long. If you'd like to wait in our lounge, I'll let you know the moment he's out of the operating theatre."

"Will he be in a public ward tonight, or do you have rooms?"

"We have semiprivate rooms in the building next door. Shall I make that arrangement for you, Mrs. Thornton?"

"Yes, thank you." Joram was only dimly aware of the activity around her, of the paging calls, the wailing of a child, the atmosphere of muted tension caused by the presence of Pretty Joe's latest. She felt a little faint; the receptionist put a bracing arm around her.

"Can you cope? Would you like to lie down?"

"No, I'll be all right."

"There's coffee in the lounge, if you'd care to have some?"

"All right."

The receptionist escorted her to the lounge. Joram searched her purse for change and dropped fivepence into the vending machine, and helped herself. The lounge was painted cream and green, and there were leprous spots of patching plaster on the walls. Framed prints of English country life didn't help much. But Joram knew that Radcliffe Infirmary was, despite its dowdy appearance, one of the great hospitals of the world. Penicillin had been discovered and first used here; the English Thalidomide babies had been brought to the hospital to be taught the use of their artificial limbs.

Joram wandered down the corridor sipping coffee. She noticed the constables again. The two by the entrance were in consultation with a plainclothesman, and outside the accident department there was some sort of row developing. More police helmets bobbed outside, and she glimpsed a man with a camera. The press had arrived.

A don this time, Joram thought, wondering if they

might be acquainted with her. That made four victims . . .
But there was a chance this woman would live.

She felt very sorry for Pretty Joe's intended victim,
but at the moment she could concentrate only on Hugh.
Two fingers gone—how would that affect his rowing? He
despised any kind of physical imperfection, wouldn't even
wear the glasses he needed to make his writing easier.
What a terrible shock this would be to Hugh.

But he was alive; he would be needing her, and that
was all Joram cared about.

THINGS HAD GONE seriously awry for Pretty Joe tonight;
that was obvious to Inspector Kilderbee as soon as he
arrived on the scene.

From the kitchen door of the flat he took in the
smashed window and the quantity of coagulating blood,
which a member of the forensic team was carefully gathering in glassine envelopes for serological analysis.

"What time did it happen?" he asked Sergeant Beer.

"Approximately seven thirty-eight P.M. this evening,
according to the key-holder, Mrs. Grimes. She lives with
her husband in the ground-floor flat."

"Do you have a report from the infirmary on Professor Ramsdell's condition?"

"Preliminary examination reveals she was severely
beaten about the face and head. She has a possibly severe
concussion, a fractured elbow, and a dislocated neck,
which is giving the most concern. She was also cut in a
number of places on the body—"

"Cut with a knife?"

"It was the opinion of the examining physicians that
most if not all of the cuts were caused by glass. The
nature of the wounds, you see, and their location—"

"Arthur," Kilderbee said to one of the detectives, "have you come up with a knife?"

"Kitchen's full of them. But not the type he's used before."

"Tag all sharp objects for examination. Will it be all right if we walk through?"

"Yes, sir, as long as you remain on the mat."

Kilderbee made his way to the window and looked down. There were droves of detectives and PC's in the garden. A neighbor was complaining that the activity was disturbing his pigeons. One detective, wearing a scuba diver's wet suit, was carefully searching the fish pool with a powerful underwater light. From other windows overlooking the block of gardens neighbors solemnly watched the police at work. But, as usual, the Inspector noted with a slight smile, some of them had their backs turned on the drama at their doorsteps and were glued to telly.

"What do you think about all this, Sergeant Beer?"

"If Professor Ramsdell had fallen through the window, or merely been pushed, odds are she would have landed on the cobbles directly beneath, or on the apron of the pool. And that surely would have been fatal."

"So the bastard picked her up and threw her out. She must have been unconscious or quite seriously dazed from the beating to allow that to happen to her."

"Unless he's an exceptionally strong man."

"He'd have to be, regardless. Professor Ramsdell is a well-endowed woman. I'd estimate five feet nine and about nine stone six." The Inspector looked over his shoulder. "This is what I make of it. They struggled back there, where the blood is. Yet apparently he didn't slash her with the knife he favors. Perhaps he tried, but she was too nimble for him. I don't believe she could have wrenched Pretty Joe's knife away from him without being cut, but she must have stuck him with something. Let's assume we're looking for a wounded man, and his wounds may need swift attention. Pass that on, Sergeant. Arthur, marks yet?"

"Nothing, sir."

"Don't neglect the undersides of the cabinets. I'll talk to the dinner guests now, Sergeant. Whom do we have waiting out there?"

Sergeant Beer consulted his notebook. "A Mr. Terry Camming, brother of the victim. His date for the evening, Madeleine Asquith, undergraduate of Paternoster College. Mr. Mark Elmes and his date, Charlotte Robsart. The unattached gentleman who has been to the loo twice because of a nervous stomach was Professor Ramsdell's intended date. His name is Paul Southard. They were invited for eight o'clock."

"The table is set for six persons. Which suggests Pretty Joe was *not* invited for eight o'clock."

The sergeant's lip curled. "Perhaps he was invited to tea and overstayed."

"I wonder."

In the living room Kilderbee introduced himself to Professor Ramsdell's guests, four of whom were seated in a row on the sofa by the fireplace. Paul Southard was standing by himself, a glass of Scotch in one hand. He looked ill and scared. Kilderbee sized him up immediately: the hearty fun-loving sort, always ready to give a party a lift and undoubtedly a lusty bloke in bed. But not dependable when it came to a crunch; he must have been the first to reach for the bottle.

"Inspector," Terry said, "I'd like to get to hospital as quickly as possible."

"Of course. This won't take but a few moments. Are you very close to your sister?"

"I'd say so."

"Where might we find Professor Ramsdell's ex-husband?"

"In Sydney, Australia. For the past six years he's been Associate Head of the Anthropology Department in the university."

"Was the divorce amicable?"

"Yes, entirely. Anne married very young, and they both

soon realized the marriage just wasn't a go." Terry was answering as civilly as he could, but his face was white and the cords of his neck stood out from tension.

"It *was* Pretty Joe, wasn't it?" the young lady known as Madeleine said almost inaudibly. The other couple clung to each other and stared at the floor.

"That is our assumption. These are routine questions that must be asked. Mr. Camming, do you think you could give me the names of all the men whom your sister has been seeing socially?"

At that Paul Southard's head came up. He took a quick swallow from his glass. Terry looked at him, then away. Didn't care for the chap at all, Kilderbee noted.

"Other than Paul here, men have always come and gone. Very few repeaters."

"Anyone in the past two or three weeks she might have taken a particular shine to?"

Terry shook his head. "I've been away for three weeks. In the States. I just returned yesterday noon."

"Well, perhaps she can tell us herself in a few hours," the Inspector said encouragingly.

Madeleine said, "D'you think Anne actually knew him?"

"Of course—how else would he have gotten in?" Charlotte Robsart said.

Terry stood up. "I'd really like to be on my way if . . ."

"Yes, quite all right."

"Inspector?"

"Yes, Mr. Southard?"

"There are news chaps outside. With cameras."

"I passed them on the way in."

"Would it be possible—" He wet his lips and met Terry's astringent gaze, then looked into his glass. "I'd like to avoid all the commotion, don't you know? The photographers . . ."

"And you don't fancy seeing your name in the paper either."

"No. I'm in a position that requires me to be—most sensitive about publicity."

Oh, got a wife stashed away, Kilderbee thought. Little nest egg in jeopardy, perhaps. "Constable!" he barked at the nearest PC.

"Sir!"

"Mr. Camming and his party are leaving for Radcliffe Infirmary. See to it that they have an impenetrable escort. There will be no words exchanged with members of the press and no photographs will be taken. Suggest an exit through the ground-floor rear, then out the front door of the flat nearest the corner."

The Inspector saw them out, then returned to survey the kitchen.

He felt elated, properly nerved up for the long night ahead. In fact, he was tingling like a dice player who has come up with a hot hand. After months of dogged work, finally they were going to knock him off. If the Ramsdell woman didn't die on them—and it seemed likely she would survive her injuries—then, by God, Pretty Joe would have to sprout wings to escape Oxford undetected!

And yet—

As he silently watched the forensic team at work, searching every inch of the kitchen for the minutest trace of their man, his policeman's instinct told him something was out of pattern, something was subtly wrong here.

It managed to worry him without appreciably cooling his enthusiasm.

"HUGH."

In the dim light Joram saw his eyelids flutter. She leaned closer to the bed.

On the other side of the opaque curtain that separated

them from the rest of the room the old man in the other bed was snoring peacefully.

"Hugh, darling."

His eyes opened, focused gradually. He saw her. He wet his lips and tried to speak.

It was three A.M. and very quiet in the hospital, except for a gurgle of water in the overhead pipes, the rubbery but not unrestful snoring. She was certain the other man wouldn't be a bother to Hugh; he was still under the influence of the post-op.

"Jory?"

"Yes . . ."

"Jory—oh, God—thirsty."

She helped him sip a little water from the pitcher off the bedside table. His eyes closed, and she thought he had nodded off again. She was fussing with the covers, tucking them in just so, when he suddenly raised his head, staring at nothing, a look of fright on his face.

"Jory—mistake. It was—didn't mean to—"

"I know all about it, Hugh. But you're going to be fine."

He twisted his head on the pillow and raised his bandaged left hand before she could prevent it. He stared at his hand until she caught his wrist and gently placed his arm by his side again.

"Gone," he said, and sighed.

"I'm afraid so, my love. But it shouldn't make that much difference to you, Hugh. Dr. Sheely said—"

Again Hugh started up, looking terrified this time. He seemed to be searching behind her for shapes in the darkness. Joram had to restrain him with both hands. She was afraid he might throw himself out of the high bed.

"The ring? You got it? The ring?"

"What?" she said, puzzled.

"Jory, where's the ring?"

"Your wedding band? Oh, I suppose— I don't really know."

His head sank despondently to the pillow. His face was

contorted, and she wondered at the size of his grief. She sought to console him.

"You can get another wedding band, Hugh darling. Rest now."

"No! Need help. You . . . got to help me, Jory."

"Of course I will."

"But you . . . don't understand. Nothing. Tell you . . . what happened."

"In the morning, Hugh. Please don't upset yourself."

"Now! *Now.*" He gripped Joram with his right hand, pulled her closer. His eyes rolled in his head; he was fighting the sedative.

"Help—me," he begged, agonized.

"You know I'll take good care of you. Haven't I always, darling? Now tell me what's bothering you. Get it off your mind so you can sleep."

Hugh told her then. He told her everything.

AT FOUR-FORTY P.M. on Thursday, almost forty-eight hours after she'd been thrown through the window, the machines monitoring Anne's vital signs indicated she was regaining consciousness.

She was in traction to correct a dislocation of the cervical spine. Tongs had been inserted into the bone of her skull; a weight was attached to the tongs by means of a pulley. There were sandbags on either side of her head to anchor it. Her right arm was in a cast. Both eyes had turned black and blue, and her split lower lip had swelled to almost twice normal size.

The first person she recognized in the room was Terry.

"Where . . . am I?" she said with difficulty.

"In hospital, Anne."

"Can't . . . move my head."

Tears ran down Terry's face. "You're not supposed to."

She ran her tongue over the swollen lip. "You need a shave," she said, frowning, and drifted off again.

By eight that night she was sufficiently wide awake to be examined by a team of doctors that included a neurosurgeon and an orthopedic specialist. Everyone else waited outside.

Dr. Price, the neurosurgeon, gave Terry the news.

"She's sustained paralysis from the site of the injury on down. Of course, we expected that. We're reasonably certain that traction will straighten the spine and no corrective surgery will be needed."

"What about the paralysis?"

"In roughly seventy percent of these cases paralysis gradually disappears as the dislocation is reduced, easing pressure on the nerves in the spinal cord. But it's difficult to say at this time how badly damaged those nerves are."

"So there's a chance she may be permanently paralyzed from the neck down?" Terry asked.

"That is a possible consequence of this type of injury."

"When will we know for sure?"

"By the end of this week some feeling should be restored below the point of injury."

"It's urgent that I speak to Professor Ramsdell," Inspector Kilderbee said. He'd had no sleep for two days; he blinked his fuming eyes to clear them.

"Yes, I quite understand. Can you make it brief?"

"I'll go along, if you don't mind," Terry said.

Anne was staring at the ceiling when they walked into the room. Her eyes flickered to Terry's face. She tried to smile, but she was too frightened.

"How bad . . . am I? Can't feel . . . *anything.*"

"That's only temporary until the traction takes effect."

"Traction?"

"Anne, this is Chief Inspector Kilderbee of the CID." Anne glanced at the policeman.

"We've met." He smiled at her; she couldn't place him. "Tuesday morning, at Paternoster. I was inquiring—"

"Ohhhh—Mary Galashields. You—found her?"

"Mary went off to Stockholm with her boy friend Lars. Wrote a letter home telling Mum about her plans, then forgot to post the letter."

Anne blinked, uninterested. She looked again at Terry, beseechingly. "What happened—to me?"

Kilderbee looked sharply at Dr. Price, who shrugged. "You have no recollection?"

"No," Anne said, struggling with a fragmented memory. "No!"

"Anne," Terry said, "Tuesday night you were—someone got into your flat and tried—"

"He tried to kill you, Professor Ramsdell. Perhaps he was there, waiting, when you arrived home. However he got in, there was a struggle in your kitchen. You wounded him—or so we believed. Does that help you?"

"No! I don't . . . remember!"

"Then he must have knocked you unconscious. Once you were unconscious he lifted you and flung you through the window in your breakfast alcove."

"God . . . Oh, God . . ."

"You landed in the fish pool in the garden below."

"And I'm still—alive. Or am I?"

"Quick action by your neighbor Dr. Grimes prevented you from drowning."

Anne was silent, shocked. Kilderbee watched her closely, but there was no hint that any of it had come back to her.

"Did you—get him?"

"Unfortunately, no. So you see—you must try to help us."

"But I . . . *can't*." Tears welled in her eyes. "Terry—Terry—I *hurt*."

"Anne, believe me, you're going to be all right. Could it have been someone we know? Don't you recall anything that might help the police?"

"I'm—trying— Ohhhhhhhhhhh—"

"What is it, Anne?"

"I'm feeling—a bloody lot of pain in my head!"

Kilderbee said, "Professor Ramsdell, I've brought some photographs I'd like for you to—"

"Inspector, that really must be all for tonight," Terry said furiously, and the doctor nodded.

"Terry," Anne moaned. "Oh, God, what a fix I'm in!"

"I'm right here, Annie. I'll be here as long as you need me."

In the corridor outside, Kilderbee encountered Sergeant Beer. They could hear Anne crying as they walked away from the Intensive Therapy Unit.

"That tears it. She has traumatic amnesia."

Beer shook his head sympathetically. "Permanent condition?"

"Should think there's a way of removing the block. Hypnotic suggestion, when she's well enough to attempt it."

"That might be a matter of weeks."

"No. We simply can't wait. Hate to do it, but I'll have to put pressure on the doctors and on her brother. Well, Sergeant?"

"Sir?"

Kilderbee rubbed his face as if he were afraid of falling asleep standing up. "How is our Mr. Thornton getting along upstairs?"

"He has spent a comfortable day."

"That's nice."

"At the suggestion of his wife he's receiving lithium as part of his scheduled medication, one hundred milligrams daily."

"Lithium?" said Kilderbee, perking up. "Isn't that the stuff used in treatment of cyclic psychotics?"

"Manic-depressive disease, but they've also done some experimenting in the States with certain types of schizophrenics. Professor Thornton has no history of schizophrenia, but he *is* prone to spells of melancholia and severe depression, brought on by overwork. He has been treated with lithium on at least two other occasions, and it seems to work for him."

"When is he due to be discharged?" Kilderbee asked.

"He'll remain in hospital another day. Inspector, they must know by now that Professor Ramsdell survived. Hospital grapevine."

"Yes. I want the guard in this corridor doubled until he's out of here. Not that I think Thornton is foolish enough to finish his bad job while he's here."

"Still, he must be sweating bloody jellybeans."

"His wife will keep him cool. She was a nurse at one time; she probably anticipated the difficulty we're having with Professor Ramsdell. And unless the don can positively identify Thornton as her attacker—"

"Do you think his wife knows who he is?"

"She must know by now."

"And still she's willing to lie for him."

"Yes, she's lying. God knows why."

ON SUNDAY MORNING Joram was up at first light. It promised to be a clear and beautiful day; already the bells were tolling. Oxford is a city reknowned for its bells in a country where bell ringing is an art and a passion, and by now she recognized many of them. From His Ponderous Eminence Great Tom to lesser tintinnabulations, quaint as old cannon, an alchemic torrent would form, multiple pealings, throat against throat, all of it sweet and resonant and thoroughly God-fearing, redoubling in celestial echo from St. Giles to the hoary churchyard of Old Marston. She thought of all the good music they'd heard in Oxford. Turn a corner and there was always something unexpected and delightful to listen to—the notes of a harpsichord drifting from an upstairs room of Balliol, madrigals sung behind a medieval garden wall. She lovingly recalled Christmas carols in Christ Church Hall, an open-air concert in Tom Quad. On May Day they had stood shivering in two feet of mist in the Grove by Magdalen to hear the choir sing a Latin anthem.

Odd how adaptable she was, to climate and circumstance. She had been at home here and would always miss Oxford, the drizzle and the damp and the antiquities, the preposterously pleasant rituals of academia, just as she often yearned for the plains of Texas, the bellowing of herd cattle and the quick flowery springs that yielded to months of heat and torpor. The heat out there somehow intensified their loneliness; the combination could kill you, or permanently unhinge your mind. Some of the antebellum women in her family had succumbed early, spent the rest of their dotty days in rocking chairs or quiet shuttered rooms. The men, of course, had their liquor and their work to sustain them.

Joram had always looked up to the men in her family, identified with them. Of her sisters and cousins she was unique, a free spirit: the men respected her ability to ride and shoot with the best of them. They were a close-knit and fiercely protective family group.

Joram fixed breakfast for herself, not because she felt in the least hungry but because she knew she must have the food. So she ate alone in the breakfast room, looking dazedly out at crimson hedges of primrose and azalea while she thought about her great-uncle Hap.

In those days there was no name for his malady; if you mentioned it at all, you said he was subject to fits. He'd loaded his rifle one night and gone into town to shoot up a cantina full of Mexican field hands; the tally was two dead, six grievously wounded. The sheriff found him wandering and raving in the street and appropriated his empty rifle. Then the sheriff took Hap home. Nothing was said about locking him up or sending him away to the state asylum. The Mexicans, it seemed, had met with an inexplicable and unavoidable accident that had nothing at all to do with the Hap everybody in the county knew and liked.

The family saw to it that the families of the victims were provided for. A day later Hap abruptly stopped ranting and fell asleep. When he awakened it was as if he'd never had his homicidal fit at all. He was as lucid as his brother Dan, and he mostly stayed that way for the next twenty years while he worked the ranch he owned with Dan and raised a fine family. Naturally they all kept a weather eye on Hap, and when certain signs appeared (an uncharacteristic lethargy, a disinclination to eat) they immediately locked him in a tack room in the barn. There he couldn't get a weapon or do himself harm by banging his head on the walls, which had been lined with cotton-stuffed feed sacks. In Joram's family they took care of their own; no one was thrown away because of a physical or mental infirmity. It must have been dreadful during his mad spells, listening all night to the moans and screams from the barn. But the rest of the time he was useful, loving, needed. A man worth protecting.

She fixed Hugh's breakfast and carried it upstairs on a tray. He awakened when she opened the drapes.

"Hello, Jory."

She leaned over to kiss his forehead. "How did you sleep?"

"All right, I suppose."

"Hungry?"

"I think so."

She helped him to sit up and placed the tray in front of him. While he ate she sat at the foot of the bed, hands in her lap, smiling.

"It's time to think about going home," she said.

He buttered a muffin awkwardly, then spread Cooper's marmalade over it. He glanced uncertainly at Joram.

"How soon could we be ready to travel?"

"Three days. Four at the most."

"By the weekend we could be on the mountain."

"Glorious," she said, encouraging him.

Hugh rubbed his bandaged hand lightly, as if he felt a stab of pain. The pain crept into his eyes. Joram despised that, but she could deal with it.

"They'll never let me out of England, Jory."

"There's no way they can stop us."

"The police will get the information they need. Amnesia or not, they'll pry it all out of her head somehow."

"No, Hugh, they won't."

"How can you be so sure?"

"From working with Ken I know that reconstructing traumatic experiences under hypnosis is a highly dangerous practice. Unless Professor Ramsdell can positively identify you, the police don't have a case. All they have is a blood sample that matches your blood group, but it isn't conclusive evidence. Everything else they think they know is conjecture. Oh, they'll be back, they're not through with us. But you have an alibi; they must prove I'm lying."

Joram gazed calmly at him, reassuring him with her show of strength. There had been a regrettable accident; it had nothing to do with the man she loved.

His doubts persisted. "What if they found my wedding band in her kitchen?"

"It'd be all over now, bub," she said lightly. "So you see—nothing to worry about."

At last Hugh smiled, willing to believe. "Damn, I'm homesick, you know that? Clean mountain air! Miles and miles of blue sky. The best place in the world to eat, get crocked, get laid." He winked at Joram.

"The best," she agreed. "But you're going to take it easy for a while. You promised."

"I promised," Hugh said obediently. With a show of enthusiasm he cut into his herb omelet. Joram got up to pour his coffee for him and scoop a few crumbs of muffin from the spread. Hugh stopped eating and stroked her bare arm. Joram leaned against the bed, eyes half-closed.

"You're one hell of a woman, Jory," he said. "You're the best there is. I can't make it up to you, but I'm going to try."

His touch made her shudder, but it was a shudder of pure animal pleasure.

THE CLINICAL HYPNOLOGIST was a pleasant little man who wore round eyeglasses that covered half his face. He spoke softly but authoritatively. He had unhappy news for Inspector Kilderbee.

"I've now had two meetings with Professor Ramsdell," he said. "This morning I was able to satisfactorily complete a susceptibility test. She's an extremely intelligent woman, as you know, and she has significant powers of concentration. She would make a good subject for hypnosis under ordinary conditions. Because of her present infirmity and limited emotional reserve, I do not recommend placing her in a deep trance at this time. No responsible hypnologist would."

"But—"

The psychiatrist in attendance said, "I'm quite in accord with Hurley. If a reconstruction of her experience would serve a useful purpose, speed her recovery in some way, then it might be worth the gamble."

"What do you mean, useful purpose? Three young women have been murdered, she was very nearly the fourth victim, and she's the only one who can give us the information we need to arrest this maniac."

"I don't think you have a grasp of what hypnosis can

accomplish," Hurley said gently. "Suppose I worked with Professor Ramsdell for a number of weeks, gaining her full confidence, gradually taking her to Stage Forty, which is the deep-trance stage. I might then be able to suggest she return to the scene of the assault and describe all the events of that night as they happened. And if I'd done my work well, always reassuring her that she could be awake in a split second if things became too unpleasant for her, she might give it a try. I say *might,* because it would be completely up to her. If she didn't want to relive the experience she'd promptly wake up. Or if she did try, to please me, the resultant shock might be too much for her. Cardiac arrest is a distinct possibility. Do you see the risk?"

"I thought that by using drugs—"

"I first mentioned the use of sodium pentothal, or Medinal or Evipal, in view of her general paralysis and the difficulty in using standard induction methods. But there is no such thing as drug hypnosis. The drugs can induce a trance, but there is doubt in my mind that such a state will permit the effective use of suggestion."

"What are the chances she might spontaneously remember the attack?"

"Nil," the psychiatrist replied. "Oh, perhaps that's pessimistic. Say, one chance in a million."

"I see—well, that isn't quite so pessimistic, is it?"

"We're sorry, Inspector. We do understand your problem. But our chief concern must be Professor Ramsdell."

"What are her chances for a complete recovery?"

"According to the neurologists, there have been encouraging signs. It's going to be a long, hard pull, however. Much depends on how she responds to physiotherapy."

WHEN TERRY CAME in Wednesday morning Anne greeted him by raising the first two fingers of her left hand an inch or so from the bed.

"That *is* good, Anne."

"I'm told there's a machine available that projects the pages of a book on the ceiling—all I'd have to do is push a button. In another week I should be able to operate the machine myself. Terry, be a love—quickly—"

"What's the matter?"

"I've had this dreadful itching between my shoulder blades all morning. Could you slide your hand gently— that's it— Oh, what a blessed relief. That's grand."

"How are the headaches?"

"Not constant any longer. They made some sort of adjustment, a lighter weight, I think. Terry, the docs turned thumbs down on the hypnosis scheme."

"I'm glad they did."

"Well, let's be honest, I dreaded the whole idea. But that leaves our madman on the loose."

"The police have at least one important clue. They're on to someone, but of course it's hush-hush. Until they nick him the guard will remain outside, so you're not to worry."

"Oh, I'm not so concerned for myself. But some other poor girl is bound to get it. Unless," she said grimly, "I managed to knife him in the balls."

Terry grinned. "Fascinating idea. By the way, I turned down a thousand pounds this morning on your behalf."

"Thanks ever so much. Who was it this time?"

"*Sunday Mirror*. Exclusive rights your life story, exclusive photos, reply soonest, et cetera, et cetera."

"A thousand pounds. What a ruddy bore. Just let me know when Warner Brothers calls."

"What would you like me to read today? We haven't finished Sunday's *Guardian*."

"I don't want to be read to. It's time we had a very serious talk."

"About what?"

"About you, my boy. Misspending your life in this gloomy hospital. Dedicating yourself to the care of your poor invalid sister."

"Oh, shut up, you sound like Emily Brontë."

"Terry, I'm in earnest. Look, we both know I'm coming along all right, there's no cause for pessimism. But it *is* a drag. I can look forward to several weeks of lying abed, then perhaps I'll be up and around in a wheelchair or on crutches, ready for some kind of therapy program. What I'm saying is, I'll get on perfectly fine without all the attention that you know I adore. And you have work to do. Important work."

"I've been hitting the typewriter recently."

"Rubbish, you have not. You can't be nursemaid and companion all day, spend your evenings brushing off the press and who knows how many other opportunists, and hope to be productive in your spare time. That's not the way you work. Terry, what about that offer from Kingman College? Is the post still available?"

"Writer in residence? I reckon. Haven't given it much thought."

"Wire them immediately. Tell them you accept."

"I couldn't—not while you're helpless like this."

"Terry, it would enormously speed my recovery to know you were settled down to an agreeable routine and writing again. I feel bad enough having had the bad luck to tangle with a sex criminal, and I'll feel worse dragging myself through weeks of therapy while you suffer on the sidelines. I have my pride, you know. I love you very much, and I want you to stay the hell away from me until I'm on my feet again. Call me often. Write every day. But go." She was crying. "Oh, damn it!"

"Close your mouth or you'll drown," Terry said, sitting on the edge of the bed and reaching for his handkerchief.

"Will you please listen to me for once and go?"

"I always listen to you. And you're always right, aren't you?"

"Oh, Terry. Oh, God, how I'm going to miss you!"

As FAR AS Kilderbee was concerned, the report from the serologist at Scotland Yard Laboratory constituted sufficient evidence to go before the magistrate and obtain an arrest warrant. Detective Chief Superintendent McJohn disagreed.

"While there could be another man in Oxfordshire with his blood group and with the identical rhesus factor present, we can't make a satisfactory case on bloodstains alone. That sort of evidence is notoriously unreliable in magistrates' eyes. When are the Thorntons leaving the country?"

"They're booked on Pam Am flight 107, departing Heathrow 1230 hours tomorrow. It's a through flight to Atlanta, Georgia."

"Any possibility of detaining them? Some pretext or other?"

"They would justifiably raise holy hell. He's a respected man in his field, and they have connections—her side of the family, I believe—with the Court of St. James's. The Home Secretary would come down on us like a ton of brick. With all due respect, Robbie, a blood grouping common to only about four percent of the population—"

McJohn sighed. "Forget the serology report for now. What about the weapon?"

"Thornton's Jaguar was dismantled. We've gone over

every square inch of the wreck scene. We found nought that could have been used to sever his fingers. And it's obvious to anyone with half an eye that his fingers were not cut off in the accident. I know we can prove *that* in court."

"Entirely circumstantial. Since we subscribe to the theory that he carried the blade away from the flat, he must have disposed of it on the way to his staged accident. The river?"

Kilderbee shook his head. "No go, even with metal detectors. Far too much muck and rusted junk to contend with. We've combed both sides of the roadway as far as the box junction without success."

"It does seem futile, since we can't be certain of his exact route from Eversedge Road. There's the elapsed-time problem. He may well have made a detour expressly to rid himself of the weapon." Superintendent McJohn studied the big map of Oxford and the surrounding countryside that was mounted on the wall of the CID's "murder room" at the St. Aldate's Station. "Would have been a colossal piece of luck if the constables had thought to stop that red Jaguar they noticed in Bolton Place."

"Unfortunately they had no idea what sort of emergency they were responding to." Kilderbee opened two file folders on his desk. "I have the reports from the FBI and the New York City police."

"They had something on our Mr. Thornton?"

"He has a police record going back to his nineteenth year, when he was arrested for assault and battery, the outgrowth of a tavern brawl in Chapel Hill, North Carolina. Charges subsequently dismissed. Further complaints, DWI dismissed, fighting dismissed."

"A bit rough-and-tumble in his youth."

"Four years later in New York City he was questioned extensively by police investigating the death of his first wife. She either fell or jumped from the fifth-floor window of their apartment on West One Hundred and Thirteenth Street. At the time he was a doctoral candidate at Columbia University. Wife some sort of artist."

"Out the window, hey?"

"Yes, that's what I was thinking. Neighbors and friends reported they fought a lot. A case of jealous possession on her part. She took a cold chisel to him one night at a party in front of about forty witnesses—accused Thornton of funning around with a bit of quiff. For his part, he was noted for a violent temper. His alibi was provided by a young woman who claimed to be screwing Thornton in her place around the corner at the time the wife either was or wasn't defenestrated. Coroner's jury returned a verdict of death by misadventure."

"What about his alleged mental problems?"

"Shortly after his wife's death Thornton committed himself to a private psychiatric clinic. He was found to be suffering from acute melancholia. He was successfully treated and discharged. But he seems to have been afflicted, off and on, to this day. Despite an excellent reputation as a historian he lost a plummy teaching position—a close friend in Oxford heard rumors of a suicide attempt. About that time the present Mrs. Thornton came along and pulled him up by his bootstraps. He is currently in the top rank of his profession in the U.S. Head of department, noted author, distinguished societies, prizes and citations."

"Still hell with the ladies?"

"Apparently Thornton's wife allows him his innings with the birds as long as he doesn't stray too far from home and hearth. Since coming to Oxford ten months ago he's been seen in the company of at least two women other than his wife, both times in the vicinity of the cottage they rented in the Cotswolds."

"Unfortunately his women friends don't match the descriptions of the murder victims."

"He's had plenty of opportunity to get around to more

than two. Can't think of a more convenient blind for his activities than the rambling old Bodleian."

"All right. We've searched the cottage. We've searched the Banbury house. Still we can't connect Thornton with Ewa Norberg, Michaeline Prell, or Valery St. James. Our most reliable witness to his activities is suffering from amnesia and couldn't identify Thornton in the series of photos we showed her. We have what would seem to be incriminating bloodstains; he has an excellent alibi. At best we have twenty hours to drive a wedge into that alibi. How do you plan to proceed?"

"I think it's time to play dirty," Kilderbee said.

"HELLO, INSPECTOR," JORAM said a full three seconds after she opened the door.

"Good afternoon, Mrs. Thornton."

"I ought to warn you, Inspector. Because of the . . . harassment we've suffered this past week, friends advised me to consult a lawyer. And I have. His name is Edward Degnan."

"Yes, I know him. Excellent man. Have I failed to inform you of your rights at any time during this inquiry?"

"No. It's the way you've conducted your 'inquiry.' I can't think of anyone we know in Oxford who hasn't been approached by the police. That's humiliating, particularly since it's all been so vague and ominous. Hugh has not been charged with any crime. But we're leaving under a cloud just the same."

"May I come in?"

"You really don't know when to quit, do you?"

She was wearing jeans and a man's shirt to do her packing, and her hair was protected from dust by a floppy velveteen cap. The effect was urchin, unself-consciously charming. A truly handsome woman, he thought, even with her eyes glared and menacing as Medusa's. Sexuality enriched by maturity, a connoisseur's delight. He had seen how shrewdly she exercised control over herself, without neurotic overtones. Her approach to people was too direct to be labeled calculating. She would have the ability to let her guard down, become completely disarming. Yet he doubted she ever exposed an area of vulnerability.

"I have my job to do," he said, mild in the face of her indignation. "There are one or two developments I'd hoped to talk to you about."

A neatly baited hook; she cruised around it. "My husband is asleep. He hasn't fully recovered from his ordeal."

"There'll be no need to awaken him, Mrs. Thornton."

"You can't imagine how upset Hugh is, knowing that some of our acquaintances may be thinking he's the sort to go around stabbing *au pair* girls and actresses."

"Ring Mr. Degnan, by all means, if you'd like him present."

"That would be almost like admitting we were guilty of something, wouldn't it?"

He noted the collective pronoun again; her insistence on *we* intrigued him. A touch of defiance?

"By no means, Mrs. Thornton."

"Oh—all right, then. Come in."

She opened the door wider and left it for him to close as she preceded him to the drawing room. There were cartons and steamer trunks in the foyer, tagged for shipping. In the kitchen at the end of the center hall the housekeeper and a maid were packing glassware in a barrel. They were chatting and laughing. Soft music and sunlight filled the ample rooms of the house.

"Drink, Inspector? Let's see, you're partial to sherry, aren't you?"

"Yes, a little Harvey's would be welcome."

She poured one for him and one for herself, sat down opposite him in front of the fireplace.

"Now, what was it about, Inspector?"

Kilderbee made a show of consulting his book. "I believe you stated that your husband arrived home at approximately five o'clock Wednesday last, after spending the day in the Cotswolds?"

"If you have it there, that's what I said."

"It seems we've placed him in a pub in Cowley at five. Positively identified by three persons. He arrived around four, had three whiskeys in the public bar, spoke not a word—other than was necessary for him to order—and seemed deeply troubled by something. He left at about ten minutes past five. Given the condition of traffic at that time of evening, it seems unlikely he could have reached this house earlier than five twenty."

"Then I was mistaken about what time he got home," she said indifferently. "I do know we sat down to supper at quarter of six. Is that the important development you were talking about?"

"Would you look at some photographs, Mrs. Thornton?"

He opened the clasp envelope he'd brought and handed her the glossies. The first photo was of Michaeline Prell, taken just after she'd been fished out of the Thames in her air-filled, grume-spattered polythene bag.

Joram glanced at it, blanched, laid all the photos face down on the coffee table and said, "You are a prize son of a bitch, Inspector. And this is harassment. And I think I will call our lawyer."

"I was hoping you might be able to identify—"

"Hoping nothing. You wanted me to lose my lunch."

"Those girls lost their lives. That's what I want you to think about, Mrs. Thornton. Three ghastly murders."

"Get out of here."

"Not yet—and say what you will about harassment. Are you aware of the circumstances surrounding the death of your husband's first wife?"

"Good God."

"Highly suspicious circumstances, I should say."

"Natalie by all accounts was a sadistic, destructive child. And she fell from that window. She was not pushed or—"

"Thrown?"

"You've lost your mind, Inspector. I realize there's a lot of pressure on you—the police have been made to look like fools—but how can you sit there and reel off fantastic accusations against Hugh without a particle of proof?"

Kilderbee took the lump of tissue from a smaller envelope, unwrapped it and laid the wedding band on the table between them.

Joram looked at it. She blinked and, he thought, almost shuddered. He was avid to take advantage of her momentary shock. It was the one thing she and her husband could not have been sure of, the one piece of evidence to put Hugh Thornton away forever.

"The inscription," said Kilderbee, "reads 'To H. from J.' Then there's the date of course."

She looked up, staring at him. "Where . . . did you find it?"

"You must know where we found it, Mrs. Thornton."

By his careful phrasing Joram recognized that it was a trick. She looked hard at the wedding band, composing herself. But she'd already given away too much, and her cheeks were flushed.

"Hugh will be pleased. We thought it was gone for good." She reached for the ring and Kilderbee didn't stop her. She was smiling thinly. "Of course I may keep it?"

Kilderbee ignored the mockery in her tone and studied

her. Joram turned the wedding band over and over in her fingers and avoided looking at him. She was determined not to get too angry, a natural reaction following the scare he'd given her. He had been holding back the ring, waiting to spring it on her when there was no other hope of breaking her down. And Joram realized it.

"You have the opportunity now, and it may be your last opportunity, to tell the full truth about the situation you find yourself in."

Her head came up sharply, but she only smiled. "You have my statement. I have nothing else to say to you. And I'm very busy this afternoon."

"Is it worth protecting him, knowing what he's done, and what he's very likely to do in future? Don't you realize you may be in the gravest danger yourself?"

Joram got up, slipped the ring into the breast pocket of her shirt and walked to the door of the drawing room.

"I'll show you out, Inspector."

Kilderbee hesitated, then picked up his photos and his hat. His sherry stood untouched on the table. He followed Joram to the stoop, paused there to put his hat on.

So they had their man, only they didn't have him. He was somebody else's problem now.

"It's really a lovely day," Joram said, looking at the cloudless sky.

Kilderbee turned, unable to resist a last look at her. Why would she want to do it? he thought. Was it an act of will or a terrible wantonness that enabled her to protect a monster? Even now he found it difficult to believe she could be so cruelly flawed. He soothed a tic in one eyelid with the pressure of his fingers. In a few weeks, or months, another girl would turn up somewhere in a polythene bag. The Ramsdell woman would be living in fear for the rest of her life. Bound by the law, he could never say a word to her about Hugh Thornton. He felt bitter and impotent.

"I'm sorry," he said.

"Oh, you needn't be." Her voice was remote, pleasant enough. She had misread him.

"Well, then. Safe journey, Mrs. Thornton."

"Thank you, Inspector." She turned then and went back into the house and shut the door.

Part Two

GHOSTS

DRIVING ACROSS THE Tamar from Plymouth Terry found Cornwall much as he'd left it several years ago, although the west-bound traffic seemed worse; he got off the main road as quickly as possible. The early afternoon was almost unbearably bright after a passing squall. The fishing villages along the southern coast were still obsessed with the commercial aspects of their centuries-old charm: the quays had been cleared for car parks, and summer visitors were clumped around postiches of trinket booth and custard stand.

A year in the U.S. had somewhat desensitized him to the ravages of junk culture. But he was a little chagrined to discover that even the off-the-track village of Pendolthan, a collecion of whitewashed cottages that spilled riskily down a gorge to the mouth of the river and a modest quay on Gwenreath Bay, had acquired a Pixie Cottage Souvenir Shoppe. Probably the quayside inn, which featured the only decent watering hole between St. Aubyns and Fowey, had also been overrun by the insatiable mob of tourists.

Instead of driving into the village for a settling-down pint or two on the terrace of the inn, Terry crossed the bridge that arched above the flume of the Pendolthan River and continued southwest, past the great silver-gray church in Cobben, stark as ever in its setting of low rambling walls and irregular beds of glowing fuchsias. The road went along a shoulder of the coombe that lay between the oblong bulk of Shotford Hill and the narrow marsh by the estuary known as Kit Cove. Above him were the tall chimneys and roofless enginehouses that marked the sites of the played-out tin mines of Shotford; gaunt ribs of felspar or solid granite in green pasture; browsing cattle at every easy turn of the road. Soon small farms, meticulously planted in corn and barley, gave way to the higher meadows and Channel view of Tuck's Estate.

Terry was home, but he felt no elation, only the gnawing conviction that he shouldn't have come at all.

Instead of turning right inside the granite gateposts and driving on to the small manor house, he followed a hedged lane past stone huts and equipment sheds to the little dingle in the midst of an otherwise treeless slope where a spring fed a trickling stream to the marsh two hundred yards below.

Wind-twisted elm and willow trees shielded the cottage in the dingle from the strong sun. His architect father had built the place as a retreat and a workroom; it was a smaller version of a typical old thatched-roof Cornish cottage he'd seen near Truro.

The partly sunned dooryard glistened with honeysuckle, dog roses and clumps of yellow celandine. On the cobbles a cat was toying with a green snake it had found. Terry walked up to the front door and pushed it open.

The cottage had been designed primarily as work space and provided only the barest comforts, although there was a handy kitchen and a WC. The interior was very well lighted because of the skillful way his father had arranged the windows. Odors of baking lingered in the air, recalling pleasurable memories of the Cornish specialties he had enjoyed during those boyhood summers.

Terry helped himself to a beef-and-tetty pasty from a basket and followed the pungent spoor of oil paint to an easel holding a half-realized canvas. Harbor scene. He recognized the long-disused seine house, or fish cellar, in Pendolthan; and there were other, completed paintings scattered about. The portrait of a laughing Cornish child, a broken tinner's cottage on the barren tor—all these showed astonishing talent.

Just something else she'd picked up in her spare time, he thought admiringly. But where *was* Anne?

As soon as he walked outside a gun was placed against

his head, just roughly enough to convince him not to move a muscle. Terry saw another one of them, shotgun in the crook of his arm, bending over the rented MG at the gate.

"Nicely done," Terry said expressionlessly.

"Who are ye?"

"I know you, Thomas Targill, even though I'm not able to look you in the face. Don't you recognize me?"

After a moment the gun barrel was lowered from beside his ear; Terry risked a glance at the blond one-eyed man, who was now smiling in astonishment.

"Cud it be? Terry?" He pushed his pistol inside his belt and gripped Terry at the biceps with such enthusiasm that Terry winced. Thomas weighed upward of eighteen stone and undoubtedly was still a dazzling wrestler, though the ancient sport was no longer very popular in the countryside. Years ago he had patiently taught Terry the refinements of his cherished art, at a time when Terry was as grateful for the attention as he was for the education.

"I dunt see so well any more, as ye might've guessed," Thomas muttered in apology. "And how long's it bain since you've cum home? T'was at Tedwin's funeral I last had a glimpse of ye! Oh, Jan, here's no stranger, tez our own Terry, home from the U.S.A. Cum along 'ere now, meet the landlord. This bufflehead's your cousin Cunaide's eldest."

"Don't start that 'landlord' business," Terry said good-humoredly, and greeted the suddenly shy cousin who was toting the long shotgun. "So, Thomas. You're taking very good care of Anne."

"Long as she stays 'ere, no 'arm will ever cum to 'er."

"Where is she now?"

"On the strand, I spoas. She bathes every day it dunt rain."

"And how's she feeling?"

"Wisht," Thomas said with a glum shake of his head. "It do seem to me that that murderer is 'eavy on 'er mind.

She dunt sleep well, despite our lookout. Oh, but you'll be a cheerful sight! Cum, I'll take you down-along so ye be'n't challenged by anoother of our intrepid gunmen."

Below the dingle the lane dwindled to a path. Two shaggy ponies wheeled away from them and raced each other to higher ground. Thomas went ahead, walking and talking so rapidly Terry had to strain to dog his footsteps and keep up with a bardic flow of gossip about weddings, funerals and adulteries. The rich grass of mid-meadow gave way to thistle and nettle, foxglove and furze. They walked along the now moldering path and plunged into the hazy cool interior of a copse, following the brook as it widened and rippled through a swath of sandrush.

Beyond the copse an old man sat hunched on a sandy hillock with a border collie at his feet. From his post he could see all of Kit Cove. They were taking Anne's fears with utmost seriousness, Terry thought, receiving a grave nod of acknowledgment from the old man.

"Be see'n ye," Thomas said with a wave. He paused to speak briefly to the old man, then walked back the way they had come.

Terry continued down to the sand-and-shingle beach that belonged to Tuck's Estate. Except for an old fishing boat idling in the shallows of the cove and a modest changing hut, the beach and cove were empty. Herring gulls soared in from Gwenreath Bay, crying raucously. The sky was faintly marked with streaks of cloud, like milk from an overturned pail. A stiff breeze had sprung up; it rocked the boat gently at its mooring.

The door of the changing hut opened and Anne appeared, carrying the two dripping pieces of her bathing suit in one hand. She was headed for the water and didn't notice him. She wore raggedy faded blue shorts and a polka-dot halter top. She'd tied her hair back with a ribbon to keep it off her neck. She was thin but sleek; the Cornwall sun had burned her a healthy red-brown, and her hair was a shade lighter than he'd ever seen it.

Terry watched, with a chill and then with horror, as

Anne limped along, almost dragging her right foot. Now he understood why she had sounded so defeated and despondent the last time he talked to her.

"Anne!"

She turned in amazement, cried something, tried to run to him, came up lame and hobbled precariously. She fell down hard on one knee in the shingle, sobbed and cursed and laughed and got up again. Terry reached her before she could punish herself further, caught her and touched her lips with his own. Then in a fit of exuberance he lifted her straight up into the sun.

On the hillock the old man put a steadying hand on the neck of his trembling collie, fumbled in the pocket of his jacket for pipe and matches, then turned his back on the cove to smoke and doze.

"WHAT SORT OF dreams?" Terry asked.

Anne paused long enough to allow the waiter to pour Irish Mist for both of them, smiled her thanks, placed a hand tentatively on her cigarette case and decided not to smoke another so soon. She looked toward Gwenny Bay, at the skein of lights sparkling along the far shore.

"They could all be lumped into two categories," she said, "— Falling and Pursued. Falling is the most ghastly by far. I had one only last night. There I was—for some reason known only to my superego—"

"Your id."

"Is that it? I can never keep their ruddy jargon straight. But to continue with my dream, I was balancing on a window ledge outside my flat. *The* window ledge. I had ammonia and water in a bucket and a sponge in hand and I was frantically trying to clean the panes. They were very dirty, but the more I scrubbed the worse the mess. And all the time I was finding it increasingly difficult to keep my footing." Anne looked back at Terry and picked up her glass. "There's always an inevitability about it, whatever the setting. I know I *must* fall, yet I try so hard not to. Well—last night, as I said, I was cleaning panes, or scrubbing them up is more like it. Then I became aware of a face behind the glass. A haunting . . . *unseeable* . . . face. And the window began inching up. I tried to hold it down, I screamed at him, 'No, I don't recognize you, please, you must leave me alone!' But blood was dripping on the ledge, making it horribly slick, and the window rose up and up, and he reached out and—"

"Oh, Anne, that's enough."

"You do get the idea."

"Graphically. What about Pursued?"

"In *that* one someone is forever trying to run me over. A malicious child on a bicycle, a motorbike maniac. General Rommel in one of his tanks."

"General Rom— This is a leg-pull. You're taking advantage of my good nature."

"I swear to God! It *was* General Rommel."

"Well, clear enough what Pursued is all about."

"Look here, Terry, I have no deep-seated Teutonic urge to be masochistically raped."

He smiled. "Is that what I was thinking?"

"Oh, wrap up. Now, sometimes my faceless man is in Pursued. Those dreams are the worst of the lot. I wake up wringing wet, gasping for breath. Sometimes there's a momentary loss of motor control that frightens me more than the dreams." She finished her Irish Mist and looked as if she craved another. Terry beckoned the waiter over.

Anne said, with an attempt at a light touch, "What I'd most like to know is, are my dreams regressive or prophetic?"

"I don't suppose you've consulted anyone at Warneford about these dreams?"

"I haven't been up to Oxford in over two months; the dreams are a recent development of my convalescence. And really—I just couldn't. I've had more than enough to do with hospitals and nerve specialists and therapists, and I simply won't be letting myself in for a gutty course of analysis. So do give it a miss, Terrence, my love."

She swallowed a large lump of liqueur and slanted a look at him. "You needn't be smiling so indulgently. I realize I've had a bloody lot to drink tonight, but it's all because I'm with you—I'm celebrating. I haven't become a solitary boozer, thank God. And now I fancy a wander in the moonlight to clear my head."

As they left the inn Terry observed that her limp wasn't as obvious as it had been earlier. She refused to use a cane, and he didn't blame her.

"If you haven't been seeing the docs at Radcliffe on a regular basis, who's been treating you? Someone local?"

"Yes," Anne said in a discouraging tone of voice.

"Is it a pinched nerve still?"

"No one's been able to say for certain, Terry."

"I shouldn't think there'd be a physician in the neighborhood with the expertise to—"

"It may all be in my head, who knows? I limp—at times pathetically. Tonight isn't so noticeable. Well, might as well confess. I've been going to Gran Gudder."

"The witch? You're joking."

"I'm not joking," Anne said patiently, "and she is not a witch. She's a naturopath; it's a perfectly legitimate form of healing. She knows all the old neglected remedies for everything from postnasal drip to tertian ague. She may have possessed impressive psychic powers at one time. Even now she has flashes of second sight that I—find compelling."

"I hope you're not swallowing some rare old concoction she's stirred together in the dark of the moon."

"Gran's treating me with hot castor-oil packs three times a week, and I'm convinced they're helping."

Terry said reminiscently, "There were stories she kept a two-headed calf in her shed. Reuben Trevithick and I snuck up there one damp night to see for ourselves. A raven flew at our heads and scared us away. Reuben

devoutly believed the old lady had turned herself into the
bird to be rid of us. It *was* the largest raven I'd ever seen
in these parts."

"What rot. She's dour and old and lonely, but fantas-
tically knowledgeable."

"Has she read the future for you yet?"

"Yes," Anne replied. "In bits and pieces. I said she
wasn't what she used to be psychically."

"Well, then?"

"You'll scoff."

"Tell me."

They stopped near the end of the quay in the onetime
smuggler's tavern. The northwest wind had a bite to it,
and Anne crossed her bare arms. Terry took off his
jacket and draped it around her shoulders. The track of
the moon lay hugely across the bay. Below them the
village idiot scuffled along, chuckling and groaning to himself as he poked into the small boats drydocked on the
slant stones, adding to his bagged collection of bones and
bottles and bits of twine.

"Gran tells me . . . it isn't over yet. He is going to find
me, she says. She has seen the two of us, high up on a
tor, on some kind of platform or trestle—"

"At the lip of a mine?"

"I don't know. But we're there, and he— There's a
fierce struggle. Then a fire. She has seen my face in the
flames, Gran says."

"Oh, Jesus, Anne. Really."

"I knew you'd scoff," she complained, but hopelessly,
and she turned her head away.

"I'm not— Look, be rational about this. There haven't
been any more trademark murders. Either Pretty Joe has
finished his work or he's dead. He may well have died
from the wound you gave him, and it's been hushed up.
Influential family, perhaps."

"He is not dead," Anne said with dreary conviction.

"Suppose he's not. Then his needs apparently have been
served. What's to be gained by seeking you out—at great

risk? It must be evident that you'll never be able to identify him."

"Well, he can't be certain of that. *I* can't be certain it
won't all come flashing back to me some perfectly ordinary morning while I'm washing my teeth or buttering my
toast."

"Not bloody likely after all this time. Anne, why don't
you give serious consideration to going back to work?"

"Oh, no. I couldn't."

"And why not? Isn't it preferable to being stuck here in
the back of beyond?"

"I happen to love Cornwall, Terry, and—"

"Let me finish, then give me an argument. Looks to
me as if you're slowly going barmy for lack of something
to occupy your mind. Old conjure women, armed guards
surrounding you twenty-four hours a day, a plague of
nightmares—you can't live like this. You're a highly complex woman. I think you're more bored than frightened,
Anne, I really do. And intellectually you're beginning to
show signs of starvation. You just aren't yourself without
a pack of chums around having a brisk chat-up about
Bach's harmonics or Fermat's last theorem."

"Do let up," she said weakly.

"And one more thing: how long has it been since you've
had a lover?"

"There *are* limits, Terry."

"That's better. You look properly angry now."

"Take me home."

"Have you been listening to me?"

"Yes," she said. "I have. And I've known you to b-be
so wrong about s-so many things. Oh, Terrrrrrry!"

ANNE HAD HER cry out before they were halfway home. For a time she sat silently with arms folded, ignoring him. Then she gave him a couple of well-meaning glances. His answering smile earned him a conciliatory pat on the cheek.

"You are going to stay a while, aren't you? I mean, I know how you feel about the old place—"

"Oh, I don't think it's so bad; sometimes memory can be most accommodating. What are you in the mood for now? We could catch the last show at the cinema."

"No, I don't think so, not tonight. What are *you* in the mood for?"

"I might go down to the cove. Build a fire, have a naked bathe, then wrap up and lie by the fire gazing at the moon. Like the good old days."

"A romp in the buff sounds just the thing. I'll go with you."

"No, you won't, sis."

"What, shy as all that?"

"I'm not shy."

"Oh, good. I was afraid you might have picked up some weird, gloomy religion in the States."

"No. But do remind me to tell you about the snake-handling sect and the strychnine swallowers."

"Ecch. I want to go nude bathing with you again. Be an angel and humor me." Anne yawned and rested her head on the seat back. "That bawl was just what I needed; haven't felt this cozy in months. Mother occasionally had some worthwhile notions about child rearing, didn't she?"

"You mean raising us up to be naked and unashamed? I suppose."

"A couple of weeks ago I crept up into the hayloft for

95

a nap. It was nice—a sunny, tickly, drowsy sort of napping. But it wasn't the same without you, Terry."

"I reckon it wasn't."

"You were always so straight and well formed, so dear —such big paws at that age. And pale, pale lashes, and that little furry stripe down your backbone. When did it come to an end? Do you recall?"

"Don't you? You ripened almost overnight. You were thirteen and looked twenty-one. From behind I couldn't tell you and mother apart. Then I went up to school and lost what was left of my innocence."

"At ten? Really? You never told me that!"

"From looking at some very explicit pictures in a book, Annie."

"Oh. I suppose that *was* a rude shock."

"Yes. When you think about the—the simplicity and openness of our relationship at the time. We could lie together, random and teasy and sensual, and still be perfectly innocent, unknowledgeable. When I saw those other bodies, in attitudes that seemed forced and ugly to me, when I heard all the names love was called . . . I had to wonder if it was meant to be that way, instead of our way."

"Poor Terry," she crooned.

"Oh, nonsense. Every boy goes through some sort of difficult awakening. Why don't you curl up with a good book tonight?"

"I don't have a good book. Our local library apparently thinks the novel died with Thomas Hardy."

"Well, I brought along a novel you might enjoy."

"I sat on my reading glasses the other night, and besides I resent your trying to be rid of me." Terry was looking rather smug, and finally she tumbled. "You've written a new book!"

"Yup," he said.

"Oh, and aren't *you* satisfied with yourself! Why didn't you tell me? Every time we chatted on the phone you were so evasive I just thought you hadn't managed to get the balky old engine started up again. Well, I want to see it immediately!"

"Before your reading glasses are repaired?"

"I shan't mind a little eyestrain. Now, don't do this to me! It's your new novel, Terry!"

Anne fidgeted in the car while Terry went upstairs to his bedroom in the manor house for the box of manuscript. At the cottage she put off opening the box long enough to fix them each a whiskey—a very weak one for herself—and to change into a caftan. Then she piled pillows on the divan to make a reading nest for herself, adjusted the over-the-shoulder lamp beam, uncovered the script with delicacy and anticipation, read the title half aloud, nodded and plunged in. After the first couple of pages she looked up at Terry, who had drifted closer. She scowled.

"Don't loiter about looking anxious," she said. "It makes me filthy nervous when you do that."

Terry laughed, took his glass and the bottle and went for a long walk.

The rounded moon was bright and unobscured above the headland, and Terry had no difficulty seeing his way around. The nightly guard had been mounted as usual. There was a man in the gatehouse with a shotgun; another patrolled on a bicycle, rifle slung across his back, one of the many estate dogs trotting after. Anne had shown him the trip-wire alarm system that Thomas Targill had devised to protect the cottage from a possible intruder off the bay. On a night like this such precautions seemed as preposterous as the prophecies of doom with which Gran Gudder had seduced his sister. But he wouldn't try to interfere. The loyalty of his Cornish "cousins" was touching, and they didn't seem to mind the arduous hours of patrol. They were doing it for Anne, who, unlike himself, was truly one of their own.

The estate that he and Anne had jointly owned since the death of their mother included some of the richest farmland in Cornwall. Thanks to the diligence of Targill and the score of cousins who lived and worked there, Tuck's Estate showed a fine profit year after year. It was a very large farm for Cornwall, two hundred acres and a bit, entirely self-sustaining, as it had been through a number of wars.

Marian Holgate married the master of Tuck's Estate six months before the Battle of Britain, and retired there to bear her first child and wait out the war. Anne was born a few days after her father was killed by a bomb in Plymouth. In 1942 Marian wed a British army officer, who died, ingloriously, of tetanus at a camp in Scotland when Terry was only a year old. So neither of them had any memories of their fathers. Anne's maiden name was Northey; she had much preferred the sound of her married name, and kept it. Terry, with a father's name but without a father, eventually took Donald Camming's name for his own—a move that infuriated Marian Holgate.

He poured another drink on the prowl, stopped at a spigot for a splash of well water. He hadn't meant it, but his ramble had brought him to the stable yard. There was a lump like a rock in his throat as he gazed around at the nearly deserted stone-and-timber stalls. Something that looked vaguely furry in the moonlight skittered across the cobbles and disappeared in the shadow of the oak that grew in the center of the stable yard. Marian, an avid horsewoman, had ordered the stables built, but they were no longer used very often; it seemed to Terry a dismal place even beneath a softening moon. He got out of there.

After the war he and Anne had remained at Tuck's Estate much of the time while Marian resumed her career. Her notions of child rearing, always progressive and sometimes quirky, permitted the belief that her children were better off at the farm or on the road with her than in public schools. She engaged a succession of excellent tutors for them. Anne, already showing high promise as a mathematician, developed her skills under the eye of a retired professor from Heidelberg. Until it became evident that even a succession of brilliant tutors couldn't keep pace with Anne's intellectual development she and Terry were inseparable, absorbed in each other. They needed no other company.

When Anne left to attend a school for gifted children in Brussels, Terry was enrolled in a spartan public school in the north of England. He found both the regimen and the weather intolerable, contracted pneumonia, was shunted home, and was again equipped with tutors. Much of the time he was alone on the farm and miserable. Worst of all, Anne had found new interests and new friends; she was seldom at Tuck's Estate anymore, and they grew steadily apart.

Then came Marian's third marriage, to Donald Camming, an expatriate architect from the United States just beginning to make a name for himself in England and on the Continent.

Terry walked back to the cottage and looked in. Anne was deep into the manuscript.

"Think I'll go to bed," he said, yawning.

Anne rubbed her eyes but didn't look up from the page she was reading. "Yes, why don't you."

"How is it so far?"

"Don't bother me."

"If the wind holds from the northwest we could go sailing tomorrow."

"Yes. Uh-huh."

"Well, good night."

"Hm."

When he saw her again it was five thirty in the morning. She was sitting on the edge of his bed with a hand on his shoulder. She had shaken him awake.

"Wuzamatter?" Terry said. There were tear tracks on her face, visible in the steely light from the windows.

"I just woke you up to tell you that I love you and that it's going to be a very great novel. That's all I have to say. Now turn over and go back to sleep and I'll see you in a few hours." She kissed his cheek and stole out of the bedroom.

Terry butted his head into the pillow and smiled, pleased. For about half a minute he listened to the dawn birds, their chirpings like little blisters and bubbles of sound breaking through the pane. Then he fell asleep again.

DESPITE ALL THE claptrap that was published to lure mobs of tourists to the southern coast, the usual ratio in Cornwall was hours of sun to days of deluge or windy drear, even in midsummer. But for almost a week the exceptional weather held: it was gusty but fair, hot on the water when the wind slackened.

Years ago they had both learned to sail in the no-name fishing boat. Anne had done some early chipping and painting and sail mending. The boat had a single mast and a deep keel, and she was a veteran of sixty years in local waters. They sailed her back and forth across the broad bay, dodging the motorboats and water skiers, and ventured up those estuaries still inaccessible by road and thus largely untouched by the tourists who were packing every available holiday camp and roasting head to toe on the public beaches. In the good trout streams that flowed down through the vales above Gwenny Bay Terry fished for their dinner while Anne roamed and indulged her newfound passion for sketching. They talked very little during the days. But evenings, with the dimming tide at their feet, a fire blazing on the stones of an old jetty, they sat wrapped in blankets and drank mulled wine. The best of their memories bubbled easily to the surface then. And when she had her thoughts in order, Anne was able to talk about the new book.

"I know what it must have cost you to write *Second Growth*."

"I've been trying for ten years. Getting far away from England was the answer. So thanks for the push."

"Thanks for treating me so well in your book."

"I gave you a number of lumps."

"Well, you said my judgment is usually out to lunch when it comes to men, which is true, and you also said that I have this tendency to be the ball-breaker in a relationship, which I shall debate with you some other time, but otherwise I'd say I definitely came off as the good guy. God, I can't get over it! I'm going to be immortal. Just like Becky Sharp. Pass me a cigarette and fill the cup, dear."

"I'd better uncork another bottle."

"Good. I have in mind getting nicely snozzled tonight. It's been an enchanting holiday and it can't last forever— but I want it to. Now, then. I have a great deal to say for which you're going to loathe me."

"Of course. I couldn't stand the sight of you for three days after you took *Perkin* apart. And after you finished criticizing *Stoner* I spent the afternoon vomiting."

"You didn't!"

"Well, I also had a touch of the flu. Okay, go ahead. I'm braced for it."

Anne lifted a smoldering brand to light her cigarette, adjusted the flotation cushion she was sitting on and sat with chin in hand consulting the fire as if she were an oracle.

"How old were you when Donald hanged himself in the stable?"

"Fifteen and a bit."

"And you were the one who found him?"

"Yes."

"Why didn't you write it that way? Having Lawrence merely hear about the suicide doesn't seem strong enough."

"I did write it. A dozen times. I was never happy with the scene."

"It *is* a dramatic high point. All of Book One builds to Donald's death."

"Yes, I realize that," Terry muttered, mechanically flinging pebbles at the water.

"It may seem to the publishers that you're sloughing an important scene. Why don't you give it some more thought?"

"Right, I shall. What else?"

"You've left Mother out entirely. The novel isn't but half realized without her. She's the catalyst. She can't remain off-scene all the time. It's a gimmick that simply doesn't work."

"I've . . . already written enough about Marian."

"In *Half Hour,* you mean? Oh, but that wasn't Mother, that was a composite of every bitch actress who ever lived. She was so terrifying she seemed almost a caricature. Exactly right for the play, of course, but in *Second Growth* too much about her is unexplained. Why did a woman of Marian's robust appetites marry a—well, someone of Donald's sexual persuasion?"

"He was straight when she met him. That's why he fled the States, to leave all that behind him, pick up the pieces. He just had the bad luck to attract Marian."

"I suppose she made him feel very much the man to begin with. And then, when she tired of him, she rather casually destroyed him."

"Oh, no. She destroyed Donald for a specific reason. Because he'd come to mean so much to me. Because she was certain he intended seducing me. That's how her mind worked. She didn't understand our relationship at all."

"I have a rather delicate question to ask—and only because it isn't made clear in the book. Were you lovers?"

"No. I loved him—so he could have worked it, I suppose. But he was too fine and just a man; he wanted more than that for me."

For several minutes they sat and stared at the fire, and at each other. They sipped their wine and listened to the mild lapping of water on the shingle.

"Wind is backing sou'west," Anne said. "It'll rain before morning."

"The moon's bright enough. We could make it home tonight."

"Oh, let's not. It's cozy belowdecks."

"If you managed to patch all the leaks."

"Most of them, anyway."

"More wine?"

"Yes, but I'd better pee first." She got up and made her way lamely over the slippery stones a dozen feet from the fire, wriggled out of her bathing trunks beneath the blanket, gathered the blanket in one hand and tried to squat. One foot slipped out from under her and she sat down hard, wailing. Terry laughed.

"Owww, you needn't be such a bastard, you don't know how awkward it is to manage in a place like this."

Terry walked over and helped Anne up.

"Here, chin on my arm."

"Thank you," she said with injured dignity, and lowered herself. "You've no idea how I used to envy you, making water so easily over the stern of the boat with that cunning little dicky of yours."

"After all these years I find out you're suffering from organ inferiority."

"All I'm suffering from is a bruised bum." She nipped his wrist with her teeth and sighed in relief. "Terry, in the book you skip directly from Donald to me. What about the two years you lived with Mother after he killed himself?"

"That'll be another novel. Someday."

"You've never had much to say about those years."

"What is it you need to know? She took me in at a valuable age and did her best to destroy me. I'm not certain why. I wasn't even as much of a challenge as poor Donald."

"She was sick, that's all. Just another alcoholic actress on the skids. Oh, am I wetting you?"

"Actually you're catering to one of my minor perversions. I like to feel warm piss splashing my toes. In the shower I—"

Anne almost collapsed in a fit of giggling. "Oaf. Now you've given me a stricture. Help me up, please."

They walked gingerly back to the fire, her arm around his waist.

"I saw very little of Mother once I went to school," Anne said. "Yet even in her worst moods she never tried to abuse me."

"She thought your brain was one of the natural wonders of the universe. Also, I think she sensed an equal in you."

"Her equal as a ball-breaker?" Anne said teasingly.

"Even as a child you were in no way dependent on Marian. She knew she couldn't terrorize you without getting back as good as she gave."

"But she terrorized you?"

"God, yes."

"How?"

"That is the problem, isn't it? How could I let it happen? I was only sixteen, of course, I'd scarcely been let out in the world. What little I'd seen I didn't like. Then the shock of Donald's death— I really belonged in an institution, not with someone as poisonous and predatory as Marian."

"Oh, Terry. You're shaking."

"It is getting colder, I think. I'll build up the fire."

For another hour they sat by the fire, Anne snugly wrapped in her blue woolen blanket, her head in his lap.

"So I saved your life," she murmured, smothering a huge yawn.

"No doubt of that."

"I sat you down in a spare room with paper and pencil and made you write. But you gathered up all the pieces and fitted them together."

"If you hadn't flogged me through five drafts of *Perkin* I doubt the book would have been publishable. No, I owe you my life. Which is why I'm determined to repay the favor."

"Terry, not now! It's been a wonderful day and I'm so beautifully drowsy-drunk."

"Professor Truscott is beside himself with anxiety."

"Isn't that sad?"

"I received another cable yesterday."

"Another cable! He is persistent."

"He's mad for you."

"Yes, but can I live up to his expectations? After all, it *is* the Lydia Worsham Chair of Mathematics we're talking about."

"In his wildest dreams Truscott never imagined he could lure someone of your reputation to his department. It'll be quite a coup for him."

"He's rather a good man—I think we met once. In Copenhagen? Yes. His field is crystallography."

"Did I mention what your salary would be?"

"Four times what I earn at Oxford. Even if they do have money coming out of their ears, it's a bloody rip-off. But I have no shame."

Terry said encouragingly, "It's only for a year, and you'll be strictly on your own. You needn't teach at all if you don't feel like it."

"I'd feel guilty as hell if I *didn't* teach."

"Good, it's settled. I'll cable Truscott in the morning."

"Terry, I have *not* accepted! I'm still—I don't know if—"

"Trouble with you academic types, you're no good at making decisions. Look, I will if you will."

"Honestly? You don't mind spending another year in the U.S.?"

"Not at all. It's an excellent college, and I'll have plenty of opportunity to do the massive rewrite you've ordered."

She stared up at him. "That's different. If we're going to be together, then—I think I might be willing."

"Dr. and Mrs. Hollis have kindly invited you to stay at the president's home while you're in residence. You'll like the Hollises. He's a scholar and a poker player and she's amusing in a potty sort of way."

"Couldn't we share a flat or a cottage?"

"Lot of thinking you'll get done with my typewriter going at all hours. Besides—the traffic does get a bit heavy at times."

"Oh, well, I certainly wouldn't want to interfere with your love life." Anne got to her feet, pulled her blanket more tightly around her and limped off down the jetty to the moored boat.

"Where are you going? Said something, did I?"

"No. I'm just in the mood for turning in now."

"I'll be along in a few minutes to give the generator a twirl."

"No hurry."

At the end of the jetty she stripped off the blanket and folded it over one arm. She reached out with her other hand to get a good grip on the gunwale of the fishing boat. Her naked buttocks shone in darker flesh like a simulacrum of the moon. She leaped artlessly aboard and disappeared below. Terry returned his gaze to the fire. He continued to sit for a long time, stirring the embers with a stick, feeling the sharpness of the rising wind. Now and then he looked to where the fishing boat had begun to creak and sway against the anchor chain.

TWO HOURS BEFORE dawn the rain began to hammer down.

In the little cabin of the boat an electric heater, powered by the gasoline generator, kept the air dry and almost warm. A little of the rain sifted in around the hatch cover, but there wasn't enough of it to be a real annoyance. As the rain continued, the automatic bilge pump kicked over periodically. The old boat rocked and groaned most pathetically under the lash of the sou'wester, but she was capable of riding out any kind of squall in the protected estuary.

He awoke to hear Anne threshing and whining in her nightmare in the larger bunk opposite his. He rolled out of his cramped space, skin tingling, fumbled his way to her side, knelt there. She kicked off most of the blanket; from thigh to cheek she felt oily-moist and hot.

"Anne," he said comfortingly, his hands on either side of her face to check the wild tossing of her head. She gasped and wailed and came awake and instantly went rigid, feeling his hands on her.

"No, you're all right, it's me."

"Ohhhh—Terry."

He pressed back wet tendrils of hair from her forehead, meekly stroked a humid temple. Anne tilted her face to kiss the hollow of his hand. Still only marginally awake, teary, a little dazed, she reached out and grasped the hard bowl of his shoulder, stroked downward as if reassuring herself, let her hand fall to the glut of muscle just above his waist. She moved her hand a little more around toward his stomach. The rising ball of his cock touched the inside of her wrist, rebounded, touched again more strongly, inspired a crawly wave of pleasure in her loins. With the pitch of the boat she shifted in her bunk, long legs sliding together. She propped herself on one elbow and moved her head in the dark, sweetly nudging aside his still caressing hand. She found his lips with the tip of her tongue and parted them. He tasted, then kissed her. But, shy as always, he seemed to be holding back. Anne smiled and reached low while keeping his full attention with lips and flirtatious tongue, slid her hand between thigh and hefty ball dangle, and pressed gently into him with her long fingers. Terry rose as if levitated, edged into the bunk, and now possessed by his own need, bowed to her. Anne held his head voluptuously as he pressed his hard mouth against the liquorish cunt, so ennobled by their passion. She began a deliciously slow and deeply felt erotic churning. She took him, root and head, fully in hand to help him enter her.

Instead of pressing forward to complete their coupling, Terry raised up joltingly, pulled her hands away from his groin and fell backward out of the bunk.

"Terry!" she cried, shocked and humbled.

He was already on his feet, hunched, moving toward the hatch cover. On the way he grabbed a slicker and clawed his way into it. Then he was topside, in the storm, and she heard the hatch cover slamming into place.

Anne lay back in the bunk with her hands tight against her face, still in rut, unable to control her solitary squirming. It was several minutes before the ache of incompletion subsided.

Then she rose, numbly dressed in sweater and slacks, found her own rain gear, zipped herself into it, picked up an electric lantern and went topside to the rain-dancing deck.

Terry was standing with his back to her, both hands on the gunwale, rain full in his face. She held the lantern aloft to see him better.

"What's wrong? Why did you do that?"

He turned briefly. She saw the scared flash of his eyes, followed by a tight smile.

"It's the curse of our existence, no doubt about it."

"I don't feel that way. It isn't wrong for us to want each other. To need each other so badly."

He made no reply.

"Terry, why can't we be lovers again? Neither of us has ever truly loved anyone else. There's only an accident of birth blocking our way, and—why in God's name should it matter so much?"

He shook his bedraggled head and looked, by his posture, as if he were going to throw himself overboard. Anne felt a twinge of fear.

"I'm going below to make coffee. Please come in before you wash away."

Without lingering to see if he'd heard, Anne went below and hung the light. She busied herself, heart aching.

She was sitting on her bunk with her own cup of coffee, grimly determined not to cry, when finally she heard Terry opening the hatch.

Part Three

PROPHETIC DREAMS

JOHN OXLEY HOLLIS III spent a very restless night, but at his age he could stand it.

He devoted most of his wakeful hours to fretting over the itinerary he'd worked out, adding or subtracting the odd side trip and the long overview, cutting too-familiar corners and dodging all the obligatory exemplaries that he was bound to run into over a period of time anyway. Then he reviewed every detail of the engine overhaul that had required most of his day, but though he was willing to be critical of every quarter turn of the wrench and the merest speck of carburetor grit, he really couldn't come up with anything to be uptight about; his Honda CB 500 just wouldn't fail him. As for the borrowed Triumph Daytona he planned to ride, well, it was almost a new bike, and Marvin, despite his attitude of benign neglect toward things mechanical, probably hadn't had the chance to foul it up yet. If for some reason the Triumph did poop out on him, they could always ride double. Too bad he hadn't had the guts to suggest that in the first place.

Oxey briefly entertained himself with the image of the two of them streaking toward the sunset, her arms firmly clamped around his waist. But that was too much—it amounted to self-torture.

Morosely he struggled up out of his tangled bed, put something trivial but soothing on the complex tape deck which he'd built himself, clamped on earphones, and finally dozed off with Peggy Lee crooning almost subliminally in his ears.

When he awoke it was already fully light outside and the earphones were pouring forth the white sound mix from the tape he'd cued to cut in after Lee.

His neck was stiff from lying half propped up on the pillows. He reached for his Oyster on the table next to his bed. Six forty-five. Jesus, the morning was half shot already.

Oxey made for the shower, let it pour down just a few degrees above the freezing point and debated skipping the weight course for once. But he was wide awake now and stern with himself. Yeah, procrastinate this morning, and maybe tomorrow you won't feel like lifting either, and then what do you have to look forward to the rest of your life? *Skinny shoulders*. He did the weights but cheated a couple of minutes off the end of the course and went rambling downstairs to the morning room.

His mother was seated at one end of the breakfast table going over her lists for the faculty mixer. After a disappointed look around Oxey said,

"Where is she?"

Mrs. Hollis looked quizzically over the straight edge of her reading glasses.

"Professor Ramsdell, Mother," Oxey said, crossing to the glass doors.

He looked out at the ivy-clad guest house that stood two hundred feet from the main house. A humid haze in the distance promised a hot and sticky day, so it was important they get an early start. "I suppose she's still sleeping," he muttered, and pounded a fist into his palm. He went restlessly back to the table and sat near his mother, where he could keep an eye on the guest house and the crosshatch of brick walkways that met at the veranda.

"Oh, EllaMAY!" Mrs. Hollis said trillingly.

"How's the party shaping up?" Oxey asked.

"We haven't been able to get hold of the Radaways. Professor Stuart is picketing the White House and Professor Fargason is walking barefoot through Mexico hoping to find God."

"I don't think God goes there any more; too many tourists."

"Would you say Professor Wills is an alcoholic, or is he a habitual heavy drinker?"

"What's the difference, he always winds up face down in the nasturtiums."

"I don't remember anything like that happening last year."

"When they pulled him out by his feet he claimed he'd been looking for a contact lens. He got pretty hot about it."

"Let's give him the benefit of the doubt," Mrs. Hollis suggested, making a notation on one of her lists.

Ellamay came out of the kitchen and flicked a dish towel at the Siamese cat, who was sitting in the middle of the Duncan Phyfe table pretending to be bric-a-brac. The cat jumped sideways to the floor.

"Chin-Su wasn't hurting anything, Ellamay."

"Cat hairs, Mrs. Hollis. They get in the food."

"It isn't shedding season."

"Read any good books, Ellamay?" Oxey said.

"Dr. Ripley's Two Loves, by Elizabeth Proudfoot Manning. When young Dr. Ripley graduates from medical school he can have his pick of internships at the great hospitals of the U.S.—Massachusetts General, Bellevue, Houston Medical Center. But because he is infected with idealism, he chooses to go to the little clinic in West Obispee, New Hampshire, that was founded by an old friend of his father, Dr. Sam Warnecke. Dr. Ripley's father had often warned him about Doc Warnecke. He said, and I quote, 'Rip, he's crusty and cantankerous. Make a mistake and he'll spit in your eye, but meet him halfway and you'll soon discover what a warm, decent, generous human being he is.' Close quote. Did I mention that Doc Warnecke has a sensitive and beautiful daughter who loves wild birds and children? But she also harbors a tragic secret that causes her to wander in the woods and cry out in despair. Very touching. But the folks in West Obispee think she has a screw loose. You can't blame them for being insensitive, they have troubles of their own. The woolen mill closed down in 1950, and the situation has only deteriorated through the years. Because they don't

get enough to eat and don't have anything to occupy themselves with, the natives naturally tend to be sullen and suspicious of strangers. But they also get sick a lot, so they need help whether they want to admit it or not. Do you see how Elizabeth Proudfoot Manning has set the stage for young Dr. Ripley's arrival in West Obispee? Through no fault of his own he runs over the town drunk in his sports car, immediately creating enemies and ill will. That's the critical point I was at when your mother called me out of the pantry. I can hardly wait to get back to my book. You didn't want any breakfast, did you?"

"Yes."

"I'se gwine on back to de kitchen, den. I'se gwine to get shake'n wid de pots and pans."

"Jesus, Ellamay," Oxey said. He took a blueberry muffin from the warmer and buttered it.

"I heard Professor Buncie was mugged in an excavation by tomb robbers," he said to his mother.

"I know; it just isn't safe anywhere these days."

"Here she comes!" Oxey said, almost bolting out of his chair. He forced himself to sit still. Mrs. Hollis looked at him.

"Oxey, your lips are blue," she said.

"Please, please don't bring that up!" Oxey begged, feeling humiliated at the thought.

"Well—she might think you have chronic heart disease."

Oxey couldn't bear sitting any longer; he hopped up in time to meet Anne as she was crossing the veranda.

"Hi," he said, terribly casual.

"*Good* morning, Oxey. Good morning, Mrs. Hollis."

Oxey followed her inside. She was wearing sturdy boots and wheat jeans and a ribbed sleeveless top. From his vantage point she looked *un-be-liev-able* in those jeans. . . . He walked into a chair and kicked the cat who was sitting under the chair, all in one gruesome, ungainly movement.

"Oh, Oxey, did you hurt yourself?"

"No, no," he said, forcing a laugh. Smart-ass cat didn't

have to carry on that way, it was like having some miserable kid sister around. Mrs. Hollis fished under the table for the injured party. The Siamese cat lay in an ashen sprawl in her arms, feigning shock. Oxey seated Anne and trudged around the table to his own place.

Ellamay strolled out with Oxey's breakfast and confided in a whisper, "Doc Warnecke has an incurable disease. The plot thickens." She took Anne's order for scrambled eggs and Virginia ham.

Mrs. Hollis said, "I understand you're having the Grand Tour today."

"That's what Oxey tells me."

"What car will you be using, Oxey?"

"Bikes, Mom."

"Ohhhh—"

"Perfectly all right, Mrs. Hollis. I've been a bike enthusiast for years, and Oxey has made all the necessary throttle and clutch adjustments for me."

"Won't it be terribly hard on your poor back?"

"My Honda's the smoothest-riding day cruiser made."

"Try to be back in time to fog the garden. The bugs were just awful last night."

"Where's Dr. Hollis?" Anne asked.

"He had to make a quick trip to Washington, but he'll be back this evening."

"The mixer's informal," Oxey told Anne. "Come as you are." He felt a yawn building and got a hand up just in time.

"Somebody's been keeping late hours," Anne said with a smile.

"I got to fooling around with Bolzano-Weirstrass. I think I've found a valid shortcut in proving their theorem."

"I shall be most interested in having a look."

"Speaking of proofs, have you read *Problems of Cosmogony and Stellar Dynamics?*"

"Good Lord. Not in years. You have an amazing range of interests for someone your age."

"I'll be seventeen on Lincoln's Birthday," Oxey said,

anxious to get across to her that he wasn't exactly a kid any more. "Jeans wrote that the sun loses daily by radiation three hundred sixty thousand million tons of its weight. I wonder if anyone's ever challenged him on that."

"Not I."

Mrs. Hollis looked up from her lists and frowned. "How long can it last at that rate?"

"Only about another five billion years, Mother."

"Oh, good, I won't have to cancel the party."

Founded in the late 1860s by members of an offshoot of the Southern Presbyterian Church, Kingman College had survived most of its first hundred years on church funds, its primary purpose to provide a liberal arts education—but not too liberal, at that—for prospective seminarians and DCE's. It was a poor but honest place, locally celebrated for the bedrock values it taught. The college made the most of half a dozen Georgian brick buildings that were occasionally free of second mortgages and a plot of ground on the outskirts of town that could scarcely be called a campus. The town of Kingman, Tennessee, wasn't any great shucks either. It had a few fine antebellum homes, some light industry, and there was usually enough tax money to repave the main streets when the potholes got too bad. The people who lived there liked their town just the way it was. And a goodly number of them still deeply resented what Homer Kingman had done to it.

Homer was the great-grandson of the town's founding father and the first of an uncommonly sorry lot to make good. Generations of Kingmans had failed at mining, whiskey making, doctoring, philandering, undertaking, second-story work and grassroots' speculation. Homer's uncle Bradley was the family legend: in his youth he had failed with a Ford agency at a time when Henry couldn't crank out Model T's fast enough to slake a nationwide lust for them. So when Homer made good it seemed as if God finally had had an attack of conscience and was determined to redress decades of neglect of that beleaguered family.

Homer Kingman seemed to go from his refreshment stand by the Kiwanis baseball diamond to multimillionaire overnight. A classic success story, the kind that entertains more than inspires. It appeared, even to those who were fond of Homer, that luck was indeed going around goosing him in the butt. Who ever would have thought? Homer was cast in the mold of his forebears: he was born roly-poly, shortsighted and anxious to please. As a child he was so heavy he was called Double Dipper by his classmates and even by his mother, who loved him anyway. She encouraged his interest in southern-style gastronomy and often let him have the run of her kitchen. By the time he was twelve Homer could whip up a Sunday dinner that was the envy of the best nigger cooks in town, and his cakes fetched premium prices at the church bake sales. Demure ladies with parasols had been known to sulk for days after being outbid for one of Homer's beauties.

Family fortunes being what they were, Homer had to go to work while still in high school. It wasn't long before he had the sandwich concession at the Elks dances and was catering every serious poker game in the county. From there it was a short step to his stand in the park (it is still there, surrounded by a fence of polished chrome; the once-scruffy turf of Kiwanis Park has become a landscaped green within a quadrangle of expensive Mies van der Rohe buildings, the world headquarters of Kingman, Inc.). During the long summer afternoons Homer had little to do but duck an occasional foul ball and tinker with his favorite foods—hamburgers and ice cream.

No one knows who purchased the first GoldenBurger, but it's certain Homer must have packed away a ton of his deep-fried failures before he hit on the right recipe and prepared one for a friend. The GoldenBurger was an instant hit, of course. Talk about lust—the demand for GoldenBurgers continues unabated on a global scale. Once you've eaten a GoldenBurger, other burgers, though they may be charcoal-broiled and gussied up with relishes, taste like the dog's dinner.

"GoldenBurgers?" Anne said, mystified.

"You must have tried one somewhere," Oxey said. "There are Goldies all over England."

"She has peculiar tastes," Terry explained. "Escargots, squid cooked in its own ink, rubbish like that."

"GoldenBurger," Anne mused.

"Ten billion sold," Oxey said. "At an average price of fifty cents a Goldie over the years."

"Obviously there's money in it," Anne agreed. They were in the rotunda of the new administration building, looking at a scale model of the college as it had existed only twenty years before. The original poverty-stricken buildings, home for fewer than five hundred students, now served as an experimental secondary school in one corner of the hugely expanded campus. Despite the fact that Homer Kingman had barely squeaked through high school, he'd had an abiding interest in education for others, and once he committed himself to making King-man the finest small college in the country he proceeded to sink one hundred fifty million dollars of his personal fortune into the project.

"Speaking of GoldenBurgers," Terry said, "isn't it almost lunchtime?"

"It's eleven thirty," Oxey said.

"That's near enough."

"I'm not hungry," Anne said. "Can't we have a peek at the Physical Sciences building?"

"I don't think the paint's dry yet." Oxey turned to

Terry. "What's the longest you've been able to go without a GoldenBurger?"

"Four days."

"That must have been sheer hell."

"I had a cold and couldn't taste anything."

"What goes *on* here?" Anne said.

"Maybe we're wrong to turn her into a GoldenBurger freak," Oxey said.

" 'Tis a heavy responsibility."

"Oh, are they habit-forming?"

"You won't think so. Not even after you've licked the last bits of crispy batter from your fingers. It'll be at least two hours before you find yourself looking forward to your next Goldie with ever-mounting impatience."

"Nobody," said Oxey, "can eat just one Golden-Burger."

"You're a pair of flaming lunatics. Well, let's have it over with, shall we? Take me to your nearest Goldie."

Their nearest Goldie was part of a complex that demonstrated the versatility of the Kingman corporation in applying a strangle-hold on the highly mobile American consumer. There was a Kingman double-decker motel for the road-weary, a Kingman oil station, a Kingman Double-Dipper Ice Cream Shop. And, of course, the jewel in the corporate crown—GoldenBurger.

There was no great secret to preparing a Golden-Burger. Everybody knew it was a patty of select-grade beef that weighed about seven ounces. The meat was basted with a savory sauce, cooked until half done in a patented cooker that could handle a hundred patties at once. Then it was automatically removed, robed in Homer's exotic batter and deep-fried in boiling fat for another three minutes. It was served in a paper shell and looked like a toasted discus. One GoldenBurger and a bag of fries came to 79 cents. Easy enough. But imitators always faltered. *Their* southern-fried hamburgs came out fetid and doughy, shrunken or misshapen. Somewhere along the line from raw patty to crisp, rounded Goldie a mysterious marriage occurred between meat, sauce and batter. That was the great secret. And that was Homer's genius.

"Not bad," Anne remarked halfway through her first Goldie. She polished it off in excellent time, licked each fingertip delicately, unashamed of her table manners. It was *de rigueur* with a Goldie anyway. But she resisted the urge to belch.

"Oh, go on," Oxey said. "That's part of the pleasure of a Goldie. The aftertaste."

"How was it, luv? Be honest, now."

"It's sort of—I think it has a—Mmm, yes. Quite. Rather awe-inspiring."

"You're more susceptible than most," Terry said.

"I was referring to the fact that such a whopping industry has sprung up around Homer's delicacy. And there seem to be so many millions left over for Good Works."

"Homer was a genuine humanitarian," Oxey said.

"Was? Oh, dear."

"Homer passed on two years ago," Terry said.

"Indigestion?"

"Hyperallergy. A bee sting did him in."

"Who got all the loot?" Anne said with a leer.

"The Kingman Foundation." Terry glanced at Oxey. "Left a few quid to his poor old mum, didn't he?"

"Most of her money is tied up in trusts for the next two thousand years, but Philippa can come up with a million or so when she needs it. She likes to endow chairs and create new departments. Enjoys all the fuss —you know, the cocktail parties, the ceremony, the unveiling of the plaque. You're occupying one of Philippa's chairs, Anne."

"I shall very much enjoy meeting her."

"She'll be at the mixer. She wouldn't miss it. A mixer is a great place to get the goods on everybody."

TERRY HAD RETAINED the house he'd lived in during his first year at Kingman. It was located a couple of blocks from the old—north—campus of the college on a pleasant, leafy street. A relic of Grover Cleveland's day, the house was steamboat-Gothic in style, with a couple of turrets, deep-set windows, a covered porch that went almost entirely around the house and that was large enough for a roller rink. There was a detached garage that might fall down the next time the wind shifted, a fenced back yard with flower beds heavy on the marigolds, an unproductive scuppernong arbor, wisteria, holly and lilac bushes for screening, and many tall shade trees. From the back of the house there was an uninterrupted view eastward of blue mountains—the Smokies.

Anne lay in a rope hammock between two sycamores, grateful for a vagrant breeze. It was close to ninety in the shade, and sultry. Her wrists and inner thighs were sore, and she knew she'd be a stiff old horse by morning, but the bike tour had been a spell-breaker, enabling her to shake off a bad case of transatlantic limsey. She still had no idea of how well she'd fit into the scheme of things here, but Kingman College appeared to be dedicated to academic excellence. The student body was kept to a manageable size, and there was a tutorial system modeled on Oxford's. Now, if there should happen to be a chamber music group partial to Haydn, and some untrammeled minds on the faculty, and if her students proved to be quick and challenging, then—

A screen door slapped and Anne turned her head lazily. She heard Terry's typewriter again; he was still hard at it in an upstairs room. One thing about the boy, he was dedicated. He set hours for himself, and he filled them with work.

Jeanie Lyles came barefoot down the slope carrying a pitcher and glasses.

"I thought you might enjoy something cold to drink?"

"Yes, I would. Thank you, Jeanie."

Jeanie poured two glasses of lemonade and hunkered down near the hammock to taste hers. She made a face. "Too sour for you?"

"No. I like it this way."

"There's this drink I had in England. You make it with lemonade and beer."

"Shandy."

"That's it. I've been going crazy trying to think of the right word. Maybe you'd like a beer with that? There's some Miller's cold."

"No, this is super." Jeanie looked to be about twenty-six. She was deeply tanned, and she wore a scoop-neck beige peasant dress and absolutely nothing else. Her honey-blond hair was long enough for her to sit on. She was a strong-bodied mountain girl, as sparing and precise in movement as a dancer, very reticent or self-absorbed. She wasn't beautiful, but her face had depth and balance; it was alluring in its contours and shadings. When she looked directly at you it was with a smile—possibly so you wouldn't notice the strictness of her gaze. She was one of several young writers who Terry thought showed exceptional promise. He had opened his house to them day and night, providing space to work, think or brood. Anne was also reasonably certain, on short acquaintance, that Jeanie and Terry were lovers. They made no show of it, but something about their relationship was deep beyond a need for words.

"Where's Oxey?" Jeanie asked, looking around.

"Oh—Terry and I both ran out of cigarettes. Oxey said he thought he knew where he could buy a carton of Players—that's an English brand I smoke—and before I could stop him he went roaring off. He's been gone half an hour."

Jeanie moved to the crotch between the roots of one

of the trees and made herself comfortable there. "He's real fond of you."

"Overly fond, perhaps. It can be disconcerting."

"There's joy in finding somebody you can talk to when you feel you're—different. Of course, Oxey is truly different—he's a genius."

"I've gathered that. Has his health been satisfactory?"

"His health? Oh, you mean when his lips turn blue. No, he's not sick, it's some sort of metabolic flaw. It's Oxey's way of blushing."

"So that's it." Anne sipped more of her lemonade. Jeanie sat spraddle-legged and round-shouldered like a Degas girl, playing with a hard-shell beetle that lumbered across the back of her hand. From time to time she lifted her head to look intently at Anne, but not as if she expected or wanted further conversation. She would be silent by nature, intuitive, osmotic. Anne's way, when she was intrigued by someone, was to chat a lot, ask questions, and, from the variables of response, inductively form the precise mental image she sought.

"Terry tells me you're a writer."

"Oh—" Jeanie turned her head toward the house as if she hoped to catch a glimpse of him. "That isn't true. Not yet. But he's turned me on to writing, and I think that's the most valuable thing that's ever happened to me."

"Is Terry a good teacher?"

"He doesn't try to teach, in a conventional sense. We don't do little textbook exercises. Terry doesn't care how much you write, or when. He's disciplined, a professional, but he won't try to persuade anybody that his way is the right way. He has the notion that if you come around it's because you're really interested in writing. *He's* interested in what you see, how you hear, what is unique about your viewpoint. He finds out. It isn't so easy. Then he bullies you until you've written something that is *yours*. A poem, a fragment of dialogue that rings true. For two months I hung around. But I didn't write a thing. I didn't participate. I was *resisting*. Terry should have kicked me out. Why did I bother to sign up in the first place? You see, I had this hangup. Here all my life I'd been thinking that music was enough, that I could express myself as freely as I wanted through my picking. But it wasn't enough. I needed words, the power of words. So I really did want to write, but I was too chicken. Scared I wouldn't be any good at all. Terry asked for observations. Jot something down, he said. A fragment. Anything. But see it differently. It came across as a challenge—by then we were getting on each other's nerves. So I wrote a lot of drecky things. You're going to be a poet, he told me. I thought he was crazy, but the idea of it, good Lord, just hearing him say that blew my mind. Then I really knuckled down and tried, but I was bad. Shitty bad. That's when Terry got on me pretty good. We sat up all one night and he just bullied away. He made me sort out an experience I'd tried hard to forget. It was a car wreck. Two of my own people were killed, and some boys I went to school with, killed too. It was the most awful sight I'd ever seen in my life. The blood, and the mashed bodies. What sort of poetry can you make out of something like that? But I did remember this one weird thing—funny how it stuck with me after ten years. One of the boys had been thrown from the car he was riding in when it crashed head on with my uncle Lupfer's pickup. He was dead, but he was . . . sort of like in a sitting position by the side of the road? And one of his arms was hung up in this old bedspring. With that dark look of death around the eyes, he was like a burglar trying to pick the lock on the gates of heaven. That was the image that came to my mind, and around it I wrote a whole poem in about thirty minutes. Wrote it right off. Then I just sat and cried buckets, and I'm not ordinarily the crying kind."

The surprising flow of words ended as abruptly as it had begun. Jeanie blinked at Anne, then looked at her beetle, which had made its way to her elbow but had a hooky leg caught on a strand of hair. Jeanie carefully disentangled it and put it on the tree.

"Where are you from, Jeanie?"

The girl pointed to the mountainous horizon. "From the other side of the Smokies. Way the other side."

"Are you living here?" Anne asked, indicating the house.

"I stay here," Jeanie said, not troubling to emphasize the distinction. "When I'm in town." She smiled at Anne, that expressionless, masking smile. With the merest lift of a shoulder, a slight turn of her head, she could build walls. "I heard myself talking, there—hoo, Lordy, I couldn't believe it. You must think I rattle on like that all the time. But I— Really, what I was trying to do was tell you about Terry. I never have the chance to talk about him. To anybody."

"I understand."

"Finish the lemonade for me?"

"No, thank you, Jeanie. I've had enough."

"I'll just drink this little bit that's left. I've been drinking gallons of lemonade this summer, seems like. But too much of it makes my asshole itch—do you have that trouble?" Her occasional use of profanity didn't seem either vulgar or perverse. She was merely speaking plainly of a plain thing: another kind of poetry, if you wanted to look at it that way. She drank from the pitcher, tilting her head back. Her face, in a shaft of sun, was still as a pond. She closed her eyes and set the pitcher down.

"He let me read *Second Growth* before he went back to England this summer."

"It's rare for anyone to get a look at one of Terry's drafts. You must mean a great deal to him, Jeanie."

"I don't know. I'm not sure where we're at, really. Have you always been close to him?"

"Always."

"I can't imagine what that's like. I was the stranger in my family. The one who just had to cross over the mountain. I do talk too much sometimes, and that's a natural fact."

"I don't think you talk too much."

Jeanie got up then, managing it so fluidly that Anne was envious.

"Will I see you tonight?" Anne said.

"Terry asked me to go to the mixer with him. I just might go. I'd like to talk to you again, when you're not real busy. I'm in and out of here myself. Four days a week I work as a guide at the Caverns to earn some bread. There are so many things . . . I've known him a year. I don't know him at all."

"Jeanie, are you in love with Terry?"

Jeanie shrugged. "I sure don't know what else to call it. But there's so much pain in his life—"

Anne said quickly, "Not so much any more."

"I think he works real hard not to let you see it," Jeanie said with another polite smile and probing, accusatory eyes.

AFTER DINNER OXEY'S father invited him into the library for a little talk. Dr. Hollis was one of those rare birds who is both an educator and a competent administrator. He had the cheerful, somewhat overweight face of an epicure and eyebrows that looked branded on.

"What did I do?" Oxey said, taking the offensive. "I was just making conversation."

"I thought we agreed that you were to stay off *that* topic while Dr. Ramsdell is here."

"Infradian cycles?"

"You know what I mean."

"Okay. I guess I shouldn't have brought up Jack the Ripper."

"You didn't improve *my* appetite. Everyone isn't a Ghastly Crimes buff, you know."

"It's a valid subject for research. Look, I don't think Anne was upset, but I'll apologize again if—"

"No, just cool it, please. You weren't planning on making the mixer, were you?"

"Well, I— That means skip the mixer, doesn't it?"

Dr. Hollis smiled. "Why don't you take in a movie instead?"

"Okay if Marvin and I watch television upstairs?"

"That'll be okay. One more thing."

Oxey sighed.

"Don't you think you're monopolizing Dr. Ramsdell's time?"

"Oh, hell, Dad!"

"Just give that some thought," his father said mildly.

Faculty mixers didn't intrigue Oxey anyway; he'd seen too many of them, and if you couldn't get at least half-way bombed, there wasn't much fun to be had. His father wasn't too strict about his having an occasional beer, but he drew the line at hard liquor, and of course grass was beyond the pale; Oxey smoked at Marvin's house when quality stuff was to be had, which wasn't that often. Kingman College was somewhat out of the mainstream, and although the school was no longer run by the Newfound Presbyterian Church, it did retain its affiliation, and certain codes of behavior were enforced.

Oxey had begun his college career at fourteen, and he'd already soaked up much of what the excellent Physics Department had to offer him. There was no doubt about his prowess, but his father had decided he needed another year to ripen on the family vine, so Oxey was more or less marking time until he decided whether to complete his graduate studies at M.I.T. or CalTech.

Almost from the beginning Oxey's classmates had been several years older; he might have grown up lonely and traumatized but for one steady friend his own age. Marvin McSorley's IQ was adequate to get him through the day, while Oxey's was not measurable by existing methods, but they complemented each other nicely. Oxey saw to it that Marvin passed in school, and Marvin shared all the lore that came so easily to him. Marvin liked to fish, hunt, climb mountains, and despite a case of acne that was as colorful as a Tiffany lampshade, he chased the girls. He was good-natured, resolutely noncompetitive and unashamed to be found in the company of a giant intellect. He went uncomplainingly along the pathway of life that his father had blazed for him. The elder McSorley was a florist. Marvin too would be a florist. McSorley and Son. That was all right with Marvin. He liked flowers. Red ones, yellow ones, purple ones. It was a going concern, and there'd always be plenty of time for hunting and fishing.

Marvin couldn't get interested in the televised baseball game: 8 to 2 in the fifth, the Cubs were murdering the Braves. He had already mentioned a couple of times that it might be a good idea to drop around to the saddle club about nine thirty, when the girls finished working their horses. One of the girls was Marvin's cousin Beth-Alma, who was such a dedicated horse freak that she almost never went out with boys, but she and Oxey got along okay because Beth-Alma could be absolutely certain Oxey wasn't going to get funny with her. The other girl was Beth-Alma's darlin' little buddy, Daisy Burner, and Marvin was pretty sure that Daisy was a live one. He was itching to find out, but Oxey hadn't moved a muscle for half an hour. He was prone on the floor of the rumpus room with his hands locked behind his head, and he was staring at the beamed ceiling. That was Oxey's deep-think position, and Marvin knew it was hopeless to try to interrupt him.

So Marvin shot pool by himself and halfheartedly kept up with the ball game. When he was bored out of his skull he flopped down on the floor and started going through the scrapbook Oxey had consulted earlier. He'd seen the book before, but he enjoyed looking at the pictures of the girls. They were three great-looking chicks, especially the actress. He couldn't imagine wanting to kill them, much less being able actually to do it. That really grossed Marvin out, because he adored females of all ages; he was courtly and affectionate with grandmothers and snot-noses alike. Oh, that time he broke up with Peg Moffett he'd wanted to punch her in the nose, but he got over it in a hurry; he was only fourteen then and not too sure of his masculinity.

He turned to the pages of the One Who Got Away.

Looking at Anne's picture Marvin felt a pleasant little shiver, inspired in part by sexual interest. Right this minute she was walking around downstairs. After being cut up and thrown through a window—Jesus! She was the only one on earth who actually knew who he was, and she couldn't remember a thing. Oxey had attempted to explain to Marvin how the brain worked and what happened to that fragile jellylike mass when it was bounced hard around the inside of the skull, but Marvin still thought her total blackout was peculiar. Of course, if she'd had a big enough scare—that he could understand. He no longer remembered being hit by the car. It had happened when he was seven: he ran out into the street without looking and the car knocked him over. He received a mild concussion and some bad scrapes, but no broken bones. But for a year afterward they had a hard time coaxing Marvin to leave his yard; he wouldn't even walk the three blocks to school. Gradually he just got over it . . . so probably she didn't go around thinking about what had happened to her. Maybe just at night, when she was alone. Marvin knew he'd try to be alone as little as possible if he was Professor Ramsdell.

Oxey stirred and sat up, blinking his eyes as if he'd been asleep. Marvin turned over the last filled page of the scrapbook.

"No new stories? It's been a year."

"No recent victims. If my grandfather had spotted anything in the London papers, he would have mailed me a clipping right away."

"You still sending him stuff?"

"Anything that has to do with cyclical homicide. The Zodiac Killer. That new wave of stranglings up in Boston."

"Do you know why this Pretty Joe guy never tried to kill anybody else?"

"Sure don't."

"Why do you suppose he killed those chicks in the first place?"

"Because it satisfied a psychopathological need, Marv."

"That's just another way of saying he was crazy? He must be dead, then. How about all that blood he lost?"

"He could be dead. He might even have killed himself, like Jack the Ripper did."

"I thought nobody knew anything about Jack the Ripper."

"Circumstantial evidence pointed to a man named Malcolm John Druitt. The Ripper was probably in love with his mother, so—you know—he had trouble getting his rocks off with another woman. With one exception, the Ripper only killed middle-aged, alcoholic whores. They were distorted mother images, Grandpa says. And it's a good bet the Ripper had syph, which he probably caught from a whore. The last stages of cerebrospinal syphilis are characterized by extremes of puritanism, violence and macabre humor. Listen to this."

Oxey picked up a book and thumbled through it.

> " 'Two little whores, shivering with fright
> Seek a cozy doorway, in the middle of the night.
> Jack's knife flashes, then there's but one.
> And the last one's the ripest for Jack's idea of fun.'

He wrote that and mailed it to Scotland Yard before he killed Mary Jane Kelly, his last victim."

"What kind of number did he do on her?"

"He scattered chunks of Kelly all over her room."

"Yucckkk."

Oxey put the book aside. "He always cut their throats first. Then he really went to work. Pretty Joe didn't go in for dismemberment. If you're using a knife, that takes a certain amount of surgical know-how. But both the Ripper and Pretty Joe were cyclics."

"How do you mean?"

"Pretty Joe killed—or tried to kill—within twenty-four hours of the full moon. Jack the Ripper killed only on the first or the last weekend of the month, when the moon was very new or very old. Infradian cycles."

"Uh, yeah."

"It's possible, if Pretty Joe is still alive, that he's in kind of a rest period of a highly unusual cycle."

"Rest period?"

"He may have just gone to sleep."

"For a whole year?"

"I don't mean he's literally sacked out somewhere. He's probably functioning as a normal member of society. He may have forgotten all about the killings and about Professor Ramsdell. But any little thing could set him off again, start him killing."

"Like what?"

"Depends on what touched him off in the first place."

"Hey, if you loan me a couple of bucks we could take the girls to the drive-in flicks."

"I don't think Beth-Alma will want to. She'd be afraid I might go berserk and try to hold her hand."

"Loan me two bucks anyway," Marvin said. "We'll find some action somewhere."

PHILIPPA KINGMAN HAD a solid grip on Anne's left arm, only partly because she'd left her cane leaning somewhere on the crowded veranda or in the muggy garden. She was holding fast because she'd taken a liking to the distinguished visiting lecturer, the first of the Lydia Worsham professors. Which was a departure for Philippa, because, as she'd said early on, usually she didn't cotton to Limeys.

"That's probably my fault—I do have a hard time understanding people who are not from the *South*. And when you don't understand a person, you don't trust him. That's a law of human nature. Now, Anne, there was something about this entrance hall I wanted to call to your attention, but I've forgotten what it was. Oh, sure! This marble floor is the vereh same kind of marble Michelangelo used to carve his statues."

"Oh, Carrara marble," Anne murmured.

"That's right, and it costs a bundle. Now, I like hardwood floors myself—plain, old, wide, pegged boards—that's good enough for me. But Homer said the whole idea was to keep the entrance hall light and airy. And it is that. But there's so damned much of the stuff, I *swear* you'd go blind in here on a sunny day! Same reason Homer had those windows installed at the head of the landing. The architect just threw up his hands, he said you don't put Adam windows in a Georgian house, but Homer wouldn't stop fiddlin' with the plans. So we got a portico out front, and a *gal*lery across the back, and Greek columns . . . I guess you would be interested to know, since you're a mathematician, that each one of those steps to the landing is fourteen feet wide. And this whole entrance hall must be thirty foot square. That's bigger than my entire house. Actually I don't have room to sling a full-grown cat. But that's all right, it's what I'm used to. If Homer hadn't died I guess I'd've tried to live here, for his sake—after all he built it for us—but the contractors piddled, and they *piddled,* and they just wouldn't get it done, so finally I flat out and said, no thank you, that place is too rich for *my* blood. And I gave it to the college. There's close to three hundred people here tonight and I reckon if you brought 'em all inside and scattered 'em around these six rooms you could fire off a cannon without a hope of hitting somebody. That's how big this house really is, even if it don't seem like it all at once."

Out of the corner of her eye Philippa saw a houseman hustling through the dining room. Placing two fingers in her mouth, she whistled him to a dead stop. Then she looked up at Anne and whispered, "You know, I don't like to whistle at coloreds. That's not the polite way to do. But I *never* raise my voice." She smiled winsomely at the approaching houseman and said, "Are you Oscar or are you John Willie Charles?"

"I'm John Willie Charles," he said.

"Well, John Willie Charles, I surely would admire if you'd bring me a tall glass of ice tea? Anne? Oh, *sure,* you're gonna have *some*thing. Soon as we go back outside you'll sweat it all out of your body anyhow."

Anne smiled. "I believe I'll have another vodka Collins."

"Vodka Collins, yes, ma'am."

"We'll be in the parlor. Don't you let us die of thirst, now."

Philippa guided Anne through a wide flat-arched doorway into another huge room. This one had paneled bleached-oak wainscoting to the ceiling, an English moquette carpet underfoot.

"Well, we got the whole works in here!" Philippa announced. "Hepplewhite, and Chippendale—do you like Chippendale? That's a Gainsborough over the mantel. Some duke or other, I understand he was as kinky as a two-dollar garden hose. Sit down, honey. This is the place to be. It's cool, it's out of the hurly-burly. Don't know why they all want to stand cheek-to-jowl like that, they see each other practically every day of the school year. I don't think there's quite so many beards this year, but there's a whole lot less underwear. . . . I don't mean to be nosy, but that limp of yours, it just seemed to get worse and worse as the evening wore on. Did you do that in an accident?"

"I took—rather a nasty tumble, Philippa."

"Bless your heart!" Philippa said, leaning forward on the sofa she occupied. "I live in mortal terror I'm gonna fall get'n in or get'n out of the bathtub one of these days. That'd mean a broken pelvis for sure, and old ladies like myself, they don't ever get up again from *that* bed of pain. I'm the soul of digression, as Homer used to say. I've got a confession to make, and I'd best get on with it. Then I'll steer you right back to Professor Kedare. Incidentally, he is *not* the marrying kind."

"Confession, Philippa?"

"Well—it's no secret I've got a pot of money. An *in*decent amount. So it's been my pleasure to give the college a boost with a little gift once in a while—an infirmary, an observatory—they tell me it helps out with the taxes I have to pay. And I like to make these donations in the name of somebody who otherwise never would be heard of. So every time I pass the fountain on the south campus I'm reminded of the little girl I played with when I was a child, Asphodel Maybank. The Asphodel Maybank Memorial Fountain."

"A lovely gesture."

"Thank you. I've always admired that name. *Asphodel*. Nowadays children are named without any imagination at all. Susie. Karen. Whatever happened to the good old biblical names? Well, I suppose the Jews are still partial to 'Rebecca.' Anyhow, there's a story behind the naming of the Lydia Worsham Chair of Mathematics, and I propose to tell that story to you now. When I was ten years old my father's business required that he spend a considerable part of his time in Memphis, Tennessee. The Bluff City. In the summertime my mother and I would join him in Memphis, and we lived at the Gayoso Hotel —which, I believe, is long gone now, but in those days it was quite a distinguished address. The Gayoso was located in the heart of town, and there was a nice little park not far away where we'd have picnics on Sunday afternoons, high up on the bluff overlooking the river. But most of the time, not having a soul my own age to play with, I was lonesome. I took long walks by myself, just out of boredom, you know. One afternoon I found myself on this quiet little street near the river. All the houses were in the New Orleans style—they stood back from the street behind high walls and iron fences, and you never saw a soul in the middle of the day unless it was a colored maid in the garden clipping flowers.

"The gutters were still brimful from a big rain the night before, and I was walking along staring at the beautiful shuttered houses and wishing I could get inside one just to gawk around. Well, God is always listening, isn't he? He sent a delivery wagon along at that vereh moment to splash muddy water all over my pretty dress. I started to cry. I stood there splattered head to toe and just bawled. Next thing I knew this high-yella maid had me by the hand and she was leading me up the path to the house where she worked. 'Don't you worry about a thing,' she told me, 'we'll have that dress good as new in next to no time.' She took me right on in, and the inside of that house was the grandest I'd ever seen, just as grand as the Gayoso lobby, except the Gayoso didn't have statues of naked women.

"She set me down in the parlor and had me take off my filthy dress. Then she gave it to another maid to be cleaned and went away and brought me back a glass of cold fruit punch. While I was drinking that a lady came in, a white woman, and I never saw such silks in my life! Oh, she was fine-looking, but there was something scary about her until she smiled. I couldn't take my eyes off her. She said, 'I understand you had a little accident.' I nodded but I couldn't say a word. She took out a little purse then and opened it and gave me two buffalo nickels. 'Buy yourself some ice cream on the way home,' she told me, and smiled again, and left the parlor. Now, you know, a nigra is mighty particular about who she works for. And when I looked at the high-yella maid she was just *beaming*. 'That was Miss Lydia Worsham,' she said. 'And this is her house. And it's the *best* house in Memphis, Tennessee.' Of course at that age I didn't know what a whorehouse was. But I never will forget how happy I was going back to the hotel that afternoon, with my dress cleaned and ironed like new and an ice cream cone in my hand. I always wanted to do something nice for Lydia Worsham, and now I think maybe I have. I hope you're not scandalized."

"I feel singularly honored, Philippa."

"Oh, I am so *parched*. Where do you suppose that John Willie Charles is?"

At that particular moment John Willie Charles was having trouble with his sister-in-law Ellamay.

"I just came in to get a glass of ice tea for Miz Kingman," he said. "I don't know nothing about your paring knife."

"Paring knife?" Ellamay said. "I'm not talking about a paring knife. It's a French chef's knife, and it was on the table when I went to the pantry, right there in plain sight. I was using it to dice up the mushrooms."

They both looked at the butcher-block table in the center of the big kitchen. No knife.

"Ellamay, I just this second walked in here. Why don't you ask Oscar or Minnie about it?"

"Because they are outside minding the bar, where they are supposed to be. They are not in here goofing off."

"I'm just gonna pour this glass of ice tea for Miz Kingman and then I'm gonna get out of your kitchen too.

You're in some kind of ugly mood tonight, you know that?"

"I don't have to be doing this. I don't have to be standing here at nine thirty in the evening making hors d'oeuvres. I could be enjoying my sunset years in my own room over my boy Renfro's machine shop in Texarkana. I could be on welfare in New York City and playing tambourine at the Lenox Avenue Temple of the Burning Bush. It's a ten-dollar chef's knife that's missing. Solingen steel. And it didn't just up and walk out of here all by itself."

"Somebody took it, then," John Willie Charles said wearily.

"Well, you see if you can't find out who, and get it back."

ABOUT ELEVEN O'CLOCK a storm blew up, and that ended the mixer, which had begun to die of attrition anyway. The remaining guests ran for their cars while paper napkins and leaves whipped around their heads. It rained pungently for thirty minutes, then the rain tapered off in a departing rumble of thunder.

Anne opened the casement windows of the guest house to let the freshened air in. She changed into a caftan and reached for her violin, in a mood to tackle Dvorak. Before she was well into the concerto she realized her violin was suffering from the dampness. And, instead of singing together, she and the violin seemed to be subtly quarreling. Her attack was too timid; she was thinking instead of feeling, even where she usually felt most confident of her intonation. She struggled for the virtuoso shadings that the difficult piece demanded.

It just wasn't on, so she quit in disgust. She was even

more disgusted when some dull sod outside began to applaud her miserable efforts.

Ordinarily she would have turned out the lights and gone to bed, but he continued to clap loudly and, it seemed to Anne, sarcastically. Her Leo pride was offended and her temper flared. She went to the front door, yanked it open, looked out.

The guest house faced a little paved road that had no other houses along it. Across the way there were several acres of arboretum, part of the Kingman campus. The effect of the rain on the sweltering air had produced a rather heavy mist through which a lamp at her gate glowed with cold intensity. The Triumph Spitfire that Terry had given Anne for her birthday was parked just outside the gate. There was another squatty car in the road, on the arboretum side.

And at that distance, perhaps sixty feet, she could just make out her admirer; he was scarcely more than a shadow in the mist.

"Don't stop!" he cried, aggrieved. "Why'd you stop?" He began to clap again.

Time for all good little college professors to be home in their beds, Anne thought. She said, a little too loudly, "If you knew anything at all about the violin you'd know I was having a wretched go. Now why don't you pack it in and go along home—I'm not in the mood."

He stoped his silly applauding and leaned heavily against his car.

"Hey," he said, "I'm *serious*. I may be a musical nebbish, but I really like your playing."

"Thank you. And good night."

"Wait! Hold on there, hold everything, I've got a great little idea."

"Spare me."

"No, no—now, just stay put."

He hunched over his car, pulled something from the front seat, held it up. A bottle of whatever he'd been drinking too much of. He reached in again, came up with a couple of wine glasses that tinkled provokingly in his hand.

"I always like to have a—I SAY, I ALWAYS SLEEP BETTER IF I HAVE A DRINK WITH A BEAUTIFUL WOMAN BEFORE I TURN IN."

"Will you please— Look, I'm not going to have a drink with you, so—"

"This is a great bottle of wine. Château Haut-Brion. Twenty years old. I SAY, IT'S TWENTY YEARS OLD! I'VE BEEN SAVING IT FOR A VERY SPECIAL—"

"All right, stop shouting. Just get into your car and—"

"I've *been* sitting in my car," he complained. "For the last hour. It's no use. All it does is—" And he made a pathetic gargling noise in his throat.

Good grief, Anne thought, but she felt helpless. If he really was having car trouble, then she supposed she ought to ring up a garage. But the telephone in the guest house hadn't been hooked up yet. And she wasn't about to go to the main house and run the risk of waking everyone.

That is, if the Hollises had managed to remain asleep through this outrage.

He had placed the glasses on the bonnet of his car and was struggling to get the cork out of the bottle with a simple corkscrew. Anne reluctantly drifted down the walk to the gate. He pulled the cork and celebrated with a yell.

"Shush!" Anne said, and then she smiled.

She could see him better now. Light glistened on the rimless spectacles he wore. He was a hearteningly handsome chap, very broad through the shoulders. His pleasure in pouring excellent wine for the two of them on a misty midnight seemed quite genuine.

It was the larky kind of thing Anne thoroughly enjoyed. Perhaps he wasn't such a lout after all.

"Come and get it," he urged her, holding out her glass.

"If you promise, *swear* you won't raise your voice again or make any more fuss."

"Oh, ah do. Ah swear it. On the fam-ily Bible."

"Just *one* glass. And then—well, we shall have to do something about your car."

"No hurry. Got a little wet, that's all. The wiring's half shot. She's an old junker, but I do love her dearly."

Anne opened the gate and crossed the wet macadam. She stopped beside his battered little Sunbeam.

With a hint of ceremony he handed the glass of Château Haut-Brion across the bonnet. He used his left hand. And in the light from the lamp behind her Anne saw that two fingers were missing.

She took the glass. He picked up his own, still with the left hand.

"To old times, and the best of friends," he proposed, smiling.

Their glasses clinked together, a chilly sound in the night.

"Have we met?" Anne said, amused but faintly puzzled.

"I must not have made much of an impression the first time," he said, his smile broader than before.

He put his right hand up on the bonnet then, and she saw the knife in it.

GRRRRRRRRRRRRRRRRRRRRRRRRRRRRRRRRRRIPPPPPPPUPUPUPUP!

Oxey's four-banger Honda came around the corner a hundred yards away, and they both looked at the head lamp bobbing in the mist. Oxey had geared down for his turn into the garage, but when he saw company in the lane he changed his mind and rode toward them. Anne sipped her wine appreciatively. Hugh Thornton laid his knife on the Sunbeam's bonnet and continued to smile.

"Hi," Oxey said, idling, blipping the engine. "What's happening?"

"We're having a nightcap," Hugh told him.

"His car won't start," Anne said.

"Oh." Oxey shut his Honda off and came over. "What are you drinking?"

"Rare old wine, Oxey," Hugh replied. "Want some?"

"No, thanks, I just had a Tastee-Freez. Driving the Sunbeam tonight?"

"She's like an olddd dog—ever so often you got to git her out and give her some exercise."

"What were you doing with the knife?"

"I thought it might help to scrape some of the green crud off the battery-cable terminals. But you know how much *I* know about cars."

"It probably wouldn't help," Oxey said. "Why don't I see if I can get her started?"

"Okay." Hugh put his glass down, picked up the knife and tossed it into the back of the Sunbeam.

"Might'nt it be dangerous having that loose back there?" Anne said.

"Oh, it's just a fish-gutting knife. Not much of a useful edge any more."

They stood together on the grass while Oxey got behind the wheel of the Sunbeam and tried to coax a start. He failed three times, got out and requested a flashlight. Hugh told him where to look.

"How's your wine holding out?" he asked Anne. "Let me give you a splash more there. It won't keep."

"No, it certainly won't. I have an idea."

"Fire away."

"Why don't I run you home in my car?"

"I hate to put you out like that."

"The very least I can do. You serve an extraordinary wine."

"I can't pose as an expert on the grape. I told Ralph at the liquor store that I wanted something calculated to please a demanding woman."

Oxey gave him an over-the-shoulder look and raised the bonnet of the car.

"I'm still at a loss for your name."

"Hugh Thornton."

A good name, she thought. Solid. Masculine. Suited him.

"And the circumstances of our last meeting continue to elude me."

"Oxford, almost two years ago."

"Oh?"

"I was on my sabbatical. We met one night at the Turf."

"In the midst of the usual pandemonium, no doubt."

"I wasn't wearing glasses then—maybe that's throwing you."

"Umm, could be. I shouldn't think I'd forget your eyes. Or that indentation on the bridge of your nose, like a slot in a screw. Were we standing as close as this?"

"Closer."

"What did we chat about?"

"The incidence of dwarfism among later Merovingian royalty. Pathetic fallacy in the novels of Jacqueline Susann. Spanish dancing."

"I don't think you've had as much to drink as you pretend."

"Wrong. I don't get tongue-tied and I don't fall over. But I do wild and improbable things."

"So we met at the Turf. I was having minor dental surgery autumn two years ago. I must have been numb from the neck up that night."

He rolled some wine over his tongue and looked away from her for a moment. "How does it shape up under there, Oxey?"

"I don't know—the alternator belt is loose, for one thing, and these ignition wires are frayed and damp. Maybe in the morning I could—"

"Hell, no, I don't want you to bother. I'll call Charley at the Gulf Station in the morning. She'll be all right sitting here overnight, don't you think?"

Oxey backed out from under the bonnet and reached for his pocket handkerchief. "Nobody uses this road unless they're going over by the golf course to make out. I'll set out a couple of reflectors just in case."

He slammed the bonnet down, looked at Hugh Thornton, looked at Anne. "Want me to go along?" he said to her.

"There's no need, Oxey."

"Well—see you in the morning." He got on his Honda and rode it back to the garage.

"Let me give you some more wine, Anne."

"Oh, absolutely not! I don't think I—Well, all right, then. This is very posh, and I must say I've all but forgot how I buggered poor Dvorak. I'll just fetch my keys. Would you care to wait in the car?"

By the time she returned Hugh had made himself comfortable in the front seat of the coupe.

"Nice," he said. "Right out of the showroom?"

"Practically. A bit pricey, but I'm daft about it. My brother Terry surprised me with it on my birthday."

"He's the novelist."

"Right. Do you know him?"

"To say hello to."

"Where am I going?"

"Oh—to the stop light, hang a left, hang a right. I'll tell you from there."

If he'd been half drunk before, or playing drunk for her benefit, he was sober now, but tense and less congenial. He took off his glasses and put them in his shirt pocket.

"Did you enjoy your stay in Oxford?"

"Sure," he said, with a grimace, as if he loathed small talk. "I got a book out of it. How did Truscott manage to lure you away from Paternoster? Money? With your reputation you could do better at Harvard or Berkeley. And you wouldn't be buried way off in the sticks."

"I like it here. Don't you?"

"I'm a country boy at heart, Anne. Are we going to let a third of a bottle of damned good wine go to waste?"

"I shall definitely have to pass this time. Until I stop seeing double halos around the street lamps."

"Hasn't affected your driving any. You're good."

"Thank you. Why didn't I see you at the mixer?"

"Faculty brawls bore me shitless. I went out to the Highway Patrol pistol range and shot a couple hundred rounds. Have you ever fired a .44 Magnum?"

"Nor any other type of weapon."

"It's a real thrill. Talk about power! *Smack.* Anyway, I planned to hit the mixer just before it ended, after my esteemed colleagues had taken their Sunday hack at you and failed. I didn't count on the cloudburst. So I had nothing to do for the better part of an hour but sit in my little car with my knees against my chest and rain dripping down the back of my neck. In a situation like that, unless I'm waiting for ducks, I get morose. And a morose Thornton is a pitiful sight indeed. So I packed away a little vodka while I was waiting. About half a fifth. Then the rain stopped and the sonata began."

"Concerto."

"I want to hear it again. Soon."

"Are you married, Hugh?"

"Yes, I am. Damned good marriage. I mean, I don't feel like I'm staked down on an anthill. But the fact of my marriage has absolutely nothing to do with you and me."

"You assume a very great deal."

"It's the secret of my success, Anne. Now, you see where that rail fence is? That's my place. Just turn in through the gate."

Anne did as she was told. The paved road cut through a piney woods. A plank bridge spanned a creek and a rippling flood. The sky had cleared. The boreal moon was riding high.

"Stop here," Hugh said.

She glanced at him, surprised, but stopped. There was no house in sight.

He reached over and turned off the engine.

Anne, after a moment, put out her hand to turn the key again. Hugh blocked her.

Anne sat back, lips compressed, and stared out her window. His reflection was there, like a face on dark water. She watched as he tipped the bottle of wine and drank off what was left of it.

"You come very close to self-parody at times," she said. "And there's no fun in that."

He sighed and thought it over. "I admit I'm not myself tonight."

"You needn't press so hard. I can't be overpowered. Seduced, but not overpowered."

"All right," he said. "Then I'll seduce you."

"Well, you already have."

Hugh cranked down the window on his side and hurled the bottle into the underbrush. They heard the faraway barking of dogs. "My mutts," he said affectionately. He didn't have to look to know how carefully he was being watched, with the sidewise scrutiny of a cardsharp. He took out his glasses and slipped them on again. He smiled gently, confounded by his own obtuseness.

"Sometimes you don't have to do anything, or say a word. So it's purely visceral, is that it? Do you always trust your gut reactions?"

"I don't trust them; I've learned to live with them."

"Damn," he said. He reached out almost timidly and touched the back of Anne's hand. She turned the hand over, and he clasped it, but didn't try to assert himself. Anne appreciated that. The drinking and driving had given her a touch of the collywobbles, and just being held so placidly was greatly soothing.

"House is just up ahead," he murmured.

Anne started the car, drove around a couple of wooded bends and came to a simple saltbox house in a hilly clearing of some four acres. The house and the low outbuildings—a kennel, a stable—were enclosed by stylish split-rail fencing. A waterfall poured brilliantly in the moonlight. Anne drove past it and up to the front of the house.

The porch lights were on and a big severe-looking dog guarded the door. He was a Plott cur, Hugh explained, a strong, dangerous mix of Plott and redbone hounds. Other dogs were making a belligerent fuss. The bear-hunting dog looked keenly at the car without a sound. He probably could've eaten it in three gulps.

"I'll call you," Hugh said.

"I don't have a phone. Just come."

"Tomorrow night? Around nine?"

"Yes."

"Good night, Anne."

"Good night, Hugh."

He stood on the porch rubbing behind the Plott cur's ears and watched until the taillights of her car disappeared in the dark concavity of woods. Then he and his furry red dog went inside.

Lights in the living room, no lights in the step-down den. He paused at the bar, but only because he was experiencing the onset of a clavus. He needed ice. He quickly got out the ice and wrapped it in a towel and held the freezing compress against the back of his neck. So many headaches lately; the big mean ones could age him a year. He went down and lay in the welcome darkness of the den, faintly watched his wife at work in the studio beyond. The door was open a few inches and she had heard him come in. She was smiling. The studio was no more than a tacked-on greenhouse built by the previous owners. Joram did her sculpting there. Her hands were quick and sure tonight; she was modeling a bust of a friend.

Presently Joram cleaned the clay of her hands and took off her smock. She dressed the uncompleted bust in wet cloth, lit a cigarette and joined Hugh in the den.

He made a sound, a half groan. Joram put a sympathetic hand on his forehead, not saying anything, but her question was plain.

"I'm going to do it," Hugh said. "But it'll take a little time."

ONE NIGHT SHORTLY after the new term began, Oxey walked over to Terry's house, which was five minutes away on the other side of the arboretum. Terry's first seminar in creative writing was under way, a get-acquainted session for old and new students. They'd dragged chairs out to the porch to augment the wicker furniture and the chain-hung wooden gliders. There was beer aplenty, good talk and laughter. Terry's second novel had just been published in the United States, and it was on *The New York Times*'s New and Recommended list. Oxey figured Terry must be feeling pretty good about that.

He skirted the porch and took the back stairs to the third-floor atelier.

A painter owned the house, but he now spent most of his elderly days in the warmer climate of San Miguel de Allende. Terry had economically transformed the floor-through atelier into a writer's roost. He'd installed a functional gray metal desk in the north-facing oriel, flanked it with two powerful bullet lamps. One wall contained bookshelves knocked together from weathered old cedar boards rescued from a barn demolition. Colorful Naugahyde pillows were scattered around the paint-stippled floor. Around the walls he'd hung his favorite lithographs and woodcuts. There was a water bed in a partly screened alcove. The toilet, washstand and ball-and-claw tub were in a far corner under a skylight, surrounded by pots of tall green fern but otherwise not shielded from view.

Jeanie Lyles, still wearing her Dark Ridge Caverns guide uniform, was snoozing on the water bed.

Oxey didn't know how long the seminar would last, but judging from the sounds of good fellowship drifting up from the porch, they were primed to keep it up until long past midnight. He looked through Terry's collection of tape cartridges, selected a show album, plugged in the cartridge, plugged earphones into the jack so Jeanie wouldn't be disturbed.

While he listened he idly looked over the contents of Terry's desk. Copies of the first reviews had arrived. They were, for the most part, written by fellow novelists. "Victor Batchford Simms is the author of a novel, *Stopgap,* and Professor of English at Weedpatch U." Whoopee. It was a flourishing form of literary vampirism. *Mr. Camming's second novel is a curious disappointment . . .* Oh, fuck, Oxey thought, and he picked up the box that contained Terry Camming's third novel.

About an hour later, when the music ran out, Oxey raised his head, feeling vague as feathers, a little dazed. He always read very fast but with total absorption, and it took him a few seconds to recover a sense of his surroundings.

Jeanie had awakened and was hanging up her uniform in the closet. She crossed to the bed, quite breathtakingly naked before the moonlit window. She seemed restricted to her own reveries as she prepared to put on a pair of beltless Levi's. She bent at the waist to step into them. Oxey took in the commodious sway of her breasts, the foxy mask of corn-silk pubic hair, and lowered his head quickly to indulge in a wet dream of honeyed soul kisses and penetralia. He was rewarded with a bulge that undoubtedly would prove embarrassing if Jeanie came his way, so he put the thought of her out of his head and the manuscript aside and went to choose another tape cartridge.

He was standing by the desk trying to get interested in a transvestite rock album when Jeanie came up behind him, dropped a friendly hand on his shoulder, lifted one earphone and said, "Your lips are blue."

"Oh, uh—hi, Jeanie."

"Want some coffee?"

"Yeh, guess I do."

"Right back."

Oxey decided not to listen to anything. He slumped back down on a pillow and read until Jeanie reappeared with two mugs of coffee, heavy on the cream and sugar for Oxey.

She'd put on a holey white Kingman A.D. T-shirt; the *i* in "Kingman" sort of obscured one of her nipples, but the other protruded puckishly between the *A* and the *D*. They were rosebud-firm, almost pointed, as choice as anything he'd seen in the dollar glossy magazines, and Oxey sighed a deep internal sigh, tired of being taken for brotherly granted by beautiful women.

"I don't think you should be reading that," she said, sitting cross-legged on the floor.

"I guess not. But I'm almost through."

"You read fast."

"How much of this is autobiographical, Jeanie?"

"Oh—I don't think he's made any of it up, actually. But there's probably a lot left out."

"It's some book."

"Sure God is."

"When do you think they'll call it quits downstairs?"

"Little while. They're getting awful gassy now, talking about Na-bok-ov."

Jeanie went to fetch her banjo. She picked out "The Cuckoo" and "Wild Bill Jones," sang the words to herself in a soughing voice while Oxey completed his reading of *Second Growth*. He replaced the manuscript on Terry's desk and looked out the window, still involved in the novel, vexed and dreaming. He turned and went to the bookshelves and took down a couple of heavy leather-bound scrapbooks with Marian Holgate's name inscribed in gold on the covers.

Oxey was going slowly through the black pages when Jeanie put her banjo away and came to kneel beside him.

"What have you got there?"

"The mother."

"Oh. How far back do these clippings go?"

"Late forties in this book."

"Here she is with Richard Burton. Isn't that Richard Burton? He looks about twenty years old."

"Ralph Richardson. Michael Redgrave. Philip Rackstraw."

"I've seen that movie on television. Change the hairstyle, and who do you think she looks like?"

"Anne."

"It's a real close resemblance. I can't feature her as some kind of monster. But she was wicked as the governess in that movie."

"Maybe it's just Terry who thinks she was a monster."

"With good reason."

"I wonder if his stepfather was the only reason," Oxey said.

Terry tramped up the inner stairs and reached the atelier looking tank-drunk and hollow-eyed but dimly pleased with things. He kissed Jeanie's offered cheek, glanced at the book Oxey was idling through and sprawled nearby.

"Your mother won a lot of awards for acting."

"She was good. Her talent never failed, even after she failed as a woman."

"How did she do that?" Oxey said.

Terry looked at him, and then through him, so Oxey decided it was time to shut up. He replaced the scrapbooks on the shelf where he'd found them.

"How are the reviews of *Stoner?*"

"Mostly favorable," Terry said. "The heavyweights haven't checked in yet. I talked to my editor today. He said Hardwicke is doing me for the *New York Review of Books* and Pritchett for *The New Yorker.*"

"I read Simms."

Terry yawned. "Oh, Simms. He has a knack for the pitiless irrelevancy."

"It was a bullshit review," Oxey said darkly. "After I write my first novel I'm going to have it privately printed and secretly distributed to library shelves by old men wearing knapsacks."

"Well, I think that's the way publishers do it now, Oxey."

Terry was restless; he got up and prowled, creating tensions. Jeanie looked long and thoughtfully at Oxey, who said, "Terry, I brought you some of the poems and stories the writer's group at the state hospital have been turning out."

"I'll read them in the morning. When are we going?"

"Thursday—okay?"

"Fine."

"The administrative assistant up there is a heck of a nice guy. Ken Bidwell. He's Hugh Thornton's stepson."

Terry stopped pacing. "Is he?"

Now that the name of Thornton had been evoked, there was much more on the top of Oxey's tongue, but Terry's attitude wasn't encouraging. So Oxey said, mumbling, "I guess I ought to be getting home."

Jeanie counted his footsteps until she couldn't hear him going down any more; she lay back and counted the moths circumnavigating the white ceiling fixture suspended above her. She said to the motionless Terry, "That Hugh Thornton zeroed in on me about three years ago."

"Did he?"

"I could have fallen for him. He has a lecher's eye for women, and perfect pitch. There are times in your life when you're in the mood for somebody like that."

"How extraordinary."

"There are girls who say he's terrific in bed," Jeanie continued, with an afterglow of malice that surprised her. "Is he seeing a lot of your sister?"

"You're a right bitch tonight," he said hatefully.

Jeanie sat up and rocked herself. "Go away, Jeanie," she crooned. "Go bang your pretty head on a cement sidewalk, Jeanie."

"No. Bloody hell. Don't go away."

"Why not? Do you need me for anything?"

"I'm not in the mood for a row, that's all."

She was suddenly remorseful. "Terry? Touch me?"

He came over and sat down at her side, facing her.
Jeanie put her chin on his shoulder like a hound would.
He traced her pebbly backbone with his fingers, and she
felt him softening. She looked into his eyes, like blue oil
mystically burning. She seized him by the ears and gave
him a slapdash bollixy loving that ultimately made him
smile.

"Yes, bitch. And you want to know why? My lips are
flaky and that tooth of mine is twinging again and I'm
constipated. I hate my job, it's too cold down there even
in summertime and I get stone bruises. I just feel sort of
turdy and cunt-funky and demoralized. I'd like a cold gin
and bitter lemon in a tall glass, and a soapy hot bath.
Then you know what? I'd like another gin and bitter.
And then I'd like for you to dry me off with a big old
towel, rough as you know how to be. Then I want to
break out the mineral oil and have you rub it all over me
and rub it up into me too, and I'll do the same for you.
Then I want to get on that water bed slippery and loving
and come all night with you, man."

Terry responded instantly, as if he intended rape on the
spot, and Jeanie was so eager he was able to conceal the
sham for several minutes. But then she pushed his hands
away and sat up, naked back to him, and put her head in
her hands. Unsure of herself, scared of entrapment, she
shook him off.

"No—*that* isn't loving, it's fine-tuning. Terry, it doesn't
work for me if it doesn't work for you."

"I'm sorry—tonight I—"

"Tonight; every night. How long is this going to go on?"

"Jeanie?"

She shook him off again and rose, dourly in heat, arms
crossed on her breasts.

"I waited all summer for you, Terry. What's happened?
I just *can't* wait any more." She walked to the water bed
and collapsed on it, floated low in pain and sorrow.

After a while Jeanie heard Terry go out and he didn't
come back.

Poor
Anne
who
sleeps
to dream
and
dreams
her
deaths
of bloody
disconnection
Death's
Anne
must
kill
the
hatted man
she'll
slice him
to
perfection
so
it's
chop
his fingers
lop
his bones
chop ye
coldly
through
his groans,
Death's Anne:
yes
rabid

chopping's
done
him in
but
wait
look here
who's
this
who dies
upon
the
floor
in gutty
exculpation—
dies
weeping
on
the
floor?

Enough!
I'll
wake
I shall
not
sleep
through
one more
visitation:
for
I cannot
bear
to see
Death's
stare
in
the eyes
of

my
Terry-O—
my sweet
my
darling
Terry-O

OXEY WAS ON the tennis court at first light, trying to work an annoying hitch out of his serve, when he heard glass breaking in the guest house and heard Anne cry out.

He dropped his racket and raced for the back door, which was closest. He saw her hand nastily hung up in a broken pane of glass, saw blood dripping; she sobbed.

"Anne—careful—don't try to move, you'll make it worse." He got a firm grip on her hand so she wouldn't yank it out of there in a moment of panic and do considerably more damage. A shard of glass was wedged into the flesh of her wrist beside the ulna. It hadn't severed an artery or the bleeding would have been torrential; hopefully the shard had missed the ulnar nerve as well. Oxey freed her wrist and she stepped back, clamping the wound with the heel of her other hand, pressing the bloodied arm against her breast.

Oxey opened the door and entered the kitchen.

Anne was leaning against the fridge. Her eyes were open, but Oxey was distressed by the somnambulistic look of her, the stark tremors, her attitude of ongoing trauma. Despite her concentration on the wound, blood continued to drip; blood skimmed in bright drops down the glazed surface of the trifling nightgown she wore, glistened on the brusque shadow of her pudendum. She breathed unrythmically, abruptly, each breath sounding harshly against her palate.

"Anne?"

"Dunno," she said, "dunno what I—"

"Anne, do you have anything I can make a bandage with?"

Oxey was already casting around the kitchen. There was a stack of dish towels beside the sink. He picked one up; it smelled clean from the dryer. He used a piece of it for a pad to hold the lips of the cut together, the remainder to bind her wrist tightly. By then she was more responsive.

"How are your fingers?" he asked. "Can you make a fist?"

Wincing, Anne made a satisfactory fist for him.

"I guess you didn't cut anything vital, but you ought to have stitches."

"Feel so foolish."

"What happened?"

"I dunno. Dreaming again. Terrible dreams. But I've never *walked* before—"

Anne looked around the kitchen. Two or three drawers hung open. She seemed puzzled. She glanced at the bloodstain over her breast; it was twice the size of the waxy brown daub of nipple and areola.

She raised her head and met Oxey's eyes. He gazed back at her with commendable self-possession. Anne tugged at one earlobe, a ritual of embarrassment.

"I *am* asking a lot of you this morning, but could you make coffee?"

"Sure, Anne."

"I'll get dressed."

Oxey put the coffee on. It was fully light now, but the sounds of dawn had been stifled in a heavy mist. It seemed sad as a stillbirth outside.

While he was waiting on Anne he examined the broken pane in the door. Apparently she'd put her fist right through it. Trying to get out? He opened the door and noticed the handle of a bread knife that had fallen into a clump of petunias by the path.

He retrieved the knife and was replacing it in the right drawer when he saw the ugly gouge across the simulated oak doors of the upper cabinet.

Oxey wondered what had possessed her to do that, and he was a little disturbed by the violence implicit in that slash. What if she'd broken the glass without getting caught on the jagged piece, and what if he'd come busting into the kitchen while she still had the knife in hand? While she was still . . . dreaming?

He shut the drawer as Anne returned to the kitchen. She'd put on lace-up boots, a mid-calf skirt and a charcoal Scottish sweater. Her face had a warmer color now.

Oxey poured coffee for her.

"You'd make a fine doctor," she said.

"I've thought about going into medicine. Space medicine, maybe—that'll be an important field in the next thirty years. How's the wrist?"

"Hurts like the devil."

"They may want to give you an antitetanus shot."

"I'll faint. I mean that—I'll faint dead away. Needles! You had just better be standing behind me—that's a warning."

"Sure," Oxey said with a curling of his lip.

"How did you happen to be up at this hour?"

"There's this dumb tennis tournament. My coach has been entering me every year since I was twelve, and I always get my brains beat out. I'm slow, that's the whole trouble. Girls who can't hit a lick can beat me, I'm so slow."

"I'll just bet you're slow with the girls," Anne said admiringly. "Is there no one very special in your life, Oxey?"

"I've mostly been around—older women. Twenty-five. Thirty."

Anne nodded. "Big-sister relationships."

"Yeh," Oxey said dismally.

"There must surely be a girl your own age who is aware of your fine qualities."

"The heck with that, I'd just like somebody I could—"

"Hmm, yes. I see. That *is* the important thing, isn't it?"

"I don't know how important it is, but sometimes it's all I can think about."

"What about Beth-Alma? Charming girl—that blasé spice of freckles and those pigtails."

"Once in a while I think Beth-Alma really digs me. The other night we were all over at Marvin's watching TV in the den. Marvin and Daisy went out to the greenhouse to have a look at the orchids his old man grows and—you know—to fool around, so Beth-Alma and I were alone. We watched a Vincent Price horror movie, you know what they're like—"

"Corn on the macabre."

"Yeh, but I think Beth-Alma was really scared. I put my arm around her, not actually touching her, and she—Jesus, I couldn't believe it—Beth-Alma moved closer to me."

"Moved closer, yes—"

"So I could hold her if I wanted to. I held her good and tight. And she—snuggled. That's when I knew it would be the easiest thing in the world to kiss her, all I had to do was lean over a little bit—"

"Oh, good! You kissed Beth-Alma."

"No. When I leaned over I could smell manure on her boots, and then I didn't want to any more."

"Oxey!"

"I can't help it. Anything that has to do with horses just turns me off. And all she *cares* about is horses. Hopeless. It's really hopeless!"

The cut on Anne's wrist required four stitches, and the antitetanus shot also seemed called for. She received all shots with face tautly averted, her lower lip sucked bloodless between her teeth. She held Oxey's hand with astonishing strength. Obviously she hadn't been kidding about her aversion to needles. Holding her protectively made Oxey's head swim; by comparison kissing Beth-Alma seemed a vapid and insignificant act.

They had breakfast at a pancake house. Anne ordered with gusto but ate sparingly.

"Well, shall I come and cheer you on today?"

"Won't be much fun. I'm playing Billy Chalk, he's seeded second. We're scheduled for four o'clock on the college courts, if you really want to."

"I'll have a look at my schedule, but I'm sure I can make it." Anne cut her blueberry pancake with a fork and said dolefully, "What I'd really like right now is a shot of bourbon."

"Bourbon?"

"Yes. Extraordinary thing, I never cared for whiskey, but I've lately developed a taste for the local varieties. Especially sour mash and—what do they call it, the clear kind?"

"White lightning," Oxey said. "I hope you haven't been drinking that stuff—no fooling, it can kill you if it's made wrong. Some of those moonshiners run their stuff through old automobile radiators, it's full of lead salts."

"Hugh must be scrupulous about his sources. He's been drinking shine for years, and never a morning after."

"Has he?"

Anne smiled, made uncomfortable by his tone.

"Oxey—now don't hang a face, don't be chuffed. He's someone I need right now."

Oxey swallowed hotly and said nothing, pretending unusual interest in an angry little blister on the heel of his left hand.

"I value your friendship," Anne continued. "I think you know that. Oxey, true friends tolerate each other's idiosyncrasies and especially their failings."

"Why does it have to be—that guy?"

"Men happen to women; women happen to men. I don't know that any of us ever have a choice."

"He's married."

"I don't want to *marry* him, Oxey. I just have to be with him for a while. It's the kind of relationship I'm always—tumbling into, but it'll be over just as quickly.

He'll fade away. But *you* never will. We have the same degree of Gemini rising, don't we? Well, that makes us more than just friends. It's a Karmic affinity. In the most exalted sense of the word, we're soul mates. If you pick any more at that it's certain to become infected. Lick it. Spittle is a natural healer. I learned that from an old woman who did my back some good."

Belief in Karma isn't rational. And astrology is—"

"Unscientific? Oh, so bloody-minded this morning. There is something fascinating about science. One gets such wholesale returns of conjecture out of such a trifling investment of fact."

"Mark Twain?"

"Mathematics, the so-called 'pure' science, labors under a formidable load of imponderables and unprovables. What is the general formula for testing whether a given number is a prime?"

"There isn't one. I don't understand—if you don't love him, how—"

"Do you love Beth-Alma?"

"No. But I—"

"Exactly. And that pretty well covers the subject of sex, except for some mechanical details you'll rather much enjoy getting the hang of yourself. Would you like the rest of my blueberry pancake?"

"Uh, yeh, I can always eat another blueberry pancake."

KEN BIDWELL HAD the eyebrows, mustache and beard of a Bouvier des Flandres. He wore glasses with heavy black frames, a woven leather bracelet, Levi's and high-top work shoes of yellow leather. His one concession to his milieu was an unpressed white jacket with *Dr. Bidwell* semiscripted on the pen pocket.

"Welcome to Tellochee, Mr. Camming. I haven't read your latest novel, but I'm certainly going to. I suppose Oxey has told you about our little writer's group."

"I've been impressed by some of the work I've seen."

"A few words of encouragement from you will go a mighty long way. I can't pretend we're going to turn out any Faulkners or Eudora Weltys. But it's the very act of creation we're interested in, as a means of analyzing functional psychopathology and purely for heuristic purposes. Actually, the writer's group is Dr. Middlemarch's brainchild—he's our behaviorist—but he's been out these past few days with tonsilitis. We're meeting on the south lawn—it's cooler there today than it is inside."

Tellochee State Hospital occupied a hundred acres on the last high plain before the mountains. At two o'clock the sun was broiling, but thunderheads towered to forty thousand feet over the Smokies. Where they walked across the crisped end-of-summer lawns the air was like dusty crystal.

"A few of our buildings go back to Civil War days," Bidwell pointed out, "but I think we have a first-rate facility here. We're making great strides in psychopharmacology. Dr. Rescher has done important work in the parametric studies of serology. We all coexist peacefully at Tellochee. *Cherchez la cause* and everyone has something to contribute, whether he's a geneticist or a developmentalist or a neurophysiologist like myself."

Oxey said, "Dr. Bidwell just finished a scenario on latent new sense modalities for NASA. It involves electrode implants for astronauts."

"Within ten years electrode implants in the brain will be as common as pacemakers in the heart," Bidwell enthused.

"Why?"

"A characteristic of brain function is the screening mechanism that prevents an overload of sensory channels. The implants could act as stimulus barriers in some cases of paranoia, or as circadian regulators for astronauts—the possibilities are endless."

"It could also lead to intentional manipulation of behavior. Dangerous procedure, that."

"We're certainly not interested in creating zombies; our goal must always be the fulfillment of human potential through the elimination of aberrant and compulsive behavior."

"Take away my compulsion to write," Terry said with unwonted severity, "and you take away my usefulness."

Bidwell smiled politely, as if he were accustomed to being misunderstood, and changed the subject. "Have you had much to do with mental patients?"

"I reckon I'll be able to cope."

"It's unlikely that any of this group will do or say anything disconcerting. Most of them are normal, by institutional standards; they simply are not adaptive to the outside world."

"You might fill me in on a couple of people whose work I particularly fancied. Abigail Weems?"

"Oh, Sister Jacobus. Of course she's not really of the Order any more—she renounced her vows after she destroyed God."

"Did what?"

"Some say God is dead; Abigail accepts full responsibility for that. Seems she was working in the kitchen of the convent one evening, and she happened to drop a heavy crock of soup on the floor. She inadvertently cursed God, and in time, according to Abigail, God sickened and died."

"An awesome burden for her to bear."

"You won't think so when you meet her. There aren't many smiles around here, but when Abby is on the upswing she often laughs, and sometimes she'll even joke about the reason why she left the Order—cloisterphobia. We all like Abigail. I suspect we have absolutely no chance of helping her."

"Rhoda Franklin?"

"You mean Rhoda and Reba. They're Siamese twins. Except Reba is invisible."

"Like that, huh?"

"Lately they've been feuding. I don't know what Reba did, but Rhoda is really chapped off at her."

"How about Valley John Powell?"

"Valley John is our firebug. A few years ago he burned up twenty thousand acres of the Pisgah National Forest. Disregarding his mania, he's one of the most charming men you'll ever meet."

"And one of the most talented."

"He could barely read and write when he came here. Lately Oxey has been slipping him Chaucer and Mark Twain."

Oxey had a clear favorite among the dozen patients who made up the writer's group, and as Terry's meeting with them ran its course he could see that Terry was also very much taken with Valley John Powell.

He was seventy or so, with a wide, humane smile that revealed a clutter of teeth like a roomful of broken statuary. He talked very little during the meeting, but he kept his eyes on Terry and nodded pleasantly now and then. He asked no questions and seemed mildly embarrassed by the one compliment that Terry aimed at him.

After the meeting Oxey waited with Valley John while Terry sat on a bench talking to a woman who had caught his eye. She wore many colorful sashes and scarves but sat with her head cocked to one side in a state of clownish catatonia, like a parrot in molt. Terry patted her shoulder after a while and left; she moved her head just enough to watch him as he joined the others.

The three of them drove into the town of Tellochee in Terry's Ford camper.

"This truck of yours has got a lot of pahr," said Valley John appreciatively.

"They build them like miniature tanks."

"Set you back right much?"

"Twelve thousand."

"Could've used a fine shocked-up truck like this one when I was a-haul'n blockade whiskey. Wouldn't be much fer speed, but with them hefty steel bumper guards it'd do fine for ram'n and wreck'n."

"Did you make whiskey?" Oxey asked him.

"Pert near all my life. I don't recommend it as purely a business proposition. There's all that grain to tote around, sometimes you got to carry a whole still on your back, and it's hot dirty work back up in the woods. See all them scars on my arms? Them's burn scars. Worse kinda burn they is. Skin just sticks to that hot boil'n metal and peels right off. But I'll tell you fellas. You make it right, like they don't hardly do this day 'n time, no sugar 'n shorts, you just go and get yourself fresh white corn like Holcomb Prolific, and build yourself a still out of the pure copper, not tin nor ahrn—that'll give your whiskey a whang taste fer sure—and then you watch your whiskey and stir it and make sure the fahr don't get too hot, and by 'n by you'll have yourself ten gallons of high shot that's worth all the bother."

"Guess we'll have to settle for hot fudge sundaes today, Valley John."

"If they's anything I like better'n a new dollar bill or a red-haired pussy it's a fudge sundae. No, I reckon I never liked nothing better than a red-haired pussy woman, because somehow er 'nother I married four a *them*. I was married five times altogether. Took me fifty years to learn to live with a woman. But I guess that ain't such a bad accomplishment in so short a time."

When they were settled down at a corner table of the drugstore in Tellochee, Terry asked him how long he'd been at the hospital.

"Well now, Terry, I never counted it all up, because it don't matter to me. I'm seventy-six years old and the hospital is home now, it'll be home till the day I die."

"Don't say that," Terry said with such sharpness that Oxey gave him a surprised look. But Valley John wasn't offended.

"Fer one thing, it ain't such a bad place to fetch up in. Now, they's plenty folks in there that is sorely touched, and they got to be kept under lock and key, but they's heap a others like myself, one reason er 'nother they just ain't much fit fer live'n on the outside. That don't mean they ain't good people in their own separate ways. Maybe they could let me go sometime and I could stay with one of my married daughters in Elizabethton or down there in Asheville, North Carolina, but shoot, who's to say I wouldn't start no more fahrs ever?—so I'd just be a constant source of worry to 'em. They do write me pert regular, and they send me money so I can buy smokes—I need m'smokes like kids need a mudhole to play in. No, sir, I don't complain. I'm happy. What kind of place was it they had you at, Terry?"

Terry looked stunned, but Valley John smiled benignly and scraped around in his tulip dish for the last of the chocolate sauce and marshmallow.

"How did you know, Valley John?"

"Lots a little things told me. You just got tighter 'n a tick because of them fences and all that chain-link window dress'n—it's something happens to the eyes of a fella when he's been inside and comes back. Oh, I've seed it plenty of times. Then there's how you talk to us. You take that nigger boy Buxtehude who writes poetry, I reckon they ain't one word in a thousand he says that don't come out smart or sarcastic, but you knowed how to handle him just right. And poor Clara—she's the one wears them gypsy clothes? She don't look up fer nobody or nuth'n, and I seed her turn her head for you."

"I suffered a nervous collapse when my mother died. I was about eighteen then. I spent two and a half years in a psychiatric clinic. Farnsworth, near London. Rather posh, actually, compared to Tellochee. But no matter how much money it costs, institutions are all alike."

"Looks like you made a right smart recovery."

"I wouldn't have if I'd stayed at Farnsworth. When my sister's marriage broke up she—accepted responsibility for me, and I was discharged. Then I took up writing. So you see, I know firsthand how helpful that can be."

Valley John held up stubby, powerful hands defined by ill luck with tools and the punishing fist fights of his youth.

"I'd be better off with a carpenter's pencil, but I do like write'n down all them stories, stories just always did come natural to me. And 'nother thing—I don't half know what's made up and what's the truth."

"That makes no difference. You just keep writing. And one day we'll put all those stories together in a book, with your name on it."

"Now, ain't that something?" Valley John said, with a shy, proud look at Oxey.

Lightning gashed the darkening sky and rain started to pour down. Terry made a dash to roll up the windows of the truck. The waitress brought another hot fudge sundae for Valley John.

"Must have loved his momma awful bad to get so upset when she died," Valley John said.

"Actually he hated her."

"Why'd he have that nervous breakdown, then?"

"I don't know. Doesn't make a lot of sense to me."

"What did the woman die of?"

"Stroke, I think. She drank a lot."

"My third wife, Elkeny, died of a stroke. She never touched a drop, because she was powerful fond of the Gospel truth. Overly fond, for a red-haired pussy woman. I believe it was the excitement of see'n a little cripple boy throw away his crutches and walk at a heal'n service that slap did her in. The Lord giveth and the Lord taketh away."

"Amen," Oxey said.

JEANIE PLAYED DOBROL, two kinds of banjo, and the Autoharp with a country-music group (three girls and a boy), and they called themselves Chobalob. Which, as Jeanie explained to Anne, was the gobble of a wild turkey in the brush. She demonstrated—*chobalobalob,* a throaty, rattling sort of sound. Jeanie was about half drunk on the Boone's Farm apple wine they were all passing around under the trees. She tried to show Anne how the button keyboard of an Autoharp dampened the strings and resulted in a distinctive tonal quality unlike that of a zither, but there was a lot of handclapping and hooraw going on, and Anne had trouble hearing even with her ear close to the resonator. The Kingman Country Music Festival had been in progress for three sultry hours, and it was only about half over. In the school's stadium a group of clog dancers from North Carolina were testing the integrity of the temporary stage. About eight thousand people had paid for seats in the stadium, but another few thousand were situated on the hillside behind the stadium, where they could hear almost as well, had plentiful shade and soft grass to loll on.

A winsome, breast-fallen maiden dropped down on one knee beside them.

"Hey, Barbry Dell. Anne, this is Barbry Dell. She fiddles. This here is Professor Anne Ramsdell, who is a concert-quality violinist—and I'm telling you some honest shit, Barbry Dell."

"Jeanie, maybe you better not guzzle any more of that wine until after we go on?"

"When's that going to be?"

"About forty-five more minutes. Hey, listen, I been down there talk'n to Merle Watson, they just got here, y'know? And Merle says Doc may want them to do 'Knob

Lick Shuffle.' So I think we ought to plan to go with something else."

" 'Bonaparte's Retreat'?"

"No, the Skillet County Band did that one already. How about 'Sparkling Brown Eyes'?"

"I'd half forget the words, it's been so long."

"We got it on tape in the bus, Jeanie."

"You want me to get my ass on down to the bus and listen to 'Sparkling Brown Eyes,' hey, Barbry Dell?"

"Sure would appreciate it. Now, you be good, y'hear? Enjoyed meeting you, Anne."

> *Too much sin'n*
> *Not enough pray'n*
> *That's what's the*
> *matter with this wurrrrld.*

Jeanie stood and dusted off her rump. She was wearing a soft buckskin dress and a black slouch hat. "Want to come along?" she said to Anne.

Anne carried Jeanie's banjo case and Jeanie carried the Autoharp under one arm. She paused to hug a man with a black shrub of beard and to kiss his little boy on the cheek, then they made their way down to the group's Winnebago motor home in the parking lot. The engine was running and the air conditioning was on. Jeanie put her own instruments in a cupboard and handed Anne a violin case.

"That's Barbry Dell's. Her granddaddy made it forty years ago, and she wouldn't trade it for any old Stradivarius you could name. That's a Tubbs bow—supposed to be pretty fair."

"Yes, it is. Would she mind if I—?"

"Help yourself."

There was the expected tacky buildup of rosin under the gut strings, which wasn't carelessness on Barbry's part; many country fiddlers believed that the accumulated rosin imparted special tonal qualities to their instruments.

After only a few moments of bowing Anne could tell that Barbry Dell's granddaddy had the eye-instinct for fine tolerances and the loving intuition of the master craftsmen. Good carrying power. High tones on the D string are convincing proof of a fiddle's tone quality, and the strong, dark-souled tones she easily produced were in keeping with the large dimensions of the chestnut-colored fiddle. Rather like a Gasparo da Salo she had once played and coveted. Anne's own Landolfi violin had cost a bit over nine thousand dollars years ago, but she would not be ashamed to appear in public with this one.

Jeanie found the tape she wanted and put it on the machine. She played "Sparkling Brown Eyes" twice, singing along on the second play.

"It'd sound better with a wah-wah pedal, but I guess we'll get by."

"I like Chobalob," Anne said.

"We've been hanging around together about four years now. There's not much money and no glory. Oh, we cut an album last year. Had a manager—I thought we might be going places. But he was so incompetent he couldn't take a piss without filling up his shoes." Jeanie sat back with her hat tilted down over her eyes. "You care for our kind of music?"

"I'm learning to appreciate it."

"There've been some good string bands here today—most of these groups are tradition-minded. But I wish you could hear the mountain music down around where I come from. Just to get there is kind of an adventure. You take the hard road to where it stops at the state line, then you pick up this clay road—that is, if it's not raining hard, nobody goes through in a gully washer without four-wheel drive and plenty of luck, and you follow the clay road maybe ten miles on into the deep cove country. And by and by you'll come to Chechero. Which is one store and one café and one gas station perched on a hill between a pile of tires gone bald from the sawmill grade and a churchyard cemetery. The church burned down before I was born and they built another one in a different place—it's some sort of local superstition. Anyhow, maybe an hour after supper in the evenings, after they've all had two desserts, one at the table and one out on the front porch, if they've got a front porch, and they've hoed the bean patch and done whatever fixing there is to do around the house, then they'll start dropping by Lon's gas station in twos and threes with mandolins, fiddles and banjos. All our best musicians—there's probably not a one of them under seventy years old. But *pick? Fiddle?* Shoo, those old boys can do it all. That's where you hear the real down-home music, in places like Chechero. But it doesn't travel so good. Even this far."

"Tell me more about Chechero."

Jeanie smiled. "Well—it's a good place to grow up to learn how to take care of yourself. I was one of twelve kids. I can plant and cook and weave, so if I never saw a dollar or another human face I could get along real fine. Let's see—I know prayers and spells for everything from stopping blood to casting out devils, and I can protect myself from a werewolf—oh, we've got them where I come from. I know just what sign is right for making a baby that'll grow up tall and strong and clear in the head, and I know how to get rid of one if I don't want it. I know a blessed lot of things, but I swear I don't know how to get Terry away from you."

"What do you mean, Jeanie?"

Jeanie's smile didn't change. "You know just exactly what I mean. When it comes to loving, people are all alike. My older brother Carl, I'd have given him my breast any time he asked, I loved him so. I don't think he ever noticed me to say scat to. And I'll tell you something else, in the mountains if a man has a lot of children and his wife dies, and he doesn't marry again, then it's sort of up to the oldest daughter to take over the chores in bed. So it doesn't bother me about you and Terry, nothing human *ever* bothers me. But I know I love him more than you do. And I want him back."

"I am not . . . sleeping with my brother, Jeanie."

"Well, who is it if it's not you? You started with him when he was only ten years old."

"Oh, Jeanie, that was—"

"I know, I know, rubbing together and hand jobs. But mama it's still called fucking, even if you didn't truly have the hang of it then. Now, don't be telling me Terry isn't getting into you regular, because I had him, had him all to myself, till he went home to England this summer. And since he's come back I've just about been going out of my mind, but he won't hardly touch me."

Despite the smile tears were streaming down Jeanie's half-concealed face. "What am I, some kind of woolly-wart old cunt you wouldn't throw to a truck driver? Are you so all-fired great in the sack? Listen, I don't even think I'd mind going tandem with you, that's how much I love Terry."

"I don't know what the matter is between you and Terry. But it has nothing to do with me."

"You're a goddamn liar."

"I don't want to fight with you, Jeanie. I have to go."

Jeanie sobbed. She sat up, and her slugnutty hat fell off. She snatched at it and hurled it. "Liar! Liar! I've seen how he looks at you!"

Anne stepped down to the sizzling asphalt of the parking lot and shut the door of the motor home. She was assaulted by the heat, by the blare of twenty loudspeakers. Her skin prickled; she felt light-headed.

> *Fly ye away from my window,*
> *little bluebird*
> *Fly ye as far as ye can*
> *away from here*
> *And let not your song*
> *fall upon my ear—*

She was fumbling in her purse for her sunglasses when she ran into Hugh.

Anne hid her eyes from him as quickly as she could, but she couldn't disguise the hard lines of distress around her mouth. He put an arm around her and she leaned against him, not giving a damn for anyone's obloquy.

> *Go spread your blue wings*
> *And I'll shed my blue tear.*

"Hey, now," he said. "You don't look too good."

"I'll be all right. Hugh? Please take me somewhere. Anywhere."

"I know just the place," he said.

BIG PLUCKY THE cur hound was making a lot of noise. He was all by himself in the echoing dawn, but to Anne, snuggled in the depths of a big feather bed, his belling was like unto the questing of thirty couple hounds. She groaned and groped for another fat pillow to pull down around her ears, discovered that Hugh was no longer in the bed with her and sat up suddenly. She shivered nakedly in the chill air of the mountain lodge and pulled the covers more tightly around her.

Hugh came in from the bathroom with a towel wrapped around his flat midsection, giving his hair a brisk rub with another towel. Big Plucky continued to bay outside.

Anne yawned. "Time is it?"

"It's soon in the morning, as they say in these parts. About twenty of seven." Hugh sat down on the bed and kissed the nape of her neck. Anne smiled and shivered again.

"How do you feel?" he asked.

"Headache. And I am sore, sore, sore. Owwwww."

"Twenty minutes in a hot shower, you'll be as good as

new. We started off drinking applejack, if you remember, then switched to the local vintage—good old Smoky Mountain strawberry wine, mixed with a little sugar and ginseng. The sugar is the reason for your headache. And the ginseng is probably responsible for your sore bottom. It's one hell of a potent aphrodisiac. They've made it illegal to dig the root in the park anymore, but there's always some ginseng to be found if you know whom to ask."

Anne put her head on his shoulder. He smelled of pine soap and strong coffee. She rubbed his head idly with one hand, tongued a drop of water from the spiky mat of graying hair on his chest. With his mutilated hand Hugh patted her rump, an affectionate and proprietary gesture.

"We certainly didn't miss a trick, did we?" Anne said somewhat moodily. "I haven't made love that way in years. Not many men want to, actually."

"You pleaded with me. In five languages. And it even sounds erotic in Russian."

"What is the *matter* with that dog?"

"A couple of boomers are driving him nuts. Red squirrels. They get Big Plucky to running in circles until he trips over his own tongue. I'll call him in. You getting up, or what?"

"Yes. At once. Give me ten minutes to bathe, and I'll soon have your breakfast on the table."

"Breakfast is my treat. I do most of the cooking up here. Take your time in the tub, I don't have to leave until eight."

Anne had thrown off the covers and was halfway to the bathroom. "Where are you going?"

"I'm the keynote speaker at the Southeastern Conference of American Historians luncheon at UT."

"Right, you did mention that. You won't be gone all day?"

"I'm afraid so. Don't worry, you won't be bored."

After her bath Anne put on low-slung corduroy pants and a plum-colored turtleneck sweater to hide a vivid suck mark at the root of her throat. Unfortunately, suck marks were unmistakable, and it often took two weeks for one to fade away, so it would be high-necked blouses and sweaters for a while. She walked barefoot down a short dark hall to the main room of the lodge, smelling hickory-cured bacon on the fire.

Hugh was busy in the island kitchen, humming, occasionally breaking into a snatch of hillbilly song. The walls of the lodge were roughhewn timber, half plastered and unpainted. The ceiling was low, heavily beamed. One wall was all glass, framed in steel, and sliding doors opened onto a screened deck that was cantilevered over a three-hundred-foot slope of nearly barren limestone.

Anne walked past Big Plucky, who was sitting near Hugh waiting for his share of the bacon, and went outside. The cove below was half filled with mist; it looked as solid as a snowbank. She shielded her eyes from the torchy brilliance of the sun rising northeasterly through conifers that formed one steep and shadowy green wall of the cove.

"Sometimes in the fall," Hugh said, "the mist will rise until it seems to be floating right outside the screen. And you don't hear a sound—not a bird, not a leaf stirring. It's eerie. But we're in for a gorgeous day. Before long you'll be able to see for miles through Smokeshade Notch, one blue cove after another all the way to Fontana Lake."

"Where are we?"

"In the middle of Smoky Mountain National Park, on one of the last holdings of private property in eight hundred square miles. Actually I own the lodge, but not the land; it's a lifetime lease. My father was a lumberman; he arranged for the lease before all his timber was incorporated into the park. Harb Turk—he's an old settler and professional poacher who lives down the road—has a similar lease, and so do the families over at Cade's Cove. Let's get after breakfast while it's hot."

Thick slices of bacon, a golden omelet, waffles soaked in long sweeten'n. Anne ate until she was afraid her eyes would bulge. Hugh handled most of the conversation. He told her that she could call birds out of hiding by kissing the back of her hand. He told her about the mature Coprinus mushroom, which was able to consume itself by secreting an enzyme that dissolved its own tissues. The cocoons on the porch, he said, were Cecropias. Each would produce a moth capable of spinning up to a mile of silk thread. The ruby-throated hummingbirds often produced three broods a year. The turtles, which came to lunch when anyone was in residence, liked fresh corn on the cob. The racoons, on the other hand, were just crazy about jellybeans.

"Uh-huh," Anne said groggily, and pushed her plate aside.

"More coffee?"

"No, thank you. That is a particularly vicious-looking bear's head on the wall. Did you kill him?"

"That one and a few others. I've been in on a lot of kills. He's one of the biggest black bears ever shot in these mountains. Weighed in at three hundred pounds. There isn't anything I'd rather do than hunt bear. Give me a few men like old Harb, a couple dozen dogs that can smell a bear fart half a mile away on a frosty morning, and we'll have ourselves a *good* time. Right, Big Plucky?"

"So many men and dogs? Doesn't seem half sporting."

"Show the lady your hard-earned scars, Big Plucky. He's a strike dog, one of the best. But I've seen even a medium-sized bear hold off a whole pack of hounds, kill a couple, until you shoot him dead. Hell, I enjoy the hunt so much I don't even mind skinning the brutes afterward. I'll even eat a piece of bear meat roasted over an open fire—and you've got to love a bear to eat him."

"Not so tasty, is it?"

"There's a famous mountain recipe for fixing bear. You drop some rocks in a pot of boiling water with the meat for several hours. Then you throw away the meat and eat the rocks."

Anne smiled and said, "You don't really enjoy the bloodletting, do you?"

Hugh gave her an odd, almost startled look, as if she were trespassing in his mind.

"Of course not. But the kill is the logical conclusion of the hunt. It's an act of good faith and not of passion. The hunt itself is a process of unlearning, of simplifying myself emotionally. In each hunt there is potential danger, but at the same time I'm reassured by trappings of ritual, the predictability of the outcome. In thirty years of study I've come to accept the fact that history is neither instructive nor predictive. We are all hostages to our psychosexual selves, therefore the future as history is written in terms of the same old random, destructive confrontations: man against man, man against himself. So I hunt bears, for the reasons given. And I also chase women, to unlearn fucking. If that makes any sense to you."

"Perhaps it does. You're not like other men in bed. I do tire of the hearty romper and the busy worker—diddle this, belabor that, tongue in, tongue out, busy, busy, busy. You can be so very still for the longest time, yet totally alive, creating awareness; and then when you move, move deeply, there's a tremendous communication of feeling. That's awfully exciting, as you may have observed. What causes your headaches?"

"Headaches?" he said.

"You've had them before, but tried to hide them from me. They seem to drain every drop of blood from your face. Last night I missed you. Found you with your head in a basin of ice water. You looked to be suffering so, I thought it best not to disturb you."

"Freezing cold is really the only thing that helps," Hugh said curtly. He got up, glanced at his watch, began to clear the table.

"Oh, no—I'll do the scullery work. You'd best be on your way to Knoxville."

Before he left Hugh gave her a mimeographed map of the area.

"This way to the Appalachian Trail and Clingmans Dome, but it's a good long hike from Smokeshade. I recommend the trail down below; it crosses the Yellowsnake here, loops around Tallalah Bog and rejoins the river just below Pitcher Falls. About four miles altogether, and there are some pretty resting places along the way. Unless you're an experienced bog walker, stay on the trail. Big Plucky is a good snake dog as well as a bear dog, but wear your high-top boots and keep an eye peeled for copperheads. I guess there's no need to worry about *Wildschwein,* although Harb tells me there have been a few around lately."

"Wild boar?"

"Locally known as Rooshians. It's a breed that could outfight a tiger, and they've only gotten smarter and tougher since they were introduced to these mountains around 1920. I have a buckshot hog rifle you could take along. Might not be a bad idea."

"Don't they usually travel and feed at night?"

"The herds do. Solitary boars sometimes get a little peculiar in the head."

"Well, if I see a tusher, I shall simply climb a tree."

Anne walked Hugh outside to his car. Sumac had begun to redden along the rutted road. There was frost in the hollows, and birds throbbed in the dense woods where sunlight cut like a razor. Clingmans Dome was castled in smoke. Below them were hushed levels of green, greenblue, burnt blue, browned gray; in the distance she could see the blacked-off side of a mountain, lobotomized by fire.

She slipped Hugh's glasses from his pocket and put them on for him. He caressed her cheek with the stumps of his left hand. As always, it was deliciously erotic, and she closed her eyes, shuddering.

"I'll be back about four with the groceries," Hugh promised.

Anne smiled up at him. He was staring at her in a curiously intense yet mindless way. She leaned against him, the top of her head nuzzling under his chin. She delicately unzipped his fly, placed her hand on the impendent cock. More tentacle than cock, she thought. They were motionless for nearly a minute; only her thumb moved, down-stroking.

"That's a friendly thing to do. Beats hell out of the usual see-you-later-kiss."

"I'm a bawd, really. A remorseless bawd."

She sighed enjoyably and released Hugh before he got to the awkward stage, zipped him up, sent him on his way with a fat slap to the rear.

Anne spent the next hour tidying up and acquainting herself somewhat with Joram Thornton.

She'd never seen Hugh's wife, had no idea what Joram looked like. She searched the many framed photographs in the lodge, but they were all of Hugh and his hunting or fishing companions. Joram Thornton's own bedroom was bright, spacious, paneled in wormy chestnut and decorated in shades of orange and yellow. It could have been a room in a first-class motel, and it had an unvisited look. Anne couldn't imagine that she spent much time at the lodge. Perhaps she had her own hideaway, her own lovers as well . . .

There might have been a clue to her personality in the several paintings mounted in a reading corner of the main room, and in a mob of terra-cotta figures on a steel-and-glass coffee table. Joram Thornton painted densely peopled folk-naïf canvases, none of which was larger than eight square inches. Farms, towns, animals, the black and white faces of Appalachia, all were meticulously miniaturized and crowded to the very edges of her canvas. Often her people were ruthlessly halved or quartered by the limits of the space she allowed for her work. Yet there was nothing ill-ordered about the compressed paintings; she always knew what she was doing.

By contrast Joram's terra-cotta figures looked quickly

made, largely unfinished. She was adroit at conveying a mood, but most of the figures seemed to be falling or losing some essential struggle with the earth in which they were shapelessly mired.

At the base of the steps going down from the deck there was a rock garden that looked to be woman's work. All the common herbs were growing there, many varieties of ferns, sedum and red trillium for accent—and pitcher plants. Joram seemed to have a special fondness for the self-sufficient little plants that fed themselves on trapped insects. Anne looked closely at one of the hollow leaves that produced a sweetish sap to lure the insects inside. All the stiff hairs growing within the leaf pointed downward, and she could see insects decaying in the rainwater that had collected inside. Attracted by the innocent scent, they had climbed in to feed, and found it impossible to climb out again.

There were a couple of six-foot staffs leaning against the stairs. Anne chose one, whistled up Big Plucky, and went off down the trail to the river below.

JORAM WAS PART of a foursome teeing off at the Kingman Country Club. Hugh recognized a couple of her chums, Bitsy Berghof and Pris Galloway, but he didn't know the other woman. He parked his Sunbeam off the road alongside the first fairway, got out, walked across the rough to the edge of the grass and waited there. Joram drove her usual hundred and ten yards off the tee, the ball slicing just at the end of its flight and landing near where he stood in the shade of a tulip poplar.

Presently they all came charging down the fairway in their golf carts.

"Heyyyyyy, Hugh," Bitsy Berghof called.

"Heyyy, Bitsy. How's old Haygood?"

"Oh, drunk and disorderly, just like always."

Joram looked over her lie and joined Hugh under the tree. She took off her sun visor and dabbed with a tissue at the perspiration on her dark forehead.

"Be a scorcher today," she said.

"Yeh."

"Cool up in the mountains?"

"There was frost last night," Hugh said. He put his arm around her waist, watched as the stranger selected a two wood and proceeded to knock the living hell out of her ball.

"Who's the pro?"

"Friend of Bitsy's from Winston-Salem. Good, isn't she?"

"You can take her."

"Oh, I don't know, I haven't been putting very well. What time shall I come tonight?"

"Joram—I don't think I can do it tonight."

She stepped away from him instantly, hung the sun visor on his shoulder and did something with her abundant hair, pulling it back behind her ears rather sharply, retying a length of ribbon to keep most of the hair off her neck. She was coloring it a walnut brown these days, but she had instructed the beautician to leave a couple of offhand streaks of white, as pure as the whites of her eyes in the mirror-finish tan that she maintained. Joram was also perspiring in a line across her bare shoulders and nape; tiny beads of water glowed against the chocolate freckles that the sun had blazed. Hugh had always been most enchanted and excited by her when she was slightly moist, from pool, tub, or the hot sun.

Joram retrived her sunshade and put it on. When she finally looked up at him it was with a smile hard enough to scratch a diamond.

"Poor Hugh," she said, not commiserating at all. "You've fallen in love with her."

His wife's displeasure saddened and thrilled him, hollowed him. He looked away.

"Hugh—now, listen to me. I want to be rid of Anne Ramsdell. Right away. You understand how important that is. It's your *life,* Hugh."

"But I—I'm not so sure we need to—"

One of the other women called to Joram. She walked away to choose a club. She hit her ball well, keenly followed its flight, then relaxed slowly and lowered the wood. She looked at Hugh again, a passing glance.

"We have to," she said, almost too softly for him to hear. "I said I would help you, didn't I?"

She climbed into the golf cart then and zipped away to pick up Bitsy Berghof. Hugh could hear the two women laughing as they drove down the fairway.

THE BOAR THAT killed Big Plucky may have been wounded by a poacher days before, or driven out of a herd by a younger, stronger boar; otherwise he probably wouldn't have been wandering alone, in daylight, by the stream below Pitcher Falls.

Big Plucky heard the tusher first as he rooted for mast beneath a lingonberry bush. The Plott cur had been walking sedately behind Anne. He almost knocked her down as he streaked past her, a single low growl audible in his throat. Then, gathering momentum, Big Plucky began to shriek in a particularly bloodcurdling way.

If the boar had been uninjured he would have made it to the hemlock ridge across the narrow stream in a couple of quick bounds. Instead he coughed his guttural battle cough and stood his ground. Big Plucky, hunt-wise but no hog fighter, had too little room in which to maneuver his boar, and the footing—spray-dampened and rotted hardwood leaves on limestone—was not to the dog's advantage. He tried to savage the already blood-flocked hindquarters of the boar, missed with his gnashing teeth, slipped and back-pedaled furiously.

Despite the treacherous ground the boar's sharp hooves and powerful legs enabled him to whirl and charge in the blink of an eye. His tusks, eight inches long, were honed razor-sharp by the grinding action of the lower canine teeth. He caught Big Plucky down low near the dog's balls and ripped him open all the way to the throat, at the same time tossing him close to six feet in the air. The hound came down in a spray of blood and gangly spill of intestines, was immediately ripped again on the ground by the three-hundred-pound boar.

Anne screamed; the boar lifted his wedgelike head and seemed to glare at her. They were approximately fifty yards apart, and there was no place for her to run. The boar backed off a few feet, lowering, raving, acting as if he meant to charge, but he was distracted by the steaming coils of Big Plucky's intestines on the ground. He began treading on the intestines with his cutting hooves as if he were killing a snake. Then he rooted in the dog's carcass. Anne turned and fled.

She was not panicked, but she had been thoroughly shocked by the power and brutality of the old boar. She made good time back along the uneven trail above the tea-colored river, but her limping half-run soon caused her lower back to ache severely. She knew that she must keep to the trail or risk getting lost in the wilderness. She looked back continually, afraid of having no warning at all should the boar decide to take out after her. It might have been saner to climb up into the crotch of a tree, but all she could think about was getting back to the lodge.

It was still difficult for her to believe Big Plucky had been killed so quickly. They had spent the better part of the day on the trail, and although he wasn't a particularly sociable animal, he was tolerant of her physical inadequacies, ready to lie down in the shade for half an hour when she needed to stop and rest. He always maintained a polite distance between them, and Anne felt he might be offended—certainly he would be puzzled—if she tried to demonstrate her growing affection for him with a pat on the head. How was she going to explain to Hugh?

She began to sob, grief-stricken, as if it was their child who had died.

After half a mile Anne couldn't force herself to keep up the pace; she slowed to a halting walk. The trail had turned away from the river, it went at a pinch through immense thickets of rhododendron and laurel. The day seemed to have darkened, and Anne wondered what time it was: probably midafternoon. In a clearing she saw that the sky was blurring over, ghost-white and gray, but she didn't think it would rain for a while.

Another twenty minutes of walking brought her to the river crossing below Smokeshade.

She had to struggle across boulders that she had taken in stride hours before. She kneeled, gasping, on the other side. A laurel switch had raised a welt on one cheek, and the backs of her hands had been scratched and gouged by thorns. She brushed away the gnats blackening the raw cuts and looked at the lodge far above her. From her vantage point about all she could see was the jutting underside of the cantilevered deck. It seemed much too riskily suspended between rock and sky, and a swift passage of dark cloud over the toy-sized house was enough to give her vertigo. She looked down, focusing on her own hands braced against the ground cushion of pine and hemlock needles.

She realized, with a sense of dread made more terrible by its unexpectedness, that she couldn't go up there. Something would happen to her if she did.

After a few moments Anne resolutely began to examine her dread, and concluded that it was feedback anxiety, complicated by exhaustion. Her dread was caused by the death of Big Plucky, and nothing more.

Instead of leaving her calmer and in control of herself, the self-analysis wrought a sudden transference—dread became fear, objectified.

It was Hugh she feared.

She was, in fact, so powerfully afraid of him, or of some lethal rage on his part, that she began to tremble coldly where she knelt. But surely he would understand what had happened. He must have lost hunting dogs before. He wouldn't blame her.

Nevertheless it was an ordeal for her to cover the last three hundred yards to the lodge, steep and treacherous walking that used her cruelly. She went up the outside stairs to the deck one dragging step at a time, expecting Hugh to appear at any moment. She was crying silently and hopelessly.

When she opened the screen door she saw that the cheery deck lanterns were lighted; the vented charcoal broiler was stocked with briquettes, which were slowly and evenly burning to the desired ashen shade. Anne dimly heard recorded music. She walked across the deck to the sliding glass doors, stopped to wipe her eyes and stepped inside.

The Sons of the Pioneers were singing mellow old Western standards at a Mužak level.

"Hugh?" she said.

There was no reply. Anne looked at herself in the glass, feeling strange and intrusive. She continued on to the island kitchen. According to the stove clock it was twenty minutes to five, much later than she had thought. Hugh had brought the groceries with him. There was a forty-eight-ounce porterhouse steak on the sink counter, and six kinds of vegetables for the salad were chilling on ice in the sink. Anne helped herself to a beer from the refrigerator and drank it greedily, scarcely pausing to taste it. Then she went looking for Hugh.

He wasn't in the lodge, and his car wasn't in the road.

She walked as far as the windowless metal shed that stood on a concrete slab in the midst of some spruce and pine seedlings a dozen yards from the lodge. There was a heavy laminated padlock on the door, and through the vents on the sides of the shed she could hear the gasoline generator that supplied power to the lodge. Above her the pines and red oaks were swaying in a strong wind. It would soon be dark.

Anne returned to the lodge, stripped in Hugh's bedroom and took a hot shower. That helped her aching back only a little and failed to lift her spirits. After she had dressed and combed her knaggy hair and put on a light makeup base to conceal the fine scratch from the laurel twig she decided to take one of the potent muscle-relaxing capsules she had brought; the pain had intensified. The medication meant fighting a woozy head for an hour or more. Usually she just curled up and slept off the effects, but she was determined to have everything ready for Hugh when he returned: potatoes in the oven, salad made, table set.

She was washing the lettuce and beginning to yawn when the stereo music stopped and she heard Hugh's voice on the speakers.

Hey, he said, *you ought to be back by now, so just thought I'd tell you it's around three forty* P.M. *my time, and, let's see, I'll set the old timer so you'll be listening to me a few minutes after five. Keep an eye on the charcoal fire, would you? What I'm going to do in a few minutes is run down to Gatlinburg before they roll up the sidewalks there and buy a couple of widgets for the generator. Nothing's seriously wrong, we'll have juice to get us through the weekend, but I like to keep that temperamental brute in tip-top working order, so it never has the slightest excuse for conking out on me. You've found the groceries —anything else you might be needing before I take off?*

"How about a big wooden salad bowl?" Anne said, smiling, feeling enormously better just for having heard his voice. It wasn't so lonely now, and Hugh sounded quite cheerful, not angry at all. No, wait— Drowsiness was creeping up on Anne; she felt vaguely disoriented, but it wasn't an unpleasant sensation. Get the straight of it now. Right. She hadn't yet told him about Big Plucky. But the hound's death didn't seem to be so terribly important any more. Anne was no longer afraid; on the contrary, she felt a powerful surge of love for Hugh Thornton. And tonight was going to be—just lovely, thank you. Lovely salad, lovely steak, lovely drinks, lovely lovely loving. Oh, it should prove to be an exceptionally fine night for loving!

. . . red wine and vinegar, seasonings. There are a hell of a lot of herbs in those squatty jars on the breakfront, Joram grows and grinds her own. Knives and things— just look in the cabinet next to the trash compactor. Have I forgotten anything?

"A FRIGGING LARGE WOODEN SALAD BOWL!" Anne shouted gleefully, and she indulged in a fit of giggles. She had to hold the counter with both hands so she wouldn't fall down.

You are going to make a salad—you'll need a bowl to toss it in. Uh, back of the pantry, on your left, should be plenty of wooden bowls, all hand-turned by the finest Cherokee craftsmen. Now I'm going to record a song for you, then I'll be on my way. I've spliced in a tape I made for some scout nephews of mine who needed to know all about Smoky Mountain flora and fauna and historical figgers. I just thought you might like hearing a human voice in the background while you work, but for chrissake don't feel obligated. The red button turns me off, the green button erases me, and the orange button consigns my soul to the devil. Love you much. See you soon.

During the ensuing half minute of silence Anne selected a bottle of red wine and a bottle of vinegar and put them on the cutting block next to the sink. She got out a bowl and began to oil it, finding herself a little clumsy but certainly adequate for the task at hand.

On top of olddddd Smokeyyyy

Hugh sang, in cornpone accents, and Anne was all smiles again. There were six big beefsteak tomatoes to slice. It would be a stupendously creative salad. Because. He deserved, who-whee, no lie: a sumbitching *masterpiece!*

> *I can love an old sweetheart*
> *Till a new one comes along*

Anne opened the cabinet next to the trash compactor and saw all the knives and choppers she could ask for magnetically attached to the inside of the door. She chose a boning knife which she judged would be excellent for producing the wafer-thin slices of tomato she wanted. It was new, high-carbon steel, mirror finish, almost a foot long. She was herself smiling on the surface of the unused blade. She tested the edge by effortlessly dividing a fat stalk of celery. Supersharp. And no time to be all thumbs, she sternly reminded herself.

She felt a cold gust of wind; outside a little rain fell in huge random drops.

Dark now. Within the hour the temperature had dropped about fifteen degrees.

Anne went out to make sure the fire was all right. The broiler hood was raised, but the glowing coals were set deeply beneath the grill, and although she could feel the heavy stirring of the rain-laden wind on the deck, there didn't seem to be any danger of sparks flying about.

Beyond the screen there was nothing to see: the mountain darkness was like a void.

She was tranquil to the point of lethargy, but the presence of the night troubled Anne. When she went back inside she left the door open only an inch and pulled the drapes across the expanse of tinted glass.

Hugh was no longer singing, and there was a slight hiss from the stereo speakers. Anne returned to the chopping block.

When he spoke it was at greater volume than he had

sung; she looked up sharply, right hand tightening convulsively on the handle of the knife.

Well, hello, Pete and Buzz! It's good to be talking to you guys again. Your aunt Joram tells me your troop will be visiting our mountains come next spring, and we sure are looking forward to that. Meanwhile I'll try to give you some background you don't always find in books, local legends and heroes. Speaking of heroes, as you probably know, Cherokee Indians were the first settlers in these parts, but I'll bet you didn't know Texas' own Sam Houston was adopted by a Cherokee chief when he was sixteen years old

He went on like that while Anne methodically sliced her tomatoes. Absorbed in her work, she only half listened.

She had begun to feel a definite distress. Her ears were ringing. That was the medicine, of course, but was it too hot in the lodge with everything closed up? She put the knife down and wiped her moist forehead on her sleeve and glanced to where the drapes were partly inflated by the wind that blew steadily through the crack between the doors.

The loss of power to the lodge was happening so gradually that, had she noticed it right away, she would have thought it was a problem with her eyes.

Outside the rain was now falling steadily.

Anne resumed with the knife.

Hugh continued speaking, but more slowly, a slur of loginess in his voice.

. . . his life old Sam thought of himself as part Cherokee. He was one of the few politicians of his day who was willing to stand up for Indian rights even though

Anne diced celery with swift, short, chopping strokes. She watched the knife avidly; its action seemed remote from her, her dreaming presence, but it was also oddly alarming, brilliant as a haunting. There was the faintest taste of blood in her mouth, but Anne felt possessed—by dreams, by a morbid anger that caused her to attack the chopping block, bringing the blade of the knife higher with almost every stroke, whacking it hard against the maple. At that point she could not have willed herself to stop.

> (Chop
> his fingers
> lop
> his bones)

The struck bottle of wine smashed in the sink, bathing the porcelain redly. Anne stood with the knife upraised, trembling, and stared at the mess. Because of the low light level the wine had begun to look darker, almost black. Anne raised her eyes to the fixture above her head. It had been harshly bright, but now it was yellow as a pumpkin, all but lightless. She heard the low-down groan of Hugh's voice.

. . . resolved to devise a system of writing for his own people

She looked wildly around the lodge. Shadows and gloom, the fiery yellow of a savage bear's eyes. The dark was coming inside; soon it would be all dark, all void, and she would be alone in that dangerous void.

The drapes over the doors filled and subsided, as if they were breathing.

Anne groaned and began to shake her head pathetically, her eyes on the drapes, on a vertical gleam of glass in the zeroing light. The tape machine had all but run down. The only sounds from the speakers were groans as terrible as her own.

> (chop ye
> coldly
> through
> his groans,
> Death's Anne)

It was the animal in her, the functioning savage, that recognized the faint pulse of reflected firelight on the glass, and it was her atavistic need to be within the circle of a fire, safe from the dark and the terrors of the dark, that drove her as far as the doors.

And then the hatted man walked in, walked dead across her tracks, his slicker a wet gleam in the bouncing light of the flashlight he was holding.

You miserable cunt

"Anne," Hugh said, "what—"

He attemped to put the light on her face, but he wasn't quick enough, and he was between her and the fire she craved. He had just a glimpse of her face, and no time at all to ponder the ferocity he saw there. The blade in her hand flashed downward.

If a billowing drape hadn't fouled her stroke, Hugh would have taken a good eight inches of steel through the neck. But the blade did enough damage to the thick muscles connecting shoulder and head to cause him to drop the light. And her headlong rush bowled him backward through the doors to the deck.

> (she'll
> slice him
> to
> perfection)

"Anne!" Hugh screamed.

She was on him already.

He rolled frantically to his left to evade a second swing of the knife, came up on the balls of his feet with his right arm hanging useless. Anne pressed, teeth bared, and swung again, missing his face by an inch. He threw himself out of the way as Anne recovered her balance like a mountain cat and came snarling and slashing. This time the blade hit the wire screen and cut through it as if it were made of paper, leaving a diagonal gap four feet long.

Hugh scrambled backward, ran into the hot grill, jerked away with a hiss of pain.

"Stop it!"

Hugh went to the wall with his good hand. He was after a poker hanging there—anything, anything at all to keep her away, even if he had to cave in her skull. But in his anxiety he missed grabbing the poker. Made clumsy by his wound, he slid along the wall and toppled a shelf crammed with bottles and jars.

One of the quart jars was filled with something highly flammable, and when it broke directly over the coals, Hugh was drenched in an exploding gush of flame.

Anne leaped backward as Hugh turned and staggered and burned ferociously. She dropped the knife and backed up until she was against the glass wall. Hugh fell but struggled up, one hand ineffectively flailing at his burning self. He turned a final sluggish time, hand dropping, began to sag as if he were burning through at the waist, retreated awkward and collapsing like a bad act leaving a lonely stage, and fell through the rip in the screen. He plunged twenty feet to the limestone below but didn't stop there; he continued to roll another hundred and fifty feet down the rutted stone until his body came to a charred, chunky, smoking stop against a windfall.

The softly falling rain finally put an end to what was left of the stubborn fire.

The deck of the lodge was also on fire, little blazing clumps here and there. The flames in the grill had once leaped almost to the roof, but now they were subsiding.

It was the sting of smoke in her nostrils and not the fascinating flames themselves that finally aroused Anne. She pulled a cushion from a chaise and began, deliberately, to beat out the isolated fires.

She smothered them all, then sank to the deck hugging the cushion to herself. She began to rock and sob and wistfully call for her lover.

"Terry, Terry—where are you, Terry?"

(Enough!
I'll
wake
I shall
not
sleep
through
one more
visitation.)

In the flickering light her eyes shone insensately; her voice went on for an hour.

IT'S AN OLD logging road that runs up to Smokeshade, bare shattery rock most of the way, very little mud except after days of rain, when a poorly rooted embankment will give way and inundate it. The woods are close to the sides of the road and tremendous overhead, like a springy tunnel roof, deflecting all but the hardest rain and containing the prevalent mists. Most nights, traveling four miles uphill from the draggle-tail of civilization at the park's edge to the Thornton lodge, it is foggy as a seacoast. Joram didn't often make the trip alone, and she loathed every foot of the road. It was comparatively easy going in the Jeep wagon, but she was tense and angry when she finally reached the lodge.

Angry, because it was not yet nine o'clock, and all the lights were out. Was he in bed with her? That was disappointingly cheap of Hugh.

Joram parked facing the lodge and left the headlights on in the mother-of-pearl night, left the motor running. She took the flashlight from the clip on the dashboard and got out, slam-banging, childishly enjoying her noise.

It wasn't raining, but the mist was wet enough. The air smelled brackishly of vegetation, of damp rot.

She was almost to the door when she heard, or failed to hear, something.

Joram turned the beam of her flashlight on the generator shed. A lone possum was shambling through the spruce, his back to her. The door of the shed was open. The generator wasn't running.

It happened from time to time. So he'd been trying to get the generator restarted. They had lanterns for such an emergency, however, and there was no lantern hanging in the shed as a work-light or burnishing a window of the lodge. Hugh must have heard her drive up—why hadn't he come?

Joram opened the front door and encountered blackness, cold silence. Her anger returned.

"Hugh!"

She flashed the beam inside, called him again. Asleep? With her? Joram walked in and walked down the hall to Hugh's bedroom. But no one was sleeping in Hugh's bed. She checked her own room, then began looking over the lodge in earnest.

Steak warm and bloody on the sink counter. Tomatoes sliced, lettuce wilting. Broken bottle of wine in the sink. She was frightened. She went to the deck and slid the doors open, smelled what was left of the charcoal fire, smelled scorched meat. Dingy and dreadful. She swept the light across the deck, over the salt glitter of smashed glass, and discovered Anne sitting, flinching, hiding from the light.

It was such a shock that Joram almost dropped her flashlight. Instead, she pointed the beam at the glass doors, so the double-mirrored light would illuminate Anne without blinding her.

Joram made two attempts before she could speak coherently.

"What is it?" she said. "What's happened?"

Anne trembled and continued to cover her face. Joram

placed the flashlight on a chair, same beam angle, and went to her.

"Where's Hugh?" she demanded.

When Anne refused to speak or look at her Joram reached down, took hold of her wrist and twisted it sharply, exposing one cheek. She hit Anne savagely across the face. Anne's mouth fell open, but she still wouldn't talk.

Joram went into the lodge, groped her way to the island kitchen, took down a lantern hanging there. A little kerosene in it. She used matches from her coat pocket to light the wick. Then she went to the pantry for liquor. Napoleon brandy. She splashed some in a glass, filled another glass with water, carried them to the deck. There she kneeled down beside Anne, who was rubbing her swelling jaw and leaking lip, and thrust the brandy under her nose.

Anne's head jerked up. Joram forced the brandy on her. Anne coughed and spat a lot of it up. Joram made her drink some of the water; Anne swallowed it gratefully, as if her throat was parched. The only color in her face was the fiery imprint of Joram's hard fingers.

Again Joram gave her brandy, this time putting the glass in her hand. After a few moments Anne began to sip it. She wasn't trembling so badly any more.

"I'm Joram Thornton."

"I assumed that," Anne said, barely whispering.

"You don't have to be afraid of me."

Anne looked at her, puzzled.

"I want to know where Hugh is."

"Hugh is dead."

Joram stared at Anne, and almost hit her again. Then she got up slowly, walked to a chair and sat on it. After a while she lowered her face into her hands.

"He burned," Anne said. "He fell."

She finished off the brandy and rose, but she was too wobbly to walk. She leaned against the wall and looked at Joram patiently.

After a time Joram lifted her head and let out a single muscular agonized yowl that echoed and echoed. Anne closed her eyes and clung to the wall.

"Get help," she said. "Please?"

IT WAS AFTER eleven when Terry reached Smokeshade. By that time Ken Bidwell had been there for the better part of an hour, and he had succeeded in getting the generator going again. He went out to meet Terry, wiping his hands on a gasoline-dampened rag. He smiled fitfully.

"Where's Anne?" Terry asked, stepping out of the camper.

"Asleep now. She was doing awfully well—fully coherent, although a little too matter-of-fact, I think. I gave her thirty milligrams of methaqualone to help smooth things out and to increase susceptibility. As a psychiatrist I felt a posthypnotic suggestion was called for. Often hysterical redintegration results in a phobic transference at some later date, so—"

"I want to know what's going on here!"

Bidwell stopped smiling and examined his fingernails for impacted grease. "There's been an accident. The charcoal broiler—Hugh is dead. He burned to death."

"Accident?"

"Yes. Yes, it couldn't reasonably be called anything else. I'll explain. But we should bring the body up, and that's going to be difficult."

"I want to see Anne," Terry said. "I want to see for myself that she's all right."

Bidwell took him to Hugh Thornton's room. Anne was lying on her back on the bed, covered with a red blanket. When the door opened and light from the hall fell across the bed she stirred restlessly and muttered something. She looked pale but peaceful. There were raised bruises on one cheek.

Terry looked at Bidwell. "How long will she sleep?"

"Hard to say. The longer the better."

"Where's the body?"

It took them a few minutes to get ready. Bidwell located a pair of Hugh's boots that Terry could wear with three pairs of socks. From his car he took cotton gloves, surgical masks, a tarpaulin, a rope hammock, two electric torches with sealed beams the size of automobile headlights, and a .38 caliber revolver.

They climbed slowly down the Tallalah Trail, looking over every foot of the bleak slope with the torches. The temperature was about forty degrees, but it seemed colder. The sky had begun to clear, revealing a moon three days from the full.

The faraway shine of animal eyes fixed the location of the body for them. Terry saw a tawny hunchback cat shape before Bidwell fired a shot to frighten the marauder off.

"I was afraid of that," he said woefully through his mask.

They made their way across the slope to the pine windfall, torch beams merging in a busy white glare. For a long time Terry didn't notice the body, because it didn't look like anything he was prepared to see.

Then he recognized a half-raised cindery hand that had been ravaged by predators; all the fingers had been reduced to spike ends of bone. Despite the surgical mask he was appalled by the stench. He instinctively aimed his light in another direction. Bidwell glanced at him.

"Can you do it?" he said.

"Yes, I think so," Terry said through gritted teeth.

Bidwell unrolled the tarpaulin and they lifted the disintegrating body onto it. There were half-melted bits of gold wire, like solder drippings, and two grotesque, translucent bubbles, all that was left of Thornton's glasses, embedded in the rendered face. Terry helped Bidwell tie the tarp securely at both ends. Then he leaned over the windfall, bracing himself with one hand, and threw up like a shot.

He was dazzling cold from shock until Bidwell brought out a pocket flask and urged whiskey on him. Whiskey helped. Then Terry gave Bidwell a hand lifting the body into the rope hammock. Between them they carried the swaying load back to the lodge, struggling to hold their footing on the trail, breathing explosively. They carried the remains of Hugh Thornton up to the deck and laid him down there.

Terry pulled off his mask and looked at the gap in the screening. He sat down weakly, head low, to catch his breath.

"Whom do you notify?" he asked Bidwell.

"There's no telephone here. I'll drive into Gatlinburg and call a park ranger I know. Also I'll want Dr. Cutler to sign the death certificate. He's an old family friend; there won't be many questions."

"Tell me how it happened?"

"There's a great deal you have to know before we do anything else. Would you come inside?"

Terry followed Bidwell into the lodge. Joram was sitting in her reading corner, a study in brown and white and darkest rue, holding a bottle of Calvados in one fist. She was wearing shades. She raised her head as if to look at Terry, but said nothing. Bidwell stood beside her and awkwardly put an arm around her squared shoulders.

"My husband," Joram said, not shakily but with a rasp, "had a distinguished career. I want you to know that he loved me. You'd better get that straight. I was willing to overlook his—his trifling faults, and I was proud of his great strength, his life-giving qualities, his knowledge, his accomplishments. He paid, many times over, for what he did to your sister. Yes, he suffered. And I will not allow Hugh's reputation to be destroyed now. Do you understand me?"

"I don't think so," Terry said, exasperated. "What did he do to Anne?"

"Mother," Bidwell said gently, "Terry doesn't *know* yet."

Joram coughed into a fist, awkwardly sought to uncork her brandy but seemed to lack simple coordination—or perhaps she hadn't the desire to focus on anything but her own obsessions. Bidwell took the bottle from his mother and poured a drink, looked inquiringly at Terry.

"Have some?"

"Good God, no, I only want to find out what this is about, this great *mystery* you're both so passionate about."

Joram wet her tongue with the brandy. "Two years ago," she said, "Hugh took his sabbatical in Oxford. He worked very hard while we were there, and he had his usual affairs. There was a tall Jamaican girl he found amusing, all sparkle and tease—I just happened to see him that one time with Lu-Allie. But usually I didn't pry into his affairs, you understand. And then, unfortunately, there was Isobel McCarry. Does the name mean anything to you?"

"No."

"Hugh fell very much in love with Isobel. It had never happened before. Oh, he had dozens of girls, always such splendid girls, but somehow he resisted serious involvement. I don't know why Isobel was different, why Hugh felt he couldn't live without her. He even seriously thought of—marrying her. After divorcing me, of course," Joram said with a dry, ghastly laugh. "But Isobel wasn't sure of herself. She did love him, she thought. Still, she wanted more time than Hugh was willing to give her. I suppose, once their affair had reached its critical stage, after Hugh had worked with such dedication for almost a year, worked and played and worn himself out—he— he just lost his bearings for a little while. It could easily happen, even to a man with Hugh's stamina."

"What does Isobel McCarry have to do with—"

Joram silenced him with a taut shake of her head.

"Hugh made demands; Isobel resisted. Then she told him it was over, said she couldn't see him again. Oh, I know *why*. He was too much man for her, that's all—more than she, than any of them, ever bargained for." Joram smiled again, she gloated over her uniqueness. "Anyway —I was visiting in London when Hugh's affair with Isobel came to an end. The day I returned he was at our cottage in the Cotswolds—that's where he took all of his girls. *Birds?* As they say in—jolly old England. Yes. Well, I hadn't seen Hugh, and I was worried, and finally when he did come home, for h-help, he was in such a s-state— no need to go into that. He'd spent the day drinking and brooding until he decided he just wasn't going to give Isobel up. I admit that Hugh sometimes had a temper when he drank too much. Years ago when he was younger, undisciplined, he could be ugly and violent. But he never—no, he *never* hurt anyone purposely."

"Hurt anyone? Are you trying to tell me—? Just a moment, where did Isobel McCarry live?"

Ken Bidwell answered that one. "In the flat below your sister's."

"The girl lived with her mother," Joram said. "So Hugh had never been to her flat; they always met somewhere else. On the night he went to Eversedge Road to confront Isobel, he made a very simple mistake. He found the apartment number on the mailbox, but walked up one flight too many."

"To Anne's flat."

"Yes. Hugh told me the door wasn't closed all the way. So he walked right in."

"In a mood to murder the McCarry girl," Terry said grimly.

"That isn't true!"

"He beat Anne unmercifully. He pushed her through a window. The man was a raving lunatic!"

"Hugh was almost as startled as Anne was. Of course she screamed, and Hugh grabbed her immediately. The kitchen was dark. Hugh was drunk and confused. Even as he struggled with her, he still thought it was Isobel—"

Bidwell said, "Under the circumstances Anne and Isobel McCarry would look very much alike. Anne admitted that. They were the same height and build. Hair about the same length, similar facial contours—"

"All that may be true, but he still tried to murder my sister. Why, if it was all a mistake?"

"Hugh panicked," Joram said. "Anne was fighting him tooth and claw. He fought back, knowing he was in deep trouble. All he wanted was to subdue her so he could get out of there. But Anne attacked him with a chopper, and narrowly missed killing him. She did succeed in chopping off those two fingers of his left hand. Hugh always had a horror of being less than physically perfect. As a boy he suffered a bad leg infection, and there was some talk of amputation. It was terrible for him. Then when he lost his fingers, he—he just went berserk. He told me afterward he didn't know what he was doing when he hurled Anne through that window."

"And you believed him."

"Yes."

Terry looked from Joram to Ken Bidwell. "Why are you telling me this now?" he asked. "Have you told Anne?"

"We didn't have to. It came back to her spontaneously. I'm not sure just what caused her memory to be restored, but I can make some informed guesses. Earlier I mentioned redintegration. Are you familiar with the phenomenon?"

"No."

"We know that Anne was suffering from so-called retrograde amnesia. This amnesia, covering periods of a few minutes to several days, always accompanies cases of severe concussion. But although an orderly sequence of events may be blocked from the conscious mind, our normal, untraumatized brain contains a continuous record of our existence. Every millisecond of life, every particle of human experience, is efficiently stored for retrieval, awaiting a recall stimulus. Sometimes we remember simply by willing to; the subconscious then helps out. Hypnosis can be effectively employed in certain instances of repressed trauma. Quite often what is hidden, or merely long forgotten, flashes unexpectedly through our minds, and we can't be sure what triggered the recall. That's what happened to Anne tonight. Part or perhaps all of a complex stimulus was repeated there in the kitchen while she was preparing dinner. She was chopping vegetables with a long knife. Suddenly she saw herself chopping off a man's fingers. At the time the generator was slowly failing, and darkness was closing in on her. As she continued to work at the chopping block she was flashing back almost subliminally to Oxford. She was badly frightened. I've known of cases where the stimulus was less powerful, yet the individual died from a paralyzed vagus nerve. Literally scared to death.

"In spite of her terror, Anne remembers quite well what was going on in her mind. The reflected light from the charcoal grill attracted her. She was trying to get outside to the warmth and the light of the fire when Hugh came in from the deck, stepped right in front of her. He was wearing his raincoat and his hat, just as he was that night in her Oxford apartment. I can only speculate that Hugh had been in the generator shed and had come to the lodge for a tool he needed. The door of the shed was open and the generator was shut down when Mother arrived. Well, Anne still had the carving knife in her hand. At his appearance the stimulus was complete, and her response was automatic: she attacked him with the knife."

"That's incredible."

"Anne will tell you herself," Bidwell said calmly. "She cut Hugh, although not fatally. Crippled him, I suspect. He blunderingly tried to avoid her. During their struggle the screen was ripped by the knife. Hugh fell against the wall shelf and brought that crashing down. Kerosene in a jar broke over the hot coals of the grill, and there was an explosion. Hugh—Hugh was incinerated. He was a very strong man and he stayed on his feet an amazingly long time, but—Anne couldn't have done anything to save him. He fell through the hole in the screen, and—"

The glass Joram had been holding shattered on the floor, and she doubled in her chair as if hit by violent stomach cramps.

"Mother, let me get you—"

"No, you don't! Not until this is over. Not until I'm certain Hugh won't be disgraced. Then you can knock me out—*kill* me, for all I care." She straightened and took off her dark glasses, a shy, unmasking gesture. Her face was wet. Her eyes absorbed no light; entranced by nightmare, they had a totem quality.

"You have questions," she said to Terry. "Get on with them."

"Why did he take up with Anne? What was the point of that? Or was he planning to finish what he'd started at Oxford?"

"Kill her? I suppose Hugh was desperate enough to consider that, at first. We knew what it would mean having her at Kingman; we felt it would be an enormous risk the first time she laid eyes on him. But even if she didn't remember him immediately, we were afraid it would all come back to her at a later time. So I convinced Hugh that he should approach Anne, preferably when she was alone."

"One look and she might have screamed for the police."

"Hugh felt he could handle her, once he'd set the scene," Bidwell said.

"How much did you know about this?" Terry asked him.

"Until a few days ago, nothing," he said, sounding unhappy about the situation he'd found himself in.

"So they met. And."

Joram grimaced. "From the beginning she was attracted

to Hugh, infatuated with him. That made it much easier
—or so we thought."

"Easier to do what?"

"Confess. Everything. And hope for her understanding.
For her—silence."

"After what Anne had been through? Not likely."

"They planned to tell her tonight," Bidwell said. "They
wanted me to be here, in, ah, more or less a professional
capacity."

"If Anne had become hysterical, you could've popped
a needle into her, is that the idea?"

"Despite Anne's obvious affection for Hugh, there was
no way to predict her reaction to Hugh's—confession.
She probably would not have taken it too calmly. I hoped
I might be a stabilizing influence, at least."

"I think you're guilty of misplaced ethics as well as
misplaced loyalties, Dr. Bidwell."

"You may be right. I felt I didn't have much choice
in the matter."

"Thornton is dead. And you want me to agree that
what happened in Oxford no longer matters. Well, I wish
you'd seen my sister in hospital. Battered. Paralyzed.
Frightened. I wish you had some idea of what she suffered to be able to walk again. That's why I don't give a
damn about Hugh Thornton's good name or his scholarly
reputation."

"We're forgetting about something, aren't we?" Anne
said quietly, but her voice spooked them just the same.

She was limping slowly toward them, barefoot, wrapped
in the red blanket. Terry hurried to her. She smiled up
at him. Her eyes, mildly swarmy, had a tendency to cross.
From the protection of his embrace Anne looked and
found Joram. She left Terry and walked deliberately
toward the woman.

"We're forgetting about three murdered girls," she said.
Joram rose to meet her.

"My husband did not kill those girls."

"Oh? Can you prove he didn't?"

"He told me so."

"And he wouldn't lie to you?" Anne said, her voice still deadly quiet.

"Lie? But it really has nothing to do with what he said or didn't say. He was my husband for twenty years. He was the only father Ken really knew. He could not have been a homicidal maniac."

"I have every reason to believe he was," Anne said bitterly.

"How *can* you believe it, after making love to him?"

The two women stared at each other for a few moments longer, then Anne's gaze wavered.

"I'm very thirsty—would someone bring me a glass of water?"

Joram turned away and walked as far as the doors to the deck. She seemed on the verge of going outside, as if unmindful of what she would find there. But Ken Bidwell got over to her fast, coughed and said warningly, "Mother!"

Joram turned again, stricken. Bidwell guided her to another part of the room. Apparently he wanted Terry to be alone with Anne for a little while.

Terry brought Anne the water she had requested.

"What do you want to do?" he asked in a low voice.

"Whatever is right."

"If I telephone Oxford tonight, the police will undoubtedly send a man right away."

"Do it, then."

"Anne—the whole bloody affair will be reopened in the press—and to what end?"

"I should think the parents of the dead girls could answer that one for you."

"It's been a year and a half; they've had time to forget the tragedy. Will it give them satisfaction to see it all raked up again, see the photos of the dead girls reprinted, hear it blaring on telly? I don't think so. And what will it mean to you? You must consider personal consequences."

"I don't follow."

"The story is just too sensational, it'll haunt you for years. You were the man's lover—don't you think that'll be found out? Every lurid detail will be printed somewhere. What about your profession? You hope to return to Paternoster next year."

"Yes, I—"

Ken Bidwell decided the timing was right and came over. "I don't believe we can put off calling in the authorities. We have to agree now on what we'll tell them. The truth or—"

"A fair approximation of the truth," Terry said. He was looking at Anne. She had closed her eyes. She stood mute.

"Anne?"

"All right," she whispered. "A fair approximation of the truth. Let us just have it over with."

"Bidwell?"

"The four of you were spending a pleasant evening at Smokeshade. A little after eight Hugh was preparing to put the steaks on. The accident occurred. None of you saw exactly what happened. He plunged through the screen before you could help him. Mother drove to the nearest phone and called me. When I got here we retrieved the body. It took us a long time. Then I drove into Gatlinburg to report the tragedy."

"The accident story seems a little hard to swallow."

"No one will be anxious to question it too closely." He grinned nervously at his fellow intrigants. "Stranger things have happened in these mountains. A friend of mine went fly-fishing this past summer, got tangled in his own line and drowned in only four feet of fast water, with at least three other men in hailing distance."

"Shut up, you son of a bitch," Anne said.

Part Four

PRETTY JOE

Thus it came about that, where Jekyll perhaps
might have succumbed, Hyde rose to the importance of the moment.

Robert Louis Stevenson,
Dr. Jekyll and Mr. Hyde

THE HORSE THAT Beth-Alma had selected for Oxey was out of her uncle's riding stable; Beth-Alma chose him for what she called his "rocking-chair canter." Oxey supposed that meant the quarter horse was easy to ride even after a minimum of lessons on proper horsemanship. He wasn't so sure about the riding part, but he didn't mind the lessons, because Beth-Alma was pleased and impressed with his speed in soaking up nomenclature. Also he had nothing against the horse, prosaically named Jess. Jess was old but sturdy and he didn't smell too bad, for a horse. He wasn't physically overpowering, and he didn't keep looking around in that nervous, quirky manner of the horse who thinks he might like to kick your head off if you gave him half a chance. He mostly stood very still while Oxey climbed up and down, getting the feel of the clunky stirrups and the Western saddle.

Saturday morning they had walked Jess around the saddle club ring with Beth-Alma mounted behind Oxey, arms encircling his waist so she could adjust his grip on the reins and show him the right amount of pressure to apply to the snaffle bit in Jess's mouth. Oxey thoroughly enjoyed that lesson. He particularly liked the way Beth-Alma's hands clung to his rib cage or the back of his belt. He also liked it when Beth-Alma blew her breath on the back of his steaming neck to cool him off a bit. It was the end of September, but they were having a heat wave.

On Sunday they went trail riding, which turned out to be a mistake. They set out early, and Jess was a horse who needed his sleep. Consequently he was in a grumpy mood, and when Oxey began to handle him awkwardly, Jess got rid of him at the first opportunity. He went from a canter to a dead stop at some minor obstacle and arched his back. Oxey flew over his head and landed in a downhill meadow with all the speed and grace of a stalling duck. It didn't hurt, but it shook him up. Beth-Alma came dashing back on Chantilly Queen, dismounted, called Jess an old fart, and socked him, not too hard. Jess, despite the punch in the nose, looked pleased with himself.

Oxey got up and toppled over again. Beth-Alma hastened to his side.

"Hurt?" she said.

"Dizzy."

"I've been thrown lots of times."

"Swell."

"You'll get used to it. Let's go sit down over there under the tree."

She led Oxey by the elbow to shade, then unbridled both horses so they could wander around and crop the dry grass. It was cooler by the crick. With her handkerchief Beth-Alma made a wet compress for Oxey's head.

"I guess you don't want to go riding any more today."

"Huh-uh."

"Now how do you feel?"

"I'm still a little dizzy."

"Your eyes look all right. You're not going to be a crybaby, are you?"

She bent quickly to kiss him on the mouth. Just as quickly she straightened up. They looked in different directions, amazed by the freshness of their respective views. Then they looked at each other. In addition to her brindled complexion Beth-Alma had pale gray eyes and kind of a thin mouth, but with a nice humorous shape to it. She had dimples in both cheeks. Wealth and luxury. He wanted to stroke her pink mottled nose, and so he did.

"I'm not going to make love until I'm eighteen," she said. "That's twenty more months."

"Why not?"

"Because it's a beautiful experience, and I don't believe in rushing into my beautiful experiences."

"Okay," Oxey said, tacitly agreeing to something, although he wasn't quite sure what.

After a little while they took off their boots and played in the crick, splashing each other until they were soaking wet. They walked back to the saddle club holding hands, the horses nodding along behind them.

"There you go," Beth-Alma said.

"What?"

"When you get to thinking hard, all the expression goes out of your face. It's one of those weird things about you I'll just have to get used to. I may not be as smart as you are, but I'm pretty smart. Five A's and one B last semester. I'll probably get a scholarship to Sweet Briar if I want one. Will you tell me what you're thinking sometimes? What are you thinking right now?"

"There's something I need to know. I'm not sure why I need to know. I don't even know where I can find out."

"Be that way," Beth-Alma said, but she didn't try to take her hand back.

Oxey's route home from the riding stable took him past Terry's rented house.

It was ten thirty in the morning. The Ford camper wasn't parked in the drive. Oxey slowed down as he looked the house over. Halfway down the block he circled back on his Honda, rode to the rear of the house and parked his bike out of sight, beneath the stairs, where there was a doorless tool shed formed by the basement wall, the steps angled above and a trellis covered with creeper.

He went up to the third floor and found that, as usual, the door was unlocked. He looked in surreptitiously, but no one was occupying the atelier.

The lights by Terry's desk were burning, and the ashtray was full. There was paper in the typewriter, a sentence half completed. Apparently he'd gotten up and gone somewhere in a hurry, either last night or early this morning.

Oxey sniffed the stale air around the ashtrays. Most likely it had been last night.

He needed to know if anyone else was in the house, so he went down to the second floor and looked into the so-called guest room, where Jeanie sometimes slept when she wasn't sleeping with Terry. But Jeanie wasn't around either, and there were no indigents and freeloaders on the first floor. Oxey continued on to the kitchen, helped himself to a glass of Jeanie's buttermilk from the fridge, then returned to the atelier.

There was a spacious walk-in closet between book-shelves which Terry used as a supply and storage area. Up against one wall was a trunk Oxey had always been curious about, but he had never found the opportunity to open it. Hadn't wanted to, but now that he'd done his homework at the Kingman College library, his curiosity about Terry demanded a suspension of scruples.

The trunk wasn't locked. Judging from the finger marks in the dust on the lid Terry opened it occasionally. When Oxey looked inside he found a litterateur's clutter of old manuscripts, boxes of letters and clippings, and at least thirty spiral notebooks. There was a small window in the closet above the trunk, and the angle of the morning sun provided enough illumination for Oxey to read faded ink and pencil script.

First, though, he looked through a bulky snapshot album. Faces from World War Two and shortly after. Most of the faces were unidentifiable, and it would have taken a lot of looking to pick out Anne's or Terry's father.

But the children and their famous mother were easily recognized. There they were on a boat, in front of a theatre, on a sound stage. Terry had always the same pained, quizzical expression as he faced the camera from a three-quarter stance. Anne was photogenic but aloof, or else she was smiling privately, as if she had just amused herself.

In an envelope he discovered a number of folded theatrical posters, only one of which interested him.

QUEEN'S THEATRE
Shaftesbury Avenue, London, W.1

H. M. Tennent Ltd.
presents
Philip Rackstraw   Eveleen Denning
and
Marian Holgate
in
A Flair for Danger
by
Barry Wickloe

Oxey had heard of *A Flair for Danger*. It was the play Marian Holgate had been appearing in the day she died of a massive cerebrovascular accident backstage. And Philip Rackstraw, who had teamed with Miss Holgate "in a number of well-received comedies and melodramas" (*New York Times* obituary), had discovered her body.

The notebooks contained early stories, sketches and fledgling philosophies. From the beginning Terry had dated his every page and counted every word. Midway in the first of the notebooks, begun while he was at Farnsworth, Anne had jotted criticism of his stories in the margins. In other notebooks she had rewritten heavily, simplifying, straightening out syntax. Until, gradually, four years after his start, Terry's first publishable story emerged. Give Anne a lot of credit for that. But he did, didn't he? Terry knew how much he owed his clever sister.

The letters. Some early business correspondence, an occasional kind note from an editor or fellow author. *Awfully impressed with your progress* . . . As for personal letters, the only ones Terry had received, or cared to preserve, were from Anne.

Oxey sat back against the wall, wiped his perspiring face and untied the string from a thick packet of Anne's letters. Terry had kept everything that she had written since the day she had gone away to school in Belgium.

Oxey skimmed through a lot of letters and several years. The addresses changed, changed again. Terry began getting his mail through his mother's agent. Anne wrote from Stockholm, then from Manchester. She had acquired a husband, but she didn't have much to say about married life.

Terry's address changed once more, to Farnsworth.

Oxey checked the date. Nine weeks after the death of Marian Holgate. He began reading more carefully, but Anne's preliminary letters to the institutionalized Terry were filled with trivialities, all composed with an eye to cheering him up. Later on there were many excuses for visits that had to be postponed. Finally, *Well, no use pretending any longer, Geoff and I just can't make a go of it . . .*

The light was changing again, and Oxey found the reading exceedingly dim. He almost missed the change in tone in one of the letters, the message he might have been looking for.

. . . fouled herself until she died of sheer unlivableness. You did not wish her to death, Terry. You struck no blow. But the sad truth is, as long as you refuse to accept Mother's death as natural and inevitable, you will never get well. And you will never leave Farnsworth.

Oxey paused there, rubbed his sore eyes, sank back to practice the black art of thinking.

So it was guilt, and not grief, that had delivered Terry into the hands of some expensive psychiatrists. He had hated his mother and wanted her to die, and she had accommodated him. Well. But was that enough to drive even a sensitive boy to the funny farm? Hard to believe. Yet that had to be all there was to it. Judging from the manuscript of *Second Growth,* Terry apparently had been nearing a nervous breakdown just from associating with his mother. Apparently, because Terry hadn't written much about that. And because of this omission his novel wasn't hitting on all cylinders yet.

Maybe, Oxey thought, if he just had a peek at the most recent manuscript pages—

He stifled a yawn and started to walk out of the closet, only to discover that he'd negligently trapped himself.

Anne and Terry had just appeared, and it was too late to walk boldly out and greet them. He hated being identified as a snoop even if that's what he was, trunk lid up and personal letters on the floor. Sweat rolled down his cheeks, and he backed up, making sure they wouldn't catch a glimpse of him through the space between door and jamb.

Confined to the closet: dumbass! Why hadn't he been listening? But they'd come upstairs very quietly, holding onto each other, not talking.

From where he was standing all the atelier except for the work area was within his view. Oxey hoped either they wouldn't stay long or they would go downstairs; then he'd have the chance to slip out. But they didn't seem to have anything special in mind. They both acted half dead. They just stood near the center of the atelier, counterbalanced, stilled but not passive, kinetically involved. Her fingers plucked thievishly at him, as if she were stealing reassurances. Her dry, bare mouth was near his own, but not touching. Her face looked scraped to the bone. Her flamed-out eyes had a starey, starved, egomaniacal quality that troubled Oxey. She rolled her face a little and put pressure on Terry's jawbone with her white perfectly edged teeth. Terry tensed and seemed to study this act of deliberate eroticism with a heavy mind. He held Anne by the waist as if he were holding a chair.

Oxey crept backward, gathered the letters, retied them, placed them in the trunk. He didn't try to close the trunk lid because he knew the hinges would squeal on him. He yearned to go home. The sweat was really pouring off him, adding to his discomfort. He went back to the door space because he had nothing else to do. The floorboards creaked, but he was sure they hadn't picked up the sound.

Anne and Terry were in approximately the same positions, but they had come to grips much more intensely, and now they were bare-assed naked.

Hairs prickled on the back of Oxey's neck. He couldn't believe it. Any of it. The rascally cock, the inviting groans. Naturally he couldn't look away. His lips turned an incandescent blue. It was his first voyeuristic experience, and he was surprised by how quickly and absolutely he was turned off by it. He was left with only a sickened curiosity as Terry and Anne made their way to the water bed.

Oxey stayed at the door long enough to appreciate the fact that long before today's beautiful experience they had learned each other well. Then he went back to the trunk corner, closed the lid (they were beyond hearing anything less noisy than a head-on collision in the street), and sat on the trunk trying to stay cool by keeping still.

Later on one of them screamed. Hard to tell who. Oxey bit his lip and bided his time. He watched half an hour pass on his watch. At that he got up stiffly and reconnoitered. They were both sprawled on their backs on the water bed, lustily sleeping. Or so Oxey thought. He left the closet and went immediately to the back door.

He couldn't have said what made him turn his head for a final look at the lovers. But when he did he saw that Terry had raised his own head and was staring right at him. The look in the man's eyes chilled Oxey to the marrow. He sprang out into the light without a word of explanation, clattered down three flights of steps and wheeled his Honda out of hiding.

Oxey spent the rest of his day in seclusion, depressed and appalled, avoiding others as if he were afraid of spreading plague. It was almost the first time he had doubted the worth of humanity, and only his second time to contemplate suicide—not to get even with anyone, much as she deserved it, but as an epic gesture of resignation.

Fortunately Beth-Alma called him around suppertime.

Oxey was less than gracious on the phone, but she had two brothers who sulked a lot, and she wisely didn't mind his mood. He ended up taking her to the movies.

ON TUESDAY MORNING at nine o'clock there was a memorial service for Hugh Thornton in the Kingman College chapel. No members of the family attended. He was buried that afternoon in semiprivacy in Kingsport, Tennessee, his birthplace.

Oxey and his father went directly from the service to the Knoxville airport, where they caught United's 10:45 flight to Washington. They arrived at National Airport at noon. His father took a taxi to his conference at Georgetown University and Oxey took another taxi, not to the Library of Congress, where Dr. Hollis assumed Oxey would be spending his afternoon, but to the Shoreham Hotel. He was carrying a flight bag that contained a toothbrush, a change of underwear, a Sony cassette tape recorder and a fifth of rare old Tennessee sipping whiskey that went for twelve dollars a quart, when you could find any of it.

He'd stayed at the Shoreham on several occasions and knew his way around. He bypassed an important-looking crowd of black men in flowing white robes and went directly to the elevators, not bothering to phone ahead. The last thing Oxey wanted was to give his man time to change his mind about the scheduled interview.

Oxey's uncle Steve had set up the interview. No problem. Steve was in his early thirties, the right-hand man of a syndicated Washington columnist who was nonpartisan, incorruptible, told the truth as he saw it and attended church regularly. Consequently he was considered by the political establishment to be one of the most loathsome sons of bitches on the face of the earth. Steve Hollis wasn't far behind on everyone's low-life list, but the two men had a lot of power. A phone call from either of them was an unforgettable event, like a train wreck.

During the Washington tryout of his new play, *The Clue Is Murder,* Philip Rackstraw was occupying a suite on the seventh floor of the Shoreham. There was a *Do not disturb* sign on one of the doors. Oxey checked his watch: twelve twenty, a little early. He rang the bell anyway, heard it razzing unpleasantly in the depths of the suite. That's all he heard for a couple of minutes while he continued to thumb the bell. Then a crash occurred inside: it sounded as if someone had taken a baseball bat to a loaded dishwasher. The crash was accompanied by a despairing but mellifluous cry of pain. Shuffling, mutterings behind the closed doors. Elaborate fumbling with the lock. One of the doors opened. A big-shouldered, defiantly blond man, sixty or so, peered out at him. He had the sad, red, smallish eyes of a bull elephant.

"Tinker?" he said, with a tremor of delight to animate his face. He threw the door wide open.

Oxey thought he was about to be embraced, so he backed up one step and said quickly, "I'm John Oxley Hollis and my uncle Steve Hollis set up an interview for my paper the Kingman—"

"Interview?" Philip Rackstraw searched the pockets of his dressing gown, came up with a pair of horn-rimmed glasses with round lenses, and put them on. Someone had written on one of the lenses with a magic marker in idiomatic Spanish. Oxey recognized the Spanish word for "balls," but the rest was untranslatable.

Philip Rackstraw seemed unaware of the graffiti as he stared at Oxey.

"—my paper the Kingman *Challenger,*" Oxey finished.

"Yes. I've never heard of your newspaper. What does it matter? It's all grist for the mill. Say anything you like about me as long as you spell my name right. Publicity. We only exist as long as our publicity says we do. It's been

weeks since I've seen my reflection in the bathroom mirror, but perhaps the effect may be reversible. Huge black
headlines will revive me. PHILIP RACKSTRAW EX-
ISTS. You *will* print that, as a special favor to me? Come
in, by all means. Mind where you step. There could be
almost anything underfoot. Broken glass. Vomit. A de-
composing teenybopper. I'm afraid to open the drapes
and look. Won't let the chambermaids in to change linen
or air the suite. Dare not. They would throw me out of
their fucking hotel. They'll try to, regardless. I've heard
rumors of a plot. Mice in the walls. I have friends, believe
it or not. What do you hear from Mikkelson, dear boy?
That's why you're prowling about, isn't it? Mikkelson's
sent a bloody messenger boy to cut my throat." He
laughed soothingly at Oxey's expression. "Merely twitting
you, of course. You are undoubtedly who and what you
say you are. No reason to believe otherwise, is there?"
He laughed again, shut the door behind Oxey and turned
on the light in the foyer.

It was a mini-chandelier that had been spray-painted
vermilion by an unsteady hand. The oceanic gloom in the
foyer was transmuted, to no special advantage. In the red
light Oxey noted that the carpet was piled high with un-
claimed room-service trays. There were more spray-can
graffiti on the trompe l'oeil wallpaper, on the ceiling.
Names: Cesar. Hipolito. Ramona. Messages invited rock
stars to sodomize other rock stars. There were faces, both
diabolical and stud-cool. Much of it was ornamentation,
pure rigmarole, the ultimate in subway-car neoclassic.

Philip Rackstraw waved a hand glumly at the display.
"Lot of barbarous talent in evidence. Tinker and some
of his PR friends did the whole suite. Ghetto children. He
picked them up I know not where, took full advantage of
all his wiles to smuggle them into the hotel. They're all
gone now. That's merely an assumption. Too fagged to
check all the closets after the party. Some fearsome events
were taking place. I've always been aware of the erotic
capabilities of Latin children, but new dimensions were

explored. They staged double-jointed extravaganzas. There must be a screwing gene transmittable only in the torrid zone. Oh, God, have I mentioned the zonked-out elegance of their plushy eyes? I'm counting on you, Buzz, to put nothing of what I have just said into print. On your scout's honor as a good trooper. After all, you routed me out of bed—is it fair to take advantage? I'm trembling, as you can see. I don't have my wits about me. I'll rely on your good will, only pointing out that I've always enjoyed an excellent press in this country. If you must write up our little rave, rather put it this way: Last week, in a moment of supreme weakness, the noted actor Philip Rackstraw, currently appearing in the new smash hit, insert title, at the whatever theatre it is, hosted a party in honor of his young friend and companion of several weeks' duration, Oswaldo Raymond Jesus blah blah blah, no last name given, last known address the Times Square IRT station. A number of Oswaldo's, a.k.a. Tinker's, newfound chums were pleased to attend. Slim as wraiths they were, dotted-Swiss complexions, but vellum-smooth beneath their clothes. Don't write that down. Pizza, orange soda, bubblegum and sniffy were served. The guests played 'Pin the Tail on the Donkey' before making up their own games. Here we have the sitting room. You can see what the demons did to it. Oh, well, I'll tidy up myself as soon as I'm feeling better. We'll have the interview in my bedroom, if you don't mind. I think less in bed, but more to the point."

Oxey doubted that Philip Rackstraw would be able to put the trashed room back into shape by himself. All the glossy furniture had been reduced to smithereens, and the carpet had taken the brunt of everything that the human body is capable of evacuating normally or rejecting under duress. The room smelled most powerfully of these abuses, and of other things: staled spicy food, stale hash smoke, purple perfume, abundant fucking. Oxey was so stunned he was almost willing to forget why he had come and make a dash for the door.

A telephone rang in the sitting room. It seemed incredible that anything like a telephone could have survived the pounding that the room had taken, but somewhere one was ringing brashly. Philip Rackstraw stood very still and listened, not happily. Even in the poor light Oxey could see him sweating.

"Am I going to answer it?" the actor said. "It's not a friend, if that's what you're thinking. My friends don't ring me. I have to ring them. That's an indignity I put up with for the sake of their friendship. So if it isn't a friend —and it isn't—who could it be? Under the circumstances, Buzzy, I wonder if you would consider—"

"Oxey."

"Answer the *phone,* Locksley."

"I would, but I can't—I mean, I don't see—"

"Never mind, there's an extension in the bedroom. I'll get it myself. I don't have to take any crap from Mikkelson. I have a contract. That means something in a civilized land."

He flew in a ragged panic to the bedroom, but composed himself wonderfully before taking off his glasses and speaking into the telephone. "Philip Rackstraw here," he said, aglow with star quality.

The actor listened for about half a minute, with steadily diminishing zeal, tongue bulging in one cheek. Oxey couldn't be sure, as he edged slowly into the bedroom, that anyone was on the other end of the line. Rackstraw ignored his presence. He sank to the edge of the bed and hung up.

"That was Tinker," he said. "Calling from New York. From his natural habitat. I heard a subway train in the background. He didn't say a word, but he didn't have to. He was letting me know how expendable I am. As if I didn't know already." He got up and went into the bathroom and splashed water in his face. "Tinker left me two days ago. I think. He took my Modigliani Jesus with him. He'll keep it for a while, a week perhaps, knowing I'm eating my heart out, knowing I'd do literally anything to get it back. In addition to being worth several thousand dollars, it has great sentimental value. But I'll never see it again. He'll casually walk down to the East River some afternoon and chunk it in."

Rackstraw patted his face with a towel and returned to the bedroom. "Sit anywhere you like. Could I fix you a drink?"

"No, sir, I don't drink."

"What a spot of luck, because I'm sure we're all out of booze. You didn't bring a photographer along. Do you take your own pictures? Is that what you have in the bag there? Your camera?" He laughed in a jolly way and made a quick feinting move to wrest the flight bag from Oxey's hand. Oxey let him have it.

The actor danced away with the bag, eagerly looking inside. He came up with the bottle of sipping whiskey.

"Oho!"

"I meant to tell you about that," Oxey said lamely. The whiskey had been intended as a thank-you for his uncle Steve.

"What have we here? A peace offering? Tell Mikkelson I refuse to change my stance. I've ne'er truckled. I am the star of his effing play, and he'll never see my like again. I shall remain a star long after his deceit and treachery have become bywords in the theatre. I could hurt him. Badly. I have the instincts of a scoundrel. But I also have the conscience not to indulge myself. Greatness of spirit. Largeness of soul. A man of all seasonings. I could not have lasted forty years in the theatre without those qualities. Tell Mikkelson that when you see him."

"I don't know who Mikkelson is."

Philip Rackstraw had the cap off the whiskey bottle. He found a glass with a used prophylactic in it, got rid of the prophylactic and poured a shot.

"Spoken with a touching but superfluous veracity. I'm fully onto you. Not that it matters. Where are you from, laddy buck?"

"Kingman, Tennessee."

"In Yahoo country? I was there once, touring with Katy Cornell. Who is Mikkelson, you ask? I'll play along. Terrible Tommy Mikkelson, the twenty-two-year-old genius. Portrait of the *arriviste* as a young man. Producer, director. Four straight Broadway hits to his credit. He did the nude *Little Women.* He did *Uncle Vanya* as a blackfaced minstrel show. Yuk, yuk, yuk. He's doing the Russian Revolution. Lyrics by Sondheim, choreography by Nureyev. Quick, now: Who has he brought in to replace me? Is it Sir Larry? I've heard rumors traveling up the air shaft. Sir Larry was seen walking around the lobby disguised as a lame-duck senator from North Dakota. He's a true gentleman; he'd go to any lengths to spare my feelings."

Rackstraw sprawled on the bed. "North Dakota. The Turf Daisy State. Isn't that what they call it?"

"I don't think they call North Dakota anything. Look, Mr. Rackstraw, I just wanted to ask you a few questions. But if you're too busy—"

"Busy? No, darling, I'm not busy. I suppose I shall go to rehearsal shortly. Just as if nothing had happened. Perhaps nothing *did* happen. I may be imagining it. That's the actor's recurring nightmare, you know. Being lost onstage, utterly lost, with nothing to say. The prompter might as well be a million miles away, because one can't hear him, one hears nothing except the murmur from the audience, the rising tide of whispers, the uneasiness. Disaster. Tears one's guts out. I have never before seen the curtain descend in the middle of an act. Perhaps I didn't see it; I may well have dreamed it."

Rackstraw grimaced and sipped the last of the three ounces of whiskey he'd poured for himself. He consulted the label of the bottle, which he was holding in his other hand. "Not my brand, but most enjoyable." He then poured another three ounces and made himself more comfortable.

"Shall we get on with it? I hope you're not going to ask tedious questions. I'd much rather you be obnoxious.

The usual biographical material is available in the press kit. I have one around somewhere—some glossy photos included."

"Could I have my flight bag back?" Oxey asked. "My tape recorder's in it."

"Tape recorder? Have you been putting me on tape?"

"No, sir. Not yet."

"Very well. I reserve the right to edit your tape as I see fit. Is that understood?"

"Uh-huh." Oxey retrieved his flight bag, took out the Sony and a blank tape cartridge, set up the little microphone near Philip Rackstraw.

The whiskey seemed to have had a salutary effect on the actor's nerves, if not on his sweat glands. He ran his hands through his Nazi-blond hair, smiled whimsically. "Tinker is about your size and age. Why I mistook you for him momentarily. You're much nicer-looking, however."

Oxey wondered if he should say thank you, and decided not to. He turned on the tape recorder.

Rackstraw patted the bed. "Come sit here beside me, so I don't have to shout. Save the old pipes. That rutting play. Two characters. Tour de force, but hard on the actors. I think there are only two characters. Saturday night there seemed to be a third. Where did he come from? If that was a deliberate attempt to cause me to lose my bearings, they failed miserably." He sneaked a look at the telephone and drank. He gazed at Oxey. He was breathing hard.

"Say something," he demanded.

"Wha-what is your favorite role?"

"That's covered in the press release."

"Are there any roles you haven't played that you wish—"

"I've played them all. I have no regrets."

"Uh—what is your fav——"

"Covered in the press release."

"Do you prefer—"

"Covered."

They stared at each other for almost a full minute. Oxey swallowed hard several times. Rackstraw finished his second generous shot of whiskey and poured a third.

"No more questions?"

Oxey shook his head a fraction.

Philip Rackstraw sat up and swung his legs smartly over the side of the bed.

"Suppose we fuck, then," he said pleasantly.

"No . . . sir."

The actor stood up and approached Oxey. Sweat was streaming down his face; he smelled like an acid bath. He held out the bottle of whiskey.

"You'd better have a little of this to drink. You look terrified."

"I . . . am."

"Of me?" He looked very closely at Oxey's face. Then he shrugged, stepped back and began to wiggle his ears.

Oxey didn't know what to think, but he was fascinated.

Rackstraw stopped and shook his head in exasperation. "Dammit, always works with my grandchildren. Puts them at ease with the old curmudgeon."

Oxey smiled slightly, and the actor smiled too.

"Why did you come up here? You must have had something in mind."

"Marian Holgate." He cleared his throat and said more loudly, "MAR——"

"Yes, yes, I understood you. What about Marian?"

"You worked with her a lot."

"Quite often. First ran across Marian when she was a part of that abominable all-girl Shakespearean troupe in Liverpool. Still in her teens. But she had talent even then. Marian lasted a very long time in a resolutely second-rate career. I recall seeing her play Richard Third—she exhibited a gangling villainy, like an apprentice torturer. I wanted to bang her then, but somehow never got around to it, not once in our thirty-year relationship. At her best she was difficult in those days, never willing to surrender the advantage in bed. And that was what Marian always looked for, the inguinal advantage—brass ring through some poor chap's cock. Also, there was something askew in young Marian. She was not evil, not depraved, but freakishly fatal, like a frost in a greenhouse. She buried three husbands, I daresay through no fault of her own."

"Donald Camming hanged himself."

"Oh, yes, poor Donald, the reformed pouf. Husband Number Three. I never got the straight of his suicide. Apparently he was fooling around with one of the children —although he seemed much too austere for any familial buggering. Marian must have laid down the law rather fiercely. She was changing then. You know how it is. No longer young. Hitting the bottle. I've seen it happen to so many of my colleagues. Yes, she was a right rummy bitch in those days. But never gave a moment's concern onstage. She retained her professionalism."

"There wasn't anything going on between Terry and his stepfather. She was jealous because Terry sort of worshipped Camming. She threatened to expose him to Terry as a, what you said, and Camming couldn't face that. So—"

Rackstraw pantomimed a realistic garroting with a fist at his throat. "Most interesting. You seem to know the family well."

"I know Terry."

"Do you, now? He made a name for himself. I wouldn't have given much for his chance of survival." The third shot of whiskey was almost gone. Philip Rackstraw was a chain drinker today. Take a sip, hold it in the mouth for a few seconds, swallow greedily, take another sip. "Please give Terry my kindest regards. He may choose not to acknowledge them. He hated everything about the theatre, but most of all he hated me, his mother's friend and confidant. Too bad—I rather fancied the dour little chap. Wished him well. She offered him to me, you know. Like a sweet on a plate."

The telephone rang jarringly.

Philip Rackstraw's head jerked toward it, and even Oxey reacted apprehensively. After three rings the actor composed himself, but he made no move to pick up the phone. Instead he refilled his glass, then leaned back against a bedpost with a severe smile and resumed drinking. When his glass was empty, in a twinkling, he put it on the bed and began to drink from the bottle. Apparently he intended to ignore the telephone. He put a huge amount of effort into it.

"Marian. The uses to which she put her own son would seem to contradict my claim that she was not capable of depravity. But don't judge her too narrowly. I believe there was a plausible, absorbing drama in her relationship with that . . . difficult boy which appealed to her more than the soppy dramas she was appearing in at the close of her life. Perhaps, after so long devoting herself to the uses of sex, she was at last obsessed by sex itself. Drink had thickened Marian somewhat, but it did not in the least dilute her . . . tigerish desirability. As for Terry, once seduced, he was enthralled, even though they were forced to invent an alter ego to make it halfway bearable for him. I've often thought that Marian was determined to purge him of all sexual inhibition. What else could she have had in mind when she invited me to drop around for an afternoon of troilism? She never got *that* drunk, God save her soul."

"Don't you want me to—"

"GET AWAY FROM THAT TELEPHONE! It will stop ringing. Sooner or later . . . it *will* stop. What were we—? Oh, the murders. Weren't we talking about the murders, ducks?"

"No, we—" Oxey said, and bit his tongue.

"All that unpleasantness in Oxford. Girls butchered. Haven't thought about it for a while. Headlines haunted me, though. You understand. Bloody dilemma. Perhaps I should've stepped forward then. Some doubt in my mind, you see. Strong accusation, minimum of proof. Embarrassing questions would have been asked. Not so helpful to the old career. Too many troubles already—

the divorce, bankruptcy—why call attention to a spot of nastiness in the remote past? Then, when his sister was attacked, I wondered if it couldn't've been—"

"*Terry?*"

And the phone continued to ring.

"It's Pretty Joe I'm talking about! Pretty Joe. That's what they called him. Lousy way to rid yourself of inhibitions, wouldn't you say? Of course he had to be a little schizoid already. Perhaps he gave birth to Pretty Joe himself. But Marian made up their little rutting song. How'd it go? She was prone to sing it when in her cups. Here we go, then, to the tune of 'Hobo's Lullaby.' Hope I manage to stay on key.

> See him naked by the window
> Tousled hair a pearly glow
> Lie down sweetly by your mummy
> Come to me, my prretttyyyy Joe . . ."

The telephone was on its thirty-third harrowing ring. Philip Rackstraw swigged from the bottle of whiskey, getting his chin wet. When he ran out of breath he stopped drinking and looked vacantly at Oxey.

"You might . . . ask him to sing it for you sometime. Literally dozens of verses, some of them quite charmingly erotic."

"Did Terry try to kill his mother?" Oxey said. Loudly enough, he hoped, to be heard on the tape he was making.

"Pretty! Joe! Don't you see, it's *Pretty Joe* who does the killings. I found Terry crouched naked in a corner of her dressing room, wild as a wolf boy. Knife in his hand. Marian was lying face down on the floor. Only a superficial wound on the left forearm. Stroke killed her. High blood pressure, those last few years. Suppose it was the shock of sonny boy coming on with the knife. Did them all a favor, I thought. GOD, THE TELEPHONE! WHY ARE THEY CRUCIFYING ME? Talked to him. Very patient. He was incoherent. Wolf-boy sounds. Totally

bonkers. Persuaded him to hand over the knife. Got him
into his clothes. Walked him out of the dressing room,
pushed him out the stage door. STOP. YOU MUST STOP
THAT RINGING! Back to dear Marian's dressing room.
Bandaged the arm. Laid her on the divan. I hid the knife
in my dressing room, tossed it in the Thames a few nights
later. Rang the house physician. Ambulance summoned.
They found Terry two days later, footloose in Chelsea.
No memory. Whisked him off to Farnsworth. Shock treatment. All the rage then. Don't you agree . . . I did them
a bloody important favor?"

"Why do you think Pretty Joe killed those girls in
Oxford?"

"Terry could never bring himself to kill the women he
loves. Hates. Loves. Not his mother—nor his sister. So
it's Pretty Joe's task to find substitutes."

Rackstraw turned then and threw the half-filled whiskey
bottle at the tormenting phone. The bottle struck the
telephone butt-first and knocked it to the floor. Rackstraw
pounced on the phone and began to rail in a high-pitched
voice. "DELIBERATE ATTEMPT TO SABOTAGE ME
I NEVER REHEARSED THOSE LINES   THERE
WAS NO SUCH REHEARSAL   YOU ARE ALL
OUT TO DESTROY ME   AND   I   WILL
NOT   STAND   FOR   IT."

His face was blood-suffused. He put the phone down
then and retrieved the bottle, which had a little whiskey
left in it. He sat down on the edge of the bed with the
bottle in his lap and sighed very deeply, once. His eyes
were wistfully fixed on a Seurat reproduction on the opposite wall. Pointillism. Bright dots of color: illusionary
shapes. It was a painting you could wander into, remain
lost in for days.

Oxey turned off the tape recorder and packed it in his
flight bag. Though he was within a couple of feet of
Philip Rackstraw, the actor paid him no mind. Oxey
picked up the telephone and found that the line was still
open. As he listened he thought he heard the far-off

rumble of a subway train. He put the assembled phone back on the night table.

Rackstraw was making some disconcerting sounds, and Oxey looked worriedly at him. He seemed to be snoring, but his eyes were wide open.

"Mr. Rackstraw?"

The actor didn't bat an eyelash. He went on snoring. At least the violent color had left his face. Was he smiling? Oxey couldn't be sure.

"I have to go now," Oxey mumbled.

As he let himself out of the suite he heard the telephone ringing again back there in the bedroom.

To BEHOLD THE wonders of Dark Ridge Caverns you first had to walk through a low-slung building that occupied most of a hillside acre. Part of the faked-stone-and-timber building was devoted to a cafeteria, adjacent to an attractive flagged terrace built around a couple of ancient cucumber trees. The rest of the building contained a souvenir shop. No tacky auxiliary amusements were offered—dusty pony rides, caged bears or performing porpoises. The parking lot was broad and seldom crowded with cars even in midsummer.

There was a reasonable admission charge to the caverns; a family of four could take the tour for six dollars and fifty cents. The girl guides wore yellow blazers and skirts, and they were incorrigible smilers. So were the young clerks in the shop. Somebody was always there to snatch up the odd scrap of paper that drifted to the floor. The rest rooms were sunny and smelled of mountain wildflowers. Everyone connected with the place was so pleasant and unassuming that you felt a little sorry for them, because, at the most, fifteen hundred people a day could tour the caverns—and how much profit margin was there in numbers like that? Particularly since Dark Ridge was open only six months of the year.

That was enough time, however, for the souvenir shop to gross three hundred thousand dollars annually, and the cafeteria, which featured a limited menu of fast-food items, also did handsomely. The Kingman Corporation, which owned the Caverns, could easily have afforded to let the people tour the caverns for free, but that was poor psychology. If it's free, there must be something wrong with it. The admission charge and the brochures available in twelve hundred Kingman motels created the right attitude of expectancy. Few people were disappointed with the natural wonders and the discreet showmanship. The fifty minutes they spent below was just enough time to bore the kids without antagonizing them, and get everybody's feet to hurting a little.

Terry came in from the blustery afternoon and found eight people with twenty cameras waiting by the elevator for the next tour. He paid his admission and joined them. He had his own camera, a Leica, around his neck. While he waited he kept his trench coat buttoned; it was always 63 degrees in the caverns.

Soon the freight-sized elevator appeared from the depths and they all shuffled aboard.

"We're the Montfort Camera Club," one of his fellow tour members said to Terry. "I see you have a Leica there."

"Is that what it is?" Terry said, smiling.

Their elfin tour guide told them her name was Becky, and she began her spiel as the elevator descended, very slowly, to the sixty-foot level.

Terry was the last to step off the elevator into the chamber. The Montfort Camera Club began shutter-bugging immediately as Becky led them at a brisk pace down a path of crushed rock. Terry followed at his leisure.

First stop was the Star-Spangled Grotto, which they reached in near darkness; only the path at their feet was lighted. Becky asked the camera nuts to hold off popping flashbulbs until everyone had had the opportunity to appreciate the intricate water-drip designs of the phosphorescent shapes that clung like starfish to the ultramarine walls.

Terry felt a tug at his sleeve and turned. He could just make out Jeanie standing behind him on the path, unexpected as a butterfly in her yellow blazer.

"You came," she said. "Well, here you are. Glory be."

"I said I'd come."

She stepped quickly into his arms and kissed him, ignoring the bulky camera that hung between them. When she had finished kissing Terry she laid her head on his shoulder and stroked his cheek with one hand.

"You like me again," she said with a contented sigh.

"I never stopped liking you."

"Sound really carries in here. Let's split."

"I just started the tour."

Jeanie stood on tiptoe and gave him another bruising kiss. "You get the deluxe tour today, friend."

She took him by the hand and led him to an intersecting path that wound through cobby pillars and continued across an arched stone bridge.

"Down there," she said, "in a deposit of alluvial rock, are footprints of birds, literally thousands of birds. Some of them were close kin to flamingos and herons. Nobody knows how they got there. Are you interested in looking at bird tracks? I didn't think so. In here we have the Great Cathedral; I'll just throw the light on."

The Great Cathedral was truly impressive: nearly translucent stalactites and stalagmites, amber extravasations, futuristic heights and setbacks of blazing opal, glimmers of crystalline red and blue in the distance. The vaulted roof of the cavern looked like a Fourth of July sky.

"Terrible about Professor Thornton."

"I know. I was there."

"It must have been—"

"He looked like a fried grasshopper. Like a burnt match."

"Don't. I can tell you're still upset about it."

They walked through the Cathedral and came to a stream bursting through bulked stone that was as rusty as ironwork. It was part of a subterranean watercourse that, Jeanie explained, at its widest and deepest formed an entombed lake far back in the string of caverns. They headed for this lake, passing through one rococo chamber after another.

"The Throne Room was discovered two years ago," Jeanie said, talking low so her voice wouldn't echo, "but it won't be open to the public until next spring. The lake is set right in the middle of the Throne Room. It's only about fifty feet in diameter, but some scuba divers went down to two hundred feet this summer without touching bottom. They said there were strong currents at depths of thirty feet. If they hadn't been attached to lines they would've been swept away to Lord knows where. So what've you been doing with yourself?"

"Writing," Terry said.

Jeanie switched on the work lights. Seen against the ocher stone, he looked pale and fragmentary, like a hangnail. Her heart went out to Terry.

"Of course they'll fancy it up with all kinds of colored lights to bring out the values of the quartz crystal, but you can get a fair idea of what it'll look like. Those are the thrones over there, in that fantail grotto—like solid ice, aren't they? Really dazzling."

"They certainly are."

"I can tell you're overwhelmed," Jeanie said with a nervous laugh. "This way."

She left the lights on and led Terry along a rimrock path above the black lake to an opening in the cavern wall. Fresh air poured through the winding passage that took them up and out to daylight.

They were in a deep vale edged with pine trees that seemed to float in the wind against the quick-changing

October sky. They could hear the wind moaning above their heads, but the air was more calm where they were, and warmer. Water trickled somewhere. In sunlit spaces and choice crannies they found the going soft as a featherbed underfoot from the timeless accumulation of pine needles.

"Nobody ever comes up here," Jeanie said, breaking out in sly smiles. Her hands were demurely clasped at her waist. "And can you believe it? I've got almost forty minutes before I go back to work."

"Forty minutes," he repeated, as if he were pleased.

"What I'd like to do, I'd like to get out of this blazer and the other things I don't want all stuck up with needles, and crawl into that big sweater of yours. I don't suppose you have that rabbity liner zipped into your coat? You do? Hoo, Lordy! It's going to be just like Christmas. I never got off better in my whole life. I guess there's worse things than having a rabbit-fur fetish, wouldn't you say? But it *is* your coat. So it's all up to you, whether we do or don't."

He smiled and began slowly to unbutton his trench coat. It was thickly lined with rabbit fur, all right, somewhat warm for the season. Jeanie stroked the fur, just once; her eyes went a little out of focus. She sighed and walked away from him, pulling off the yellow blazer. She laid it, folded, on a flat rock, and unzipped her skirt. She looked up at the sun, gloating, eyes aswim with tears. Her hands trembled, not from horniness, not yet, although she was very, very near it, but from her relief at having Terry back, at having him want her again. She couldn't hear him walking up behind her, but she sensed he was close. She took off her blouse. That left bra and panty hose. His hands were on her back, and he helped with the bra hooks. She didn't turn around but gave her shoulders a little shake, enjoying the cool freedom, the nervy breast play. His hands deftly rolled the panty hose to her thighs, and her nipples became hard as twigs. Jeanie took over then, stooping to finish pulling down her panty hose. She felt one of his hands at the small of her back, fingers provocatively spread, as if he were measuring, sizing up. Jeanie pulled off the panty hose one foot at a time. Her mouth had dried out. She licked a sun tear from one corner of her mouth. Then she crossed her arms over her breasts, feeling a chill that even the full stroke of the sun couldn't nullify. She turned goosily, laughing, opening her arms to him, and Pretty Joe killed her.

The shock of being struck in the solar plexus by the ten-inch chef's knife all but doubled her on the blade; every muscle in her body tensed until she shook and trembled. The expression in her eyes was one of catastrophic surprise. He gathered himself for a final thrust, and this time the blade severed the spinal cord. He let go of the knife she had slumped on and stepped quickly out of the way. Jeanie plunged face down into the pine needles. Sun glinted on the parabolic inch of blade exposed below the occipital bulge.

No movement, not a sound. He knelt and looked her sternly in the eye, as if he were convinced she might be trying to fool him. But the eye was slick and cooling, her soul beyond recall.

He got busy. He turned Jeanie on her side and pulled the knife just enough so that the blade no longer protruded from her neck. From his inside pocket he took out a pad of polythene sheeting and unfolded it, squaring it beside the body. He rolled Jeanie onto it. There was some blood on the pine needles where she had fallen, but he paid no attention. He took his stapler from another coat pocket, folded and tucked the polythene neatly, and stapled Jeanie inside.

The card came last. He stapled it to the bag. This time the message was more to the point.

WHAT MUST I DO TO MAKE YOU SEE THE ERROR OF YOUR WAYS?

Pretty Joe didn't know how to say it any more plainly than that.

He picked up the body and walked back into the passage that led to the Throne Room.

It was difficult work getting Jeanie down that narrow passage. Her face shone mistily through the double thickness of polythene. Twice he skidded and almost fell headlong before reaching the path above the deep lake in the Throne Room. Fortunately the lights were still on, otherwise he'd be feeling his way riskily, in total blackness. He had brought along a compact flashlight that he could hang around his neck or clip to his belt, but it didn't have much of a beam.

As he started down the long path with the body he heard voices echoing. He quickly put Jeanie in the only possible hiding place, wedging her in a sitting position between two smooth quartz outcroppings. She could not be seen there—unless, of course, someone came up the path from below.

The voices were more distinct: visitors were approaching the Throne Room. He scrambled back up the path to the crevice in the cavern wall, his only way out should a mob of tourists suddenly appear. But he remembered that Jeanie had told him the Throne Room was not yet open to the public.

Two girl guides entered the cavern. From where he was standing, in the deep shadow of the crevice, he could follow their progress without having to worry about being noticed. Also he could keep an eye on Jeanie, who appeared to be staring directly at him when he glanced at her.

Despite the cool of the cavern he was sweating. The girl guides were chatting about their boy friends; he couldn't make out many words in the sound-swallowing enormity of the cavern. They sat beside the lake to smoke and gab. He watched them uneasily, fidgeting.

When he looked again at Jeanie he was a little stunned to see that she wasn't staring at him any more. Her head had slumped to one side. All of her body seemed to have shifted inside the humid bag. As he watched in dismay he saw the twinkling fall of drops of water from the roof of the cavern; the drops were sliding down the surface of the polythene. They also made a wet glaze on the rounded surface of the quartz hump against which he'd propped Jeanie. In his haste to put her somewhere he hadn't noticed that the rock was wet, and now the frictionless bagged body was slowly tilting toward the sharp drop that ended at the surface of the lake some thirty feet below.

Down there the girl guides stubbed out their cigarettes on the soles of their shoes, dropped the butts into their jacket pockets. They sauntered away from the lake, still chatting.

Behind and above them Jeanie leaned out over the drop.

He couldn't try to grab her, because the girls were passing just below, and any sudden movement on his part might have fatally attracted their attention. So he watched helplessly as Jeanie's slide quickened and she fell out of the saddle of rock in which he had placed her.

As she started to roll down the slope to the lake the polythene snagged on a sharp piece of rock and tore wide open. He saw the body falling free of his improvised bag.

One of the girls clicked off the lights in the Throne Room as they walked out, and Jeanie completed her lifeless descent in darkness, rolling almost soundlessly except for the scratching of the handle of the knife against the rock. The blade was pounded through her again and once there was a solitary spark, flaming brightly as a star in an otherwise empty universe. Then she rolled into the lake with a muted splash.

He waited, petrified, in the dark, but the girls apparently hadn't heard a thing. Gradually their voices became indistinct. He took out the square flashlight that just filled his palm and thumbed it on. Its light was adequate to get him safely down the path. He went immediately to the edge of the lake and cast the flashlight beam on the rippling water. With a stronger light he might have had a glimpse of an arm or leg as Jeanie sank slowly to the current that would tug her away from the calm surface and into brawling miles of underground water.

He just couldn't believe how badly everything was working out. The idea had struck him, on his first view of the Throne Room, as having both simplicity and dignity. They would discover her, although perhaps not for a day or two, seated on one of the twin thrones in the grotto. But Jeanie was gone, never to be found. He had selected her only after a great deal of thought. He had killed her, but to no purpose.

He wiped chilly perspiration from his eyes, took a last sorrowful look at the lake, walked slowly from the Throne Room. After a while he didn't need his flashlight; the lights from other chambers guided him back to the tour beat.

As he walked and pondered, the truth of their situation became clear to him. Terry's desperate compromises had brought them to an impasse. Killing a hundred girls would in no way set them free. It was hopeless. So . . .

No more unheeded warnings. No more substitutes could be permitted.

That resolution he accepted with a fearfulness that was more characteristic of Terry than himself. (But were they ever, at any point, so totally separated, uncommunicative?) It was dark indeed where Pretty Joe now proposed to take them, darker than any cavern under the earth. And if they got in so deeply, could they hope to get out again, with their cherished freedom?

Pretty Joe's growing arrogance asserted itself. He didn't care what Terry would think. They were equals, more or less, an equality founded on accommodation. Perhaps it was true that they needed each other to survive, but Pretty Joe was now willing to test that assumption. He'd always been careful not to push Terry too far, but Terry would have to make some real sacrifices if they were to continue to get along. Terry knew what he was risking every time he made love to Anne. There was just no other way. Pretty Joe had to kill Anne; he had to do it while he was near his peak strength and Terry was relatively weak.

The Montfort Camera Club had departed, but he fell in with another tour group. Within fifteen minutes he was crossing the parking lot to the camper truck.

THE DAY AFTER his apocalyptic interview with Philip Rackstraw a subdued and anxious Oxey flew back to Knoxville with his father.

At his uncle Steve's house in Falls Church he had played the tape over and over, forgoing a night's sleep, finding about 20 percent of the actor's remarks unintelligible. But—despite the jangling telephone in the background—those crucial statements about Terry's sexual relationship with his mother, and the Pretty Joe doggerel, had come chillingly through. In legal terms Oxey wasn't sure what he had (and it was his impression that Philip Rackstraw in his present state of mind wouldn't make a satisfactory witness in court), but even an amateur psychologist could figure out that Terry—make that Pretty Joe—was highly dangerous. What most worried Oxey was the unshakable conviction that he knew *why* Joe had murdered those three girls in Oxford. One unforgettable glimpse of Anne's face the past Sunday in the atelier had told him why.

If he hadn't left his seat belt fastened, Oxey would have been jumping out in the aisle every other minute. As it was, he did enough squirming to distract his father, who was attempting to write a speech.

A part of Oxey's discomfort was due to the fact that the day before—Tuesday, the first of October—there had been a full moon at 5:40 P.M. CDT. And Pretty Joe the

Oxford butcher-boy was demonstrably a creature of the moon's phases.

Also Oxey was still very much afraid he'd made the wrong decision by not calling Anne the previous night and trying to persuade her, without being too specific, to stay as far away from Terry as she could. Of course she would have thought he was crazy, and he hadn't been able to see the wisdom of trying to play the tape for her long-distance.

Somewhere over the Blue Ridge Mountains Dr. Hollis gave up on the speech and put his writing materials away.

"Enjoyed visiting with Steve and the family, didn't you?"

"Sure," Oxey said.

"I wish we could take more trips together. I just don't see enough of you, Oxey, and I feel badly about that."

To Oxey's surprise his eyes began to fill with tears, and he quickly turned his head away from his father. He wanted very much at that moment to confide in Dr. Hollis, to play the tape and thus be partially relieved of the burden of responsibility, which was worse than guilt or any sin he could imagine. But he knew it just wasn't right. Anne should hear the tape first. Terry was her brother, and it was up to Anne to decide what to do.

That is, if Pretty Joe hadn't caught up with her already.

WHILE OXEY WAS winging home, the combined first grades of the West End Grammar School of Kingman were completing their autumn nature-studies outing at Dark Ridge State Park. By three o'clock they had collected two cardboard cartons of nuts, leaves, mosses and stones. Their teachers, Tricia Rosewald and Mary Schuyler Finch, were bedraggled but pleased. There had been only two scraped knees and one wasp sting. No one had fallen into the shallow waters of the spring and no one had thrown up all day.

"Teacher?"

"Yes, Billy Luke?" Tricia said.

"What is this?"

"Why, it's a—it looks like—I'm sure it's a squirrel's head."

"What happened to its ears and its fur and its brains?"

"That's just the skull you have there—scavenger insects ate everything else."

"Teacher!"

"What's the matter, Anita?" asked Mary Schuyler Finch.

"We want to get a drink of water and we can't, because Gary Connor is spitting in the spring."

"You tell Gary to come here to me *right now*. You tell him Mrs. Finch means business. And I'm sure it's all right to drink—his spit has probably floated away by now. Drink upstream from where he was spitting, why don't you?"

"Which way is upstream?"

"Oh, Teacher," said May Hummerston, "we still can't get a drink."

"Now what?"

"Because there's a lady swimming in the spring."

The teachers looked at each other.

240

"How long do you think she can stay under water?" Anita said to May.

"I don't know—she's been under water a *long time.*"

"My brother can hold his breath under water six minutes."

"You've got rocks in your head, Anita. You've got a *raisin* for a brain."

"I'll go see what this is all about," Tricia Rosewald said to Mary Schuyler Finch.

"Thanks. Uh—I want you girls to stay here with me while Miss Rosewald talks to the lady in the spring."

Tricia Rosewald walked down a leafy path to the spring. She saw Gary Connor standing a little way upstream, very near the source. He had a long stick in his hand and he was poking at something in the water.

"*Gary* Connor!"

The boy looked at her in consternation, then back at the bubbly water.

"What do you think you're doing?"

"I'm trying to get the lady out," Gary Connor explained. "But her foot's caught on something."

"What lady?" Tricia said, approaching him, and then in the clear green water she saw a spready flow of drowned blond hair, a gaping mouth, jelly-button eyes. A knife handle protruded just below and between the woman's ample breasts.

"Gawwwwkkk!" Tricia said. She grabbed Gary Connor by the hand and ran with him along the bank to the path, and up the path through the woods to the picnic clearing. Along the way Gary tripped over a tree root and sprawled screaming, but Tricia didn't stop for him. She just kept running, almost as fast as a man, lifting her knees high. She ran right past the startled Mary Schuyler Finch, and kept going to the bus, to wake up the driver, who was catnapping on the back seat.

Oxey dropped his father at the college, where he had a banquet to attend, and drove the car home. Before carrying the luggage to the house he knocked on Anne's door, but she wasn't there. Her car was nowhere to be seen.

His mother was in the kitchen with Ellamay.

"Did you have a good time in Washington? How are the twins?"

"They're at the age where they brush their hair a lot, and they don't want to play horsey any more. Haven't seen Anne this afternoon, have you?"

"I just walked in the door a few minutes ago."

"Ellamay?"

"She hasn't been around."

Oxey was halfway to the wall phone, intending to call Anne's office at the college, when Ellamay said, "Her brother's been looking for her too."

"Was he here?"

"Most of the afternoon. He was sitting in that truck of his, parked across the street from the cottage. I looked out three or four times, and he just sat there. So that's why I say he—"

"What time did Terry leave?"

"All I know is he was gone by four thirty."

Mrs. Hollis said, "If you're going to call Professor Ramsdell, would you remind her we're having drinks for the Yugoslav Cultural Delegation at eight thirty?"

"Sure," Oxey mumbled, and he dialed Anne's office number.

No answer.

It was now ten after five. Oxey remained in the kitchen long enough to drink a glass of iced tea, then he loped up the back stairs to his bedroom and changed his clothes. He picked up his biking helmet and the tape recorder and returned to the kitchen.

"Ellamay, I probably won't be home for dinner."

"*Now* you're telling me?"

Anne's front door wasn't locked, and Oxey walked right in. He chose a conspicuous spot for the tape recorder, appropriated one of her lipsticks and wrote a message on a bedsheet:

ANNE

I TALKED TO PHILIP RACKSTRAW
IN WASH
KNOWS WHAT REALLY HAPPENED TO
YOUR MOTHER
TERRY IS PRETTY JOE
TERRY IS *PRETTY JOE*
LISTEN TO TAPE

OXEY

After he'd rigged the sheet where his message would hit her right in the eye when she walked in the door, Oxey got his Honda out of the garage and tore over to Terry's house.

The camper truck wasn't there, and the house was closed up. It looked forbidding in the waning light of day.

No point in sticking around, Oxey thought. Terry undoubtedly was still looking for her. His own chances of finding Anne first weren't exactly even, but possibly he knew her habits and her schedule better than Terry. Tuesday was not one of her more rigidly structured days. She could be swimming in the gym or fiddling in one of the music rooms in the Fine Arts building. Or she might be playing backgammon in the Student Center. All he had to do was look for her car. But Terry was cruising right now, doing the same thing . . .

Oxey was on his way to the Student Center when he

saw Terry's big camper truck pull into the drive-in Goldie on Cove Creek Boulevard. He followed. He rode slowly past the space where Terry had parked, observing that Terry was alone.

Oxey was elated. If Terry had stopped only long enough for coffee, that would still give him the time he needed to locate Anne.

Then he had another idea. What if there was a way to make absolutely certain Pretty Joe wouldn't try to kill Anne?

Ordinarily Oxey wouldn't have considered climbing into the truck cab with a homicidal maniac. But here they were at suppertime in a jammed Goldie, cars bulging with kids, and hadn't Ken Bidwell told him many times that he had an aptitude for handling the mentally deranged? Oxey had no way of knowing just who he would be talking to, but he reminded himself that Pretty Joe killed only women, and for a purpose; he was not uncontrollably violent. What Oxey had to do was—well, he didn't know for sure. Try to reach Terry. Talk quietly, be persuasive, convince *Terry* that it wasn't really Anne's fault, that Anne was not a reincarnated Marian Holgate.

Oxey was confident that it was the mother figure Terry feared and hated, and not his own sister. Terry really loved Anne, and needed her. No matter what Pretty Joe thought.

So Oxey parked, chained up his bike and helmet and walked across the lot to the camper. Oxey rated himself only about average in physical courage, and he was shaking. Nevertheless he was able to smile at Terry when he opened the door and looked in.

"Hello, Oxey."

"Hello, Terry."

"Are you alone?"

"Uh, yeh, I sure am. How about you?"

"Yes, I'm alone."

"Maybe you don't want company. I just thought I'd—"

"No, no, get in."

Terry was wearing a rough-out jacket and Levi's. He had a day's growth of beard, but otherwise he looked entirely himself. Maybe just a little fatigued.

"Where've you strayed to?" Terry asked him. "I haven't seen you for a while. It's been more than a week, hasn't it?"

Oxey wondered about that remark, but judging from Terry's expression he wasn't being devious. So just possibly he didn't recall Oxey's attempt to sneak out of the atelier on Sunday. Or had it been Pretty Joe glaring at him from the water bed? That was almost enough to give Oxey the shakes all over again. Two men slipping unpredictably in and out of the same skin, not leaving so much as an ectoplasmic ripple in the air.

"I went to Washington yesterday with my dad. Got back about an hour ago."

"Oh, Washington."

"Have you ordered yet?"

"I was sitting here enjoying the sunset. What shall it be for you? By the way, my treat."

"Oh, no, listen, Terry—"

"I really do insist."

"Well—okay. Some fries. And a large Coke."

"No Goldie?"

"I'm really not all that hungry."

Terry rolled down the window on his side and called in the orders.

There was an orange VW parked next to him. Mom and Pop with two kids in the back. Pop was saying, "You all had better decide *right now* if you want a Chocomoca shake or a banana shake." In the car on Oxey's side, a vintage convertible with libidinous fenders, sexy tail fins and a fifties fuck-me grill, two men in work clothes were watching a National League play-off game on a tiny portable television set. The sound was turned up good and loud. Bottom of the eighth, and the Dodgers had ducks on the pond.

"What've you been up to?" Oxey said to Terry.

"How do you mean?"

"Have you done much writing?"

"No. I work very hard at it, but at the end of the day I only have a few lines down. I write the same line over and over, perhaps thirty times. Change a comma here, add a word there. I'm in a superstall phase. That happens. No use fighting it. Packed it all in yesterday. Went fishing. Came full circle. The fish weren't biting either. It's the bloody full moon."

"What about the full moon?" Oxey said, startled.

"Fish don't bite so good when the moon's full."

"So you didn't catch many fish."

"I didn't catch *any*."

A man got out of the station wagon parked in the bay directly in front of them and with a show of weariness and disgust unfolded a road map on the front fender. One of his kids leaned over the seat and tooted the horn. He went back into the wagon in a blithering dudgeon, grabbed the offending kid and smacked him. His wife screamed at him. He screamed at his wife. A gust of wind picked up his road map and sailed it halfway across the Goldie lot. He walked stolidly after his map, the back of his neck richly scarlet. Before he could get to the map a motorcycle ran over it.

"What's a squeeze play?" Terry asked.

"What?"

"A squeeze play. The telly announcer was saying something about the big squeeze play that didn't come off."

"Oh. Well, in baseball, when you have the bases loaded, and, like there's one out and you need a run to tie or win, the batter tries to drag a bunt down the first base line as the man on third breaks for the plate. If it's a good bunt, then it's practically impossible to throw the runner out at home."

"But in this instance the play failed."

"I think the Cards were probably looking for the squeeze. They saw it coming. Or else the ball was bunted in the air. Yeh, Gowdy says that's what happened. The batter couldn't execute. He—screwed it up. Terry—"

"Yes?"

"I don't want to wait on the fries and the Coke. I'll pay for them, but—it was a bad idea, I guess. Stopping. So I, what I want to do is, just run on h-home now—"

"You look as if you—"

"—don't feel too good. That's true." Oxey grinned woefully. His face was a dull copper color, green at the gills. "I don't like to travel. I get upset in airplanes. I'm still not comfortable with the idea of manned flight."

"That *is* too bad. I was hoping we— Well, never mind."

"I'll—see you around, then."

Terry was sitting sideways in the seat. He put out his hand. "Oxey? Don't go."

The mild restraint caused a very bad reaction in Oxey. "Terry, I really think I'm going to be sick. That's no lie."

"No, you must stay. Listen to me. Jeanie's dead."

Oxey stared at him. Then with what seemed like his last breath Oxey said very quietly and coldly, "What?"

Terry's hand tightened on his arm, and there was a pathetic shine of tears in his eyes.

"I'm as sorry as you are. Believe me. I feel badly, I do. I resisted. Because Jeanie was very close and dear to me. She was, Oxey. A very dear, loving girl. But—he demanded Jeanie. He said it had to be someone obviously difficult to sacrifice. No . . . easy little pickup from the side of the road. Oxey?"

"You—you can't do that anymore. Not ever again."

"But it isn't my fault."

"*His* fault?"

"Yes!"

"Don't—don't get upset, Terry. We have to protect Anne now. We have to keep Pretty Joe away from her."

"I know that," Terry said earnestly. His grip on Oxey's forearm had become painful.

A car pulling into the lot collided with a car backing out: yawlp, thud, tinkle. They both looked in the direction of the accident. There were two girls in the Ford Pinto that had been hit, and two husky boys in the other car. They appeared to know each other. They waved and laughed.

As they were watching this Terry reached into a vinyl tool caddy fixed to the door on his side and slowly withdrew a hammer. He still had hold of Oxey's arm.

"Terry," Oxey said, turning to look at him, "where is Pret——"

Pretty Joe swung the hammer and hit Oxey full in the face with it.

Oxey's head bounced off the dashboard; he cried out, but not loudly, the sound muffled by a gush of blood into his throat. Pretty Joe quickly hit him again, on top of the head, and Oxey threw up his hands to ward off further blows. More blood was streaming down his broken face. He couldn't do much to stop the attack. Pretty Joe leaned into him and pounded away with the hammer: short, vicious blows. He quickly drove Oxey down into the space between the seat and the fire wall.

Then he lowered the bloody hammer and looked around.

The men in the tail-fin car were watching TV. Everyone else seemed to be absorbed in the trivial drama created by the collision. A private cop was trying to get traffic untangled where the two cars blocked the driveway.

He turned to slip the hammer back into the tool caddy. As he did so he glanced down at the orange Volkswagen. A moon-faced little girl with red hair and heat rash was studying him as she sipped her Chocomoca shake through a straw.

Terry smiled at her.

Without a change of expression the little girl reached behind her and tugged urgently at her daddy's arm, which was hooked over the back of his seat.

"You see what he's doing all wrong there? He ought to just have them two cars pull off to the side somewhere, instead of trying to move ever'body else around them. He don't have the good sense he was born with."

"He was behind the door when they was dishing out the brains," said Rosalie's mother.

"Rosalie, would you leave go Daddy's arm? Because Daddy is trying to eat his supper, honeybunch."

Rosalie stopped clinging to him and glanced again at Terry. She had the self-righteous look of the born tattle-tale. Terry smiled again, but he was sweating. He thoughtlessly attempted to wipe his forehead with the back of his right hand. He left a streak of blood above the eyebrows. Rosalie's China-blue eyes got a little wider, and she lost her appetite for Chocomoca milk shakes. She slowly slid back away from the window and put her hand on Daddy's arm again.

"Chrissake, Rosalie—"

At that moment her brother, who was sitting with Rosalie in the back seat, drew up his leg and cruelly kicked Rosalie for intruding on his space. Rosalie began to howl and shed blobs of tears.

Terry took advantage of Rosalie's tantrum to grab a poncho from the back of the truck cab. He pushed Oxey's battered, bleeding head down between his knees and threw the poncho over him. Terry's hands were smeared with blood. He used a pocket handkerchief to wipe them clean, a chore he finished just as one of the Goldie Girls arrived with a carton of food.

"Two twenty-four with tax, sir, and we all want to say *thank you* for stopping at GoldenBurger. What did you do, swat a mosquito? God knows, they been fierce for this time of the year."

"Sorry—?"

"Little smear of blood on your forehead. No, over just a tad. *There,* you got it. Hey, are you English by any chance?"

"Yes, I am."

"I knew it! I'm crazy about the way y'all talk. Year before last my roommate up at UT, she was English. I just loved to listen to her accent. When she said 'Woody Woodpecker' it came out sounding like 'Wooooooody Woooooodpeckah.' Except I can't make it sound just like she did—but you get the idea. Being English yourself."

"Keep the change."

"I sure do thank you! Enjoy your stay. I just want you to know we're not perfect here in America—who is?— but down here in Tennessee we all still love our country, and we're not ashamed to say so. Bah now."

"Goodbye," Terry said.

He could still hear little Rosalie sobbing as he rolled up the window. He started the truck and backed slowly out of the parking bay. Night was falling fast along Cove Creek Boulevard. His hands were sweating, slipping on the wheel. He wiped them on his rough-out jacket, drank some coffee and replaced the paper cup in the carton on the seat next to him.

Terry didn't know what to do about Oxey. He'd never had a corpse on his hands before. Pretty Joe had always disposed of the girls; that was his pleasure and his responsibility. Why had Joe lashed out at Oxey? Probably he was angry because Terry had wanted to talk to someone about Jeanie. Once upon a time Terry had had some control over Pretty Joe; he could force Joe to go away when he didn't want him hanging around.

But Pretty Joe had become shockingly powerful, and reckless, and he was furious about his failure with Jeanie. So he was making Terry suffer for his own mistakes and bad temper. Pretty Joe had never liked Terry much, but he had tolerated him, while making it plain that any time he really wanted to he could take over permanently. That was Terry's dilemma, and his worst fear: a fear of limbo, while Pretty Joe put his lethal hand on the throttle and poured on the coal, and sent the human engine careening to destruction.

Why should Pretty Joe care? He was a creature of anger and frustration. He had so little to lose.

Terry thought it might appease Joe, for a while, if he

did a good job of getting rid of the body. And if he concentrated very hard on the task at hand, then he might also divert Pretty Joe's thoughts from Anne. In that interval—Terry hoped—he would surely think of something that would save his sister from Pretty Joe's compulsive wrath.

"See him naked by the window
Tousled hair a pearly glow
Lie down sweetly by your mummy
Come to me, my pretttyyy Joe . . ."

"Did Terry try to kill his mother?
"Try to kill his mother?
"Kill his mother?

"Suppose it was the shock of sonny boy/
coming on with the knife
"Shock of sonny boy coming on with

"Wolf-boy sounds.   Wolf boy Wolf

"No memory.
"No memory

"Ellamay?"

"Quite charmingly erotic
"Sing it for you some

"Yes, ma'am?"

"Erotic   erotic   erotic
    erotic

"Knife in his hand
"Face down on the floor
"Incoherent   incoherent
    quite
charm
ingly
incoherent wolf/
boysounds

"Where is Oxey?"

"Professor Ramsdell, do
you feel all right?"

"Tousled hair a pearly glow

"Try to kill his mother
    mother
Mother Mummy
sweetly by your

"Please tell me where I
can find Oxey."

"Don't you agree

"He left here a good half
hour ago. Is something
the—"

"Did them all a bloody
    important favor?

"Would you give my
apologies to the Hollises? I
shan't be able to attend the
pour after all."

"Ask him to sing it for you
"Ask him to sing it for you
"Prretttyyyy Joe
"Prretttyyyy Joe

"None of my business,
Professor Ramsdell, but
honey, why don't you sit

down for a couple of
minutes and let me pour
you a good stiff shot of
bourbon?"

"Down sweetly by your

"Oh, God. Oh, God,
Ellamay. Oh, my God, my
God—"

"(Hope I manage to stay
on key)"

THE INTERSTATE WASN'T lighted where it passed beneath
Ellistown Road, and neither was the flyover itself, which
carried only light traffic from farm to town and back
again. The sky was dark now, except for a streak of
cobalt blue in the west, and the stars were twinkling brightly. The Interstate was busy twenty-four hours a day—
always plenty of tractor trailers.

It was a long, level stretch of highway, and Terry had
been hanging around long enough to observe that the
truck drivers frequently hit seventy miles an hour traveling under the bridge. Even if one of the drivers saw the
body just before it fell to the pavement in front of him,
he would never be able to stop in time. Probably he
wouldn't stop at all after running over Oxey. Terry was
certain to be well on his way no matter what happened,
and it was likely, since Oxey was just a boy, that the
police would believe he'd been doing something extremely
foolish up there. Like trying to walk the railing. And it
should prove impossible to tell, once the body had been
mangled by a tractor trailer, that he'd also been struck
several blows with a hammer.

More than enough blows to kill him—and perhaps sufficient damage had been done to the brain so that Oxey could be presumed to be clinically dead. Unhappily for Terry, the boy was still stubbornly breathing.

Terry found this out when he pulled the poncho off Oxey and saw tiny bubbles of blood around his swollen nose. Breathing—but that didn't alter the situation; it only made Terry more squeamish. Nevertheless he turned off his small flashlight, pocketed it, spread the poncho on the seat and lifted Oxey onto it, so he would be handy when Terry needed to move quickly to dump him. He had parked his camper truck close to the rail on the right-hand side of the bridge, over the northbound lanes. From there he could see the huge trucks coming from a long way off, aglow with running lights, hear the low-down roar of the engines and the deepening tire whine. He waited, door partly open, eyes on the Interstate.

The sounds of traffic below obscured the well-tuned rumble of the mill in the sheriff's prowl car. He wasn't aware of the car at all until the sheriff threw the side-mounted spot on him from about fifty feet away. Then Terry turned quickly, slamming the door as he did so. He held up a hand to shield his eyes.

The sheriff got out of his car, put on his Stetson hat at a nifty angle and came toward Terry with the aplomb of a parade marshal, swinging a big skull-popper flashlight in one hand. Terry went to meet him.

"Y'aught to have your parking lights on if you're gonna be stopped like this."

"I was trying to save the battery."

"She break down on you?"

"No, but I heard a noise underneath, as if something was dragging."

"What part England you from?"

"Cornwall."

"Yeah. Didn't get down that far. Had some good old times in London, though. I was mil'tary police in Frankfurt, Germany, back about fifteen years ago."

"Sie sprechen Deutsch?"

"Shit, not any more I don't. I never cared enough about any kraut to want to converse with him. Of course, being in the mil'tary police, I never met your high-type kraut. I don't doubt there are some. I see you got one of these big new Fords. Prob'ly the biggest."

"Four hundred sixty cubic inches."

"Saw one just like it at Scotty's fishing camp the other day. *Powerful* mother. Don't you have a flashlight?"

"Not a very good one."

"I'll have a look underneath for you. Maybe I should see some identification? Technically you're in violation, parked here without lights, but I won't give you a ticket for that."

"Thank you," Terry said, holding out his wallet.

"You're at the college, huh? My oldest daughter went there two years before she started making babies. Okay, Mr. Camming."

The sheriff switched on his flashlight and hunkered down. Terry put his wallet away. He turned toward the truck cab and saw Oxey's bloodied hand pressed against the glass of the window.

His surprise was so unpleasant that he almost strangled on it. The sheriff was down on his knees now, having a hard look up under the truck. All he had to do was lift his head and he was going to see Oxey's hand fixed behind the glass by the glare of the spotlight.

"Nah. Don't see a thing."

"Toward the rear, I think."

"Did it sound like it might have been the tail pipe?"

"Possibly."

Terry edged toward the door of the truck.

"No, that wasn't it, these mounts are okay."

Terry opened the door a few inches, reached in and pushed Oxey's head down. Oxey groaned, but so softly that the sound was lost as a Greyhound bus snarled by on the Interstate. Terry kept a hand on Oxey, but Oxey didn't move again. Terry found it incredible that he had been able to move at all.

Disastrous, Terry thought, blinking back panicky tears. What else was going to go wrong tonight?

The sheriff got up and dusted off the knees of his khakis. "What I think it was, you snagged up some junk that was loose in the road and drug that a ways."

"Could be."

"Wouldn't hurt to get checked out at a garage. Buddy Sawtelle is still open, corner of Rutledge and the Forked Deer Pike?"

"Thank you, Sheriff."

"That's okay."

The sheriff switched off his flashlight and returned to the prowl car. Terry climbed into the camper truck and sat there with his hands tight on the wheel until the sheriff turned off his dazzling spot, hit the headlights and pulled out and around Terry with a wave of his hand.

Terry reached for the hammer.

But Oxey was unconscious on the seat, and Terry wasn't capable of smashing the helpless boy in the head. Fortunately he was able to think of a better, painless way to be rid of Oxey. It would take a little time, and he'd have to do some digging. Pretty Joe was getting impatient —Terry sensed that—but whose fault was it? That goddamn bungling Pretty Joe was responsible for the mess he was in!

He covered Oxey with the poncho. Then the tears that he had suppressed for so long began to stream down his cheeks. Terry had a crying fit, banging his clenched hands helplessly on the steering wheel. Oxey lay motionless beside him.

Finally, when Terry could see well enough to drive, he made a quick U-turn and went roaring back into the town of Kingman.

ANNE, DRIVING HER Triumph Spitfire, caught up with Terry at the intersections of Rutledge and Cove Creek Boulevard.

He was going west on Cove Creek, toward the college. She was waiting out a red light behind a pickup truck and a Buick with a little toy dog in the back window, whose eyes lighted up whenever the driver's foot was on the brake. When the light didn't change promptly and she realized that she might lose Terry, she suddenly spurted out from behind the Buick, shifted into second almost immediately, burning some expensive rubber, dodged a blue Cougar that was hanging a sharp right, and found herself on Cove Creek.

Terry was already two blocks away and she was on the wrong side of the street, driving into a tight two lanes of eastbound highway traffic. Oncoming cars honked and shrieked and their lines broke in panic; she blasted the coupe through to the proper lane, where she blind-sided an old junker traveling in her direction. She hit the other car hard enough to spin them both around in the street, the junker more or less coming apart as it hissed and wobbled to a stop against the far curb. Anne restarted the stalled engine, found her bashed-in car would run, and drove on, dragging metal and spitting sparks.

She looked for the camper truck and laid on the horn, hoping to attract Terry's attention. At the next intersection the light changed red against her; she went through it without a pause, passed two cars on the wrong side of the street and pulled up alongside Terry in the curb lane, hand on the horn again.

He glanced at her but kept driving, a little faster.

"Terry!"

Three blocks away railroad signals were clanging, flash-

257

ing red where the Southern tracks cut diagonally into Cove Creek and continued down the middle of the boulevard for about a hundred level yards, and as Anne glanced toward the signals she saw a green-and-yellow diesel engine roll into view, westbound just as they were. Ahead of them cars were stopped, waiting on the train.

But Terry didn't slow down, and she realized that he didn't intend to stop at the crossing—all he wanted now was to get away from her. It was all he'd ever wanted, really—to be left alone to work and live.

The tears in her eyes all but blinded Anne. She knew she would not have control of her half-wrecked car much longer. Smoke was pouring from a rubbed rear tire and the brakes were so far gone she was afraid to touch them, afraid of a locking skid. The whole car was vibrating, sending shock waves through her. But she stayed beside the camper truck, even when Terry veered out to pass the line of waiting cars and aimed for the narrowing space in the road a couple of hundred feet away. They were both doing close to fifty miles an hour.

Anne screamed at him, knowing he couldn't hear because of the rumbling, hooting train.

Terry roared obliviously around the front of the engine with inches to spare and disappeared down Cove Creek Boulevard.

Anne turned the wheel hard left to avoid being ground under the wheels of the train; it was her last act of control over the car. She was able to do only a little braking as the car shot across the street, across the apron of a Gulf station and into the garage, where it collided squarely with another car on the rack.

Smoke immediately filled the sports coupe. Her hands automatically released the shoulder harness.

A grease-stained man pulled her out. "Goddamn *insane* fool thing to do—"

Deafened by shock, Anne shook him off. "All right—I'm all right—"

They both stepped back as flame blossomed beneath

the wrecked car. The attendant ran for a fire extinguisher. Anne wandered outside. A Volvo was gassing up at the pumps, its owner nowhere in sight. Anne got in, anticipating keys in the ignition. She drove off, pulling away from the attached hose, quickly stepped the Volvo up to fifty miles an hour. She headed for the campus of Kingman College.

At this point Anne had no clear idea of what she was doing. She drove unfeelingly, in terror, obeying her instincts. She would go straightaway to Terry's house—but no, she'd been there already—but that was before she'd seen him on the street and gone howling witlessly after him—perhaps he was just now returning home. Of course. She must get to Terry, assure him that she could never believe he had murdered those three girls. Until the accident it had been impossible for Anne to put Philip Rackstraw's extempore accusations out of her mind, and that obscene bit of doggerel had been driving her mad with guilt.

Mercifully, the collision with the train had temporarily separated her from her reason.

Now sirens motivated her terror and reminded her that she had stolen a car. Long before she saw the police cars, their cyclonic whooping hounded her off the street and through a gate of the college, where she waited, shaking, for the cars to pass.

As soon as they were gone she proceeded, at a slower pace, to the north campus, and emerged a couple of blocks from Terry's house.

Anne saw the camper truck backed up almost to the garage when she drove by the first time. As far as she could tell, Terry was not behind the wheel, but it was foggy tonight. He had left the parking lights on. The house itself was dark.

She made her turn and came up in front of the house. Parked, got out. There were three other houses on the block, and nothing across the street but the arboretum of the college. She heard a television set. She heard an air-plane.

She heard Terry digging.

She walked, trembling, along the edge of the drive, staying on the grass. The driver's door of the camper truck was ajar. Anne glanced inside as she passed, saw a bundle on the seat, thought nothing of it. She was at-tracted by the heavy spadework Terry was doing behind the house. For some reason his nocturnal efforts intimi-dated her. She approached him quietly.

Terry was digging by lantern light in the storage space beneath the back stairs. She could make him out through the creeper-covered lattice. He'd already dug a sizable hole—the available space was roughly three feet by six feet, and Terry seemed determined to dig it all out.

Anne did not have to stand there long observing him before she realized he must be digging a grave. And she remembered the bundle on the front seat of the camper truck.

It had the effect of sobering her up, as if she'd been on a long drunk. She went immediately to the truck cab, opened the door wider, reached in and lifted the poncho from Oxey's bloody head. A couple of bluebottle flies lumbered past her, and that made her sick; she retched, but only a meager, bitter liquid ran down her chin. She had nothing left in her stomach.

Anne climbed into the truck and put her ear to Oxey's frail chest. She didn't hear anything, and then she thought she did. She sobbed and gathered Oxey in her arms and laid him on the wet grass beside the drive. She was glad she couldn't see his face too well. She wiped hopelessly at the gelatinous blood and kissed a pale untouched ear.

"Oxey. Oxey."

He was out of breath from grave-digging and not all that quiet coming up behind her. Anne turned and threw herself out of the way as the bright metal of the shovel sliced past her head and smashed the driver's window of the truck. Anne then had her first good look at Pretty

Joe. In those few seconds she had no doubts at all that it was he, and that she most certainly would never see Terry again.

His shovel had broken off an inch above the blade. Anne was on her knees in the drive, and when he grabbed her to kill her with his bare hands, she hit him in the head with the biggest stone she could lay her hands on. Then she ran for the Volvo.

Pretty Joe wiped away the blood that was running from his temple and matting in the lashes of his right eye, climbed into the camper truck, roared down the driveway and drove broadside into the Volvo before Anne could go ten feet.

The Ford had a bumper like a heavy-duty tow truck: it was made of oak planks two inches thick, and solid steel bars protected headlights and grill. There was enough power under the high hood to push the Volvo across the street and into the opposite curb as if it were a child's tricycle.

But he needed to back up in order to make another run at it, to turn the Volvo into total junk and pound Anne to jelly along with it. While he was reversing, Anne bolted from the car and ran into the arboretum. Behind her the Volvo exploded when Pretty Joe rammed it a second time. She looked back through the saffron-tinted fog as he went into reverse again; then he came grinding full tilt into the night woods after her.

There was plenty of room for Pretty Joe to maneuver in the uncluttered arboretum, where the trees and shrubs had been planted to show them off. And Anne was hobbled, unable to run very fast, to move with the quickness she needed to avoid being run down. But she realized that she was only a few hundred yards from the Hollises, and if she could make it that far, she had a chance.

Pretty Joe understood what she was up to, and he didn't waste any time coming after her.

The headlights of the Ford revealed an arched timber

footbridge that spanned a twenty-foot ravine, and Anne scrambled for it.

She was on the bridge seconds ahead of him, and it was far too narrow for the truck. But in a sense he had her trapped; Anne was only halfway across to the opposite bank when Pretty Joe drove the four-ton camper truck into the posts that supported the bridge. The structure shuddered and yawed, nearly throwing her into the shallow water of the creek below. Floor boards buckled and timbers creaked. Off balance, Anne clung to the railing. She was still trying to get to her feet when Pretty Joe took another crack at the supports and succeeded in uprooting the bridge from the bank. It plunged as a mass of jumbled planks toward the creek.

Anne rode the falling bridge most of the way down, then fell clear into three feet of water.

When she struggled out of the pool she continued downstream, falling painfully several times on the slippery flat stones of the creek bed. She heard the truck idling along above her, and the beam of the hand-operated spotlight cut through the mist to pick her out. She was losing her bearings again, not sure of where she was going, and the light terrified her. Nevertheless she was attracted by it, she had to look at it. She saw his face indistinctly above the incandescent glare.

Anne waded for the bank and pulled herself out of the water. Behind her Pretty Joe shifted gears and drove carefully down into the creek. With the spotlight out of her eyes, Anne was able to make out the distant glow of a street lamp, and she homed on it, finding a clear path. She ran again, shivering, impelled by the geared-up growl of the Ford as it wheel-walked over the rocky stream bed. Very dimly she wondered how long it would take him to drive up the rather steep bank; maybe he would become mired. But before she could gain fifty yards on him Pretty Joe was happily on her trail again, slowly churning up speed in the soft leaf mold of the arboretum floor.

By now she could see blacktop glistening in the cold blue light of a street lamp, see her own gate and the peaked tiled roof of the guest cottage.

Anne, feeling headlights hot on her back again, looked frantically around. Her head was still turned when she ran at close to top speed into a pipe-frame metal sign. She rebounded from the impact with the reverberating sign and fell, stunned, on her back. Pretty Joe was only three seconds behind her in the truck, coming fast. Instinctively she rolled over, into a narrow depression in the middle of the path; the camper truck drove directly over her and came to a sloughing stop, with one of the back wheels nearly hubcap deep in the soft loamy earth.

Anne crawled until she could walk, and walked until she could run, and ran right past the camper truck and into the street while Pretty Joe was still concentrating on getting his left rear wheel out of the earth. She heard the truck door open as if he intended coming after her on foot. But when she looked back he was half in, half out of the cab, just watching. Because they were both within sight of the main house now, and they could hear music: violin and piano duet, a sonata Anne had played often but could not now recall by name.

Anne stopped, sobbing, to stare at him. She had made it to the house and she had beaten him—what could he do but watch her go?

The hatred in his eyes was too much for her to bear for more than a moment. She stumbled on.

Ellamay was in the morning room with John Willie Charles when Anne came in off the veranda. They looked at her in genuine fright. She was caked with mud and leaf mold; bright smears of blood shone through the murk.

"Ellamay—"

"Professor Ramsdell?"

"You must—call the police for me. Do it now."

"Sit *down*, honey. Where have you been?"

It was almost like being scolded; Anne's sobs quickened to hysterical laughter.

"Ellamay, I can't—you've got to—quickly, before—please do what I say!"

"Who's that fool drive'n out there on our patio?" John Willie Charles said, his face close to the glass of the french doors.

Anne had slumped into a chair, but she turned to look just as the headlights of the camper truck lit up the glass of the doors. She heard the wide-open howl of the engine, and she knew that Pretty Joe wasn't finished with her yet.

"Get out!" she said hoarsely, trying to lift herself from the chair. "Both of you get out of here!"

"He's coming right up here on the veranda!" John Willie Charles said indignantly. He was standing there, as dazzled as a jacklighted deer, when Ellamay, who always had her wits about her, grabbed him by the arm and snatched him away.

They were both showered with smashed panes as the camper truck burst into the morning room and drove into the oak table behind which Anne had been sitting moments before. A breakfront exploded like a fragmentation bomb.

Anne was running as Pretty Joe threw the truck into reverse. He followed her through the flat-arched doorway into the marbled entrance hall.

In the parlor across the way the musicians had stopped playing, and she could see thirty bewildered faces turned toward her. She leaped for the fourteen-foot staircase.

Again Pretty Joe missed her only by inches; he braked the huge camper into a hard skid on the marble floor, a back wheel bumping over the lowest step as Anne climbed out of the way. Pretty Joe gunned the engine and mashed the brake, slewed dangerously on the slick floor as statuary disintegrated in his path, and ended up aimed at the stairs.

Anne had been watching when she should have been running, but she was certain he wouldn't—he couldn't possibly—the staircase couldn't support a truck that size.

Pretty Joe didn't seem to realize that. He drove straight for her.

The stairs held. Anne leaped over the balustrade to escape being smashed against it. She fell screaming to the marble floor as the truck hurtled up the last few steps to the landing, drove straight through the windows there and out onto the groaning balcony.

The balcony wasn't as stoutly constructed as the staircase. It started to crumble almost immediately under the weight of the truck. But Pretty Joe was already in reverse, and as the Corinthian columns buckled and toppled and most of the balcony floor fell like an avalanche onto the veranda below, the truck backed safely inside.

Dr. Hollis and two other men picked Anne up. She had sprained or fractured an ankle in her fall and was crying piteously. They lugged her into the parlor as Pretty Joe came bumpity-bump back down the stairs after her.

The house was shuddering now from the impact of the balcony falling in ruins, from the pounding weight of the truck on the staircase.

The heavy parlor doors were slammed shut seconds before Joe drove into them, but for once the truck didn't have the necessary momentum. The solid oak doors splintered but held.

In the entrance hall the ceiling was coming down.

"Get out!" Anne cried as they laid her on a sofa in the parlor. The thirty or so guests corralled there hadn't made a move to clear the house. Now they began leaping through windows onto the front lawn.

Pretty Joe didn't try the doors again; he came through the wall, which was easier, despite the wainscoting. As he did so, wiring was torn loose, the lights went out, smoke and dust filled the parlor and part of the ceiling fell in chunks. Anne covered her head with her arms. Beside the sofa Dr. Hollis went down, even as he tried to protect her; he lay half buried in debris.

The truck bulldozed a grand piano into the fireplace. Then Pretty Joe backed off and took a leisurely look around just as the last of the trapped guests were jumping through the windows.

Flames crackled in the walls of the battered house.

In the choking darkened room Anne rolled off the sofa. Shocked and hurting, she began to crawl toward the parlor doors.

Pretty Joe flicked on the hand-cranked spotlight and searched methodically for her.

He found her clinging to the damaged doors, which had been parted a couple of inches by the impact with the truck. She was trying to pry them farther apart, but they were stuck fast in their tracks.

The light grazed Anne, came back to hover like a ghost. She worked harder, gasping. Clawing.

Pretty Joe made a backing turn, and then he drove very slowly toward the doors. There was no place she could go on one foot. She stuck with the doors, fighting to release them. Pretty Joe hesitated, then drove forward.

At last Anne gave up. She turned numbly and just waited for him, her back to the doors.

With an expert's touch he pinned her flat with the heavy bumper, set the brake, got out. He had in his hand another of the chef's knives that he favored.

He leaned on the front fender of the truck, intent, not smiling, not caring to speak, and watched her squirm.

Pretty Joe.

Pretty Joe?

No, she thought. *I won't believe it*.

An unstable psychoneurotic creation, powerful only in his craze for retribution.

Call Terry, she thought, struggling. *Call him back. Hurry!*

In Cornwall one long-ago spring she had partially fallen through the rotted wooden cover of an old well. Precariously stuck, she had seen her brother, far ahead, walking obliviously over the crest of a hill.

Call him back!

"Terry!" Anne shouted.

It disturbed his concentration. He shook his head fractiously.

"Terry, I'm stuck! Get me out, Terry! I want my brother! Don't let him do it, Terry! Help me!"

He raised the knife, but she saw the flash of doubt in his eyes.

"Hurry, Terry! Stop him!"

His hand flicked out like a duelist's, the point of the knife coming to rest between her breasts. Anne sobbed but didn't flinch or look away. Again she said, softly but firmly, "You can't let him, Terry."

There was a change in his eyes. She smiled gratefully.

"Terry."

"Yes."

"Is—isn't there another way?"

"Yes. There's another way."

"Wouldn't it be better? After all you've suffered?"

He shrugged, pale and uncaring. "It might be better."

"Please let me help you."

She dared then to put her free hand on his hand, the one that held the knife.

Terry sighed. "No, I think I can manage. For once."

"All right, Terry. Whatever you wish."

He looked around at the smoke and the ruins and smiled remorsefully. "Pretty Joe made a right mess of things again, didn't he?" Tears ran down his cheeks. He withdrew the knife, put his knife hand on the fender.

"I'm hurt, Terry."

"I know. I'm sorry. Someone will be along to help you, won't they?" He leaned over and kissed her muddy cheek. "I should hurry. He comes and goes, you know. Wouldn't want him coming back just yet."

"But I want you to—"

"Goodbye," Terry said, and at that instant she realized what he was thinking, had been thinking all along. Anne reached for him, reached short and screaming as he raised the chef's knife and placed the blade with great accuracy and then drew it through his spouting throat with enough strength to nearly decapitate himself.

Epilogue

ANNE

THE GIRLS OXEY met on the train from Lisbon to Cascais spoke a little English, and they were willing to talk to him once they determined that he wasn't trying to pick either of them up. They were sisters, and they lived in Mexico City, where their father had been posted as second secretary to the Portuguese ambassador. Because they were only visiting in Cascais, they hadn't heard of the *escola* at the Quinta Oberon. The oldest girl, a stunning dark-eyed blonde named Henriqueta, was crazy about Johnny Cash, and she felt certain, since both Oxey and Johnny Cash lived in the state of Tennessee, that they must be friends and neighbors. Oxey replied that he often saw *Senhor* Cash riding by his windows on summer mornings, mounted on a Tennessee stud and strumming his guitar, and that *Senhor* Cash never failed to wave a big hello. The girls were thrilled and smiled happily, and when they all got off the train by the blue sea they allowed Oxey to buy them fruit drinks at a sidewalk café a couple of blocks from the station.

Henriqueta made inquiries for him, and came back shaking her head.

"Oppy, there is no more the school. Is all—can you dig it?—shut up."

"Doesn't anyone live there?"

"Living there, yes, someones, but no *escola*."

She had secured directions to the *quinta,* which Oxey only half understood in translation as they huddled over the map of the region that he'd brought with him. Henriqueta made a dot with a pencil above the coast road to Cabo Raso. "Quinta Oberon." She looked curiously at Oxey, who wondered what the proprietor of the café had been telling her about the place. Or the woman who owned it.

"I don't see a road to the *quinta*."

"Road, yes. Very bad road."

Oxey walked the girls home to a pleasant little *solar* tucked away in the blooming hills above the fishing village. Then he returned to rent a Vespa motor scooter from the local garage. It was hot for February in this corner of Portugal, temperature in the seventies and not much of a breeze off the calm Atlantic. He rode west and presently came to an unmarked road that wound upward past a few small homes through dense cypress and dragon trees to a large house he could just make out from below. A small river crossed and recrossed the road and had washed it out in places. He decided to walk his scooter rather than risk a tumble. But it was hot work in the midday sun. Sub-tropical vegetation had closed in rather thickly on the narrow road, and the massive stone-and-masonry *portão* was all but overgrown by tree-sized ferns.

There was a red Ferrari parked in a shed opposite the gate. Carved creatures, half lion and half serpent, arched protectively over the wooden door in the gate. Finding no means of announcing himself, Oxey left the scooter by the *portão* and walked in. Four flights of stone steps led up to the cliff house through a *quintais* that had been badly neglected. A fallen palm tree across his path had been down for at least a year.

On the level below the terrace of the house he came upon a scabby swimming pool with patched sides and perhaps a foot of evil-looking water in the bottom. A young man was painting in a pavilion at one end of the pool.

He was about Oxey's age, blond and lean, with a dished-out face that radiated unkindness. He wore a pair of shorts and rope sandals. He looked sharply at Oxey but said nothing as he continued to paint. Oxey smiled at him, and after a while he walked over to the pavilion, which had a tiled roof turned up at the eaves in the Chinese manner. So did the roof of the main house. It was believed to protect the inhabitants from malevolent spirits—and the blue stripe painted around the cornice of the house also deterred flies and witches.

"What do you want?" the painter said. German or Austrian accent, Oxey noted, and introduced himself.

"I asked what you wanted. I do not need to know your name."

"Is this the Quinta Oberon?"

"Yes."

"Well, that's just what I wanted. I wanted to find the Quinta Oberon." He looked at the painting the young man was working on, a portrait of a Nazarene fisherman's wife done in the style of Gustav Klimt. He was glared at for peeking, but Oxey didn't care.

The young man might then have progressed from glaring to physical intimidation—he looked the type to fly off the handle. But he took in Oxey's slightly battered nose, the small scars that divided one eyebrow and impinged on Oxey's upper lip, and realized that Oxey had twenty pounds on him. Oxey never hit anyone, but he looked as if he would at the slightest provocation, so the young man began to put away his paints.

"My working days are very precious to me. I cannot work if I am interrupted."

"Nobody told me about you," Oxey said.

The young man smiled sulkily as he lifted his canvas from the easel, and Oxey had another look at it.

"She seldom sees anyone; she doesn't give interviews. So you are wasting your time coming here."

"I don't think I'm wasting my time, Hugo. Do you always sign your name first, before you do the painting? That's very interesting. Where is Anne?"

"In bed, perhaps. She has not been well."

"If you're going up to the house, would you mind telling her I'm here? I don't have any angles, I'm just a friend."

"Then wake her yourself," Hugo said. "She always sleeps on her stomach, and she much prefers to be awakened in this manner." He made a corkscrew gesture in the air with his middle finger. "And it does not matter to her who does the awakening. It is skill that counts." He folded the easel and walked down the hill, canvas in one hand, tools in the other.

Oxey went up to the spacious terrace. Paint was flaking off the white wrought-iron patio furniture and the canvas-topped dining pavilion needed a good scrubbing to get rid of some winter mildew. But the square stones of the terrace had been recently hosed and swept, the hedges were trimmed, and there were flowers everywhere. He heard hedge clippers around the corner of the main house, followed the sounds past dovecote and carriage house until he discovered Anne, barefoot, industriously trimming topiary by a purling fountain.

She was thin and brown and looked fit, at least from where Oxey stood. But she was facing three-quarters away from him as she reached up to clip a sprig of hedge, and all he could really see were the unsubtle angles of her face, not the features. He walked across the paved courtyard, and when Anne heard his boots she turned in surprise, frowned at him, then slipped the sunglasses riding on the crown of her head down over her eyes. Prescription lenses, he thought. Once she could see him clearly she just stood there with the clippers hanging from one hand, mouth open anticly, as if her jaw had come unhinged.

"Oxey?"

"Hello, Anne."

"But you—*how*—I never expected—"

"You should have expected me, soon as you quit writing."

She took a faltering step back, appearing helpless to defend herself against even the most amiable rebuke. She closed her eyes briefly; behind the lenses of her glasses the downcast lashes looked like husks in amber.

"I thought it might be time," she said.

"It wasn't time," Oxey replied, now having a critical look at her. He saw that it was possible she had been physically unwell for many months. Too many bones showed, and what flesh there was retained bruises like yellow underpainting beneath her tan. Hers was a truant thinness; she resembled a child going through the most ungainly and botched-up phase of her growth. Her face was grooved rather than lined, and there was a raw redness at the root of her nose that troubled him. Or maybe she was just getting over a lingering cold.

Anne opened her eyes and laughed then, but it was a stilted laugh, and as if she was aware that her pleasure seemed mechanical, she threw her arms around him, still holding the hedge clippers, and gave him a hard affectionate embrace.

"I can't believe the size of you! I might not have known you at all except for the eyes. *They* haven't changed. Where did you get such beautiful rippling muscles?"

"I've been doing a lot of wrestling—hundred seventy-four-pound class."

"Wrestling! I'll wager you're a tiger."

"Well, I'm still not very quick."

"How can you just pop up in Portugal in the middle of winter? Aren't you supposed to be at college?"

"I have a couple of papers to write, but no more classes until I start med school in the fall. So I decided, you know, I really needed to get away."

"And see old friends? Well, it's marvelous that you came, but you ought to have given warning. We're literally going to the dogs around here. You must have noticed the shape the pool is in. I've tried repeatedly to have the leaks repaired. No go. And the *quintais*— We've had trouble getting a couple who would work out, that's all. If *she's* a good housekeeper, then *he's* a poor gardener and a worse chauffeur . . ."

Oxey smiled. "Why don't you put Hugo to work, he looks old enough."

"Hugo! Have you met Hugo already?"

"Oh, sure."

"Let's get out of the sun," Anne suggested, leading him back to the terrace. "Medical school, did you say? So you finally opted for medicine."

"Yeh, but I don't think I'll practice, it's research that interests me."

"And how is your family—?"

From below they heard the spirited rumble of the red Ferrari as Hugo jockeyed it out of the shed. Anne left Oxey and hastened to the edge of the terrace, where she was in time to see Hugo depart in a mile-high huff.

His leaving seemed to upset her. She glanced at Oxey as if hoping for an explanation.

"I interrupted him while he was painting. I didn't know any better."

"Oh. He's had great difficulty buckling down—I hope he won't go off on a tear now. Time is so short. He works slowly and we must be ready for the Biennale."

"Is he that good?"

"Hugo is a genius," Anne declared, waving him to a chair as she headed for the house. "Have you had lunch? Amalie will bring us something. Won't be but a moment."

Long after the youthful maid had wheeled out a cart containing an effervescent melon, thinly sliced smoked ham, sardines and a carafe of vin rosé Anne reappeared. She had bathed and put on a skirt and peasant blouse and jangle-jewelry and a darker pair of shades, but even so she was detectably high—on cocaine, Oxey was sure; he would not believe she was fool enough to snort heroin. She drank a lot of the Setúbal wine and ignored the luncheon. They chatted through a long and changeless afternoon. Anne made coy excursions to the house and came back recharged, lips loosely together, laughter high and forced and an affront to his nerves. The co-ed school, she explained, had been a shaky proposition all along. The superchildren whom she preferred and had culled from lists of rejects from less tolerant institutions proved predictably hard to handle. She hinted at a minor scandal that hadn't done them any good. Her remaining few students had departed Christmas a year ago. All save Hugo, the *enfant terrible*.

It became clear to Oxey that the chief reason for the school's failure had been Anne's single-minded interest in Hugo. She spoke of his peccadilloes with feverish candor and no trace of regret—of calculated but hair-raising suicide attempts, of gambling sprees in the casino of Estoril and episodes of reckless driving. Toward evening they toured Hugo's studio in the renovated carriage house. Obviously he had talent, but he was not a big producer —a few sketches, canvases drastically incomplete. Anne spoke wistfully of two paintings snapped up months ago at a fashionable London gallery, and requests for more. But there was a musty air of failure in Hugo's studio, of talent struggling hopelessly with self-indulgence and more demonic urges. Hugo's temperament and baleful influence had left its mark everywhere. There was only the one servant girl, Anne confessed, because money was low. And even when they did have money at unpredictable intervals (royalties from the continuing sale of Terry's books were a principal source of income), no one in the nearby villages wanted to work at Quinta Oberon.

As night fell, Hugo's continued absence and, perhaps, her dwindling hoard of coke, made Anne fretful. She could deal with specters of her own devise but not the memories that Oxey occasioned. Having him around was an ordeal for her. But she worked just that much harder to make him feel welcome. She squandered energy preparing an elaborately authentic Portuguese meal—*bacalao* and spring lamprey in wine—but again she couldn't eat. Finally she couldn't speak either, and they both fell sadly silent. The night was chilly; a wind off the Atlantic guttered the flames of the candles on their table. Oxey saw tears in her eyes.

"They did a good job on your face," Anne said. "Not too perfect—men do wear scars well. Do you want to stay tonight? I wish you would."

"I'll stay."

"I can't sleep with you. You don't want to, anyway. Oh, not very much. Did you want to before you came?"

"I thought about it," Oxey said with a gentle smile, "for four years." He snuffed out the candles and held one of her jumpy hands, in love with her as always, but feeling no passion.

"I exist on the best terms I could arrange, Oxey. I need Hugo. Things are a bit iffy at the moment, but he's going to be a brilliant success. I'm really quite happy. You must believe that."

In the middle of the night Oxey was awakened by Hugo's voice. He didn't understand the language, but the shrill tones indicated Hugo was having a nasty tantrum. He sat nervously on the edge of the bed in his undershorts. He didn't hear Anne until suddenly she screamed in pain, hurt cruelly and unexpectedly. He leaped down from the bed and was at the door before he could control himself. Picking a fight with Hugo would not make things better for Anne, so he went trembling back to the bed and lay there sleeplessly for an hour or more. He didn't hear either of them again.

It was barely light in the east, only about four thirty in the morning, when he dressed and went out. The door to Anne's room was partly open. He looked in and saw her sitting on a low sofa. Hugo was on the floor, head in her lap, and he appeared to be asleep. She stroked his head languidly. Oxey thought he saw Anne look at him, but she didn't turn her head or lift her hand, and so he left without saying goodbye.

How to stay healthy all the time.

> "*I can recommend this book for authoritative answers to questions that continually come up about health and how to live.*"—Harry J. Johnson, M.D., Chairman, Medical Board Director, Life Extension Institute.

Wouldn't it be wonderful if your whole family could stay healthy all the time?

It may now be possible, thanks to PREVENTIVE MEDICINE. This is the modern approach to health care. Its goal is to prevent illness before it even has a chance to strike!

A new book called THE FAMILY BOOK OF PREVENTIVE MEDICINE shows how you can take advantage of this preventive approach, and make it an everyday reality for yourself and your family. More than 700 pages long—and written in clear, simple language.

TELLS YOU ALL ABOUT THE LATEST MEDICAL ADVANCES

For example, the new knowledge of risk factors in disease is a vital tool of preventive medicine. With it, your doctor might pinpoint you as, say, a high heart attack risk long *before* your heart actually gives you *any trouble*. He could then prescribe certain changes in your diet and habits—perhaps very minor ones—that could remove the danger entirely. This would be preventive medicine at its ideal best! But even if a disease has already taken root, new diagnostic techniques can reveal its presence earlier than ever before. And, as a rule, the sooner a disease is discovered, the more easily it is cured.

SEND NO MONEY—10 DAYS' FREE EXAMINATION

Mail the coupon below, and THE FAMILY BOOK OF PREVENTIVE MEDICINE will be sent to you for free examination. Then, if you are not convinced that it can help you protect the health of your entire family, return it within 10 days and owe nothing. Otherwise, we will bill you for $12.95 plus mailing costs. At all bookstores, or write to Simon and Schuster, Dept. S-53, 630 Fifth Ave., New York, N.Y. 10020.

SIMON AND SCHUSTER, Dept. S-53
630 Fifth Ave., New York, N.Y. 10020

Please send me on approval a copy of THE FAMILY BOOK OF PREVENTIVE MEDICINE. If not convinced that this book belongs permanently in my home, I may return it within 10 days and owe nothing. Otherwise, you will bill me for $12.95, plus mailing costs.

Name...

Address..

City..State..............Zip...........

☐ SAVE. Enclose $12.95 now, and publisher pays mailing costs. Same 10-day return privilege with full refund guaranteed. (New York residents please add applicable sales tax.)

LOOK FOR THESE GREAT POCKET 📖 BOOK BESTSELLERS AT YOUR FAVORITE BOOKSTORE

THE PIRATE • Harold Robbins	
YOU CAN SAY THAT AGAIN, SAM! • Sam Levenson	
THE BEST • Peter Passell & Leonard Ross	
CROCKERY COOKING • Paula Franklin	
SHARP PRACTICE • John Farris	
JUDY GARLAND • Anne Edwards	
SPY STORY • Len Deighton	
HARLEQUIN • Morris West	
THE SILVER BEARS • Paul E. Erdman	
FORBIDDEN FLOWERS: **More Women's Sexual Fantasies** • Nancy Friday	
MURDER ON THE ORIENT EXPRESS • Agatha Christie	
THE JOY OF SEX • Alex Comfort	
RETURN JOURNEY • R. F. Delderfield	
THE TEACHINGS OF DON JUAN • Carlos Castaneda	
JOURNEY TO IXTLAN • Carlos Castaneda	
A SEPARATE REALITY • Carlos Castaneda	
TEN LITTLE INDIANS • Agatha Christie	
BABY AND CHILD CARE • Dr. Benjamin Spock	
BODY LANGUAGE • Julius Fast	
THE MERRIAM-WEBSTER DICTIONARY (Newly Revised)	